THE LOYALTIES

OF

LIEUTENANT HAWK

GORDON B. CLARK

Map by Barbara Neeson

Long Point Press
Spruce Head, Maine

This is a fiction, though some resemblances to both the living and the dead, and some similarity to worldly accouterments of our world, are intended.

ISBN 0-9661371-2-4
Library of Congress Catologue Card Number 98-094263

Printed by Odyssey Press, Inc.
Dover, New Hampshire

LONG POINT PRESS
P.O.BOX 143
SPRUCE HEAD, ME. 04859

GORDON B. CLARK of South Portland, Maine, enlisted in the Air Corps in 1942, and after flying in the Mediterranean, CBI and European theaters, was discharged in Germany in 1946.

Returning to civilian life, Clark graduated from Rollins College, Mexico City College and the University of Maine at Orono. He has published poetry, one novel and edited literary magazines over his years at the University of Maine at Augusta while helping interested students understand and appreciate writing.

WORKS BY GORDON B. CLARK

SARAH'S GORILLA　　(poetry)

NAKED SIN　　(novel)

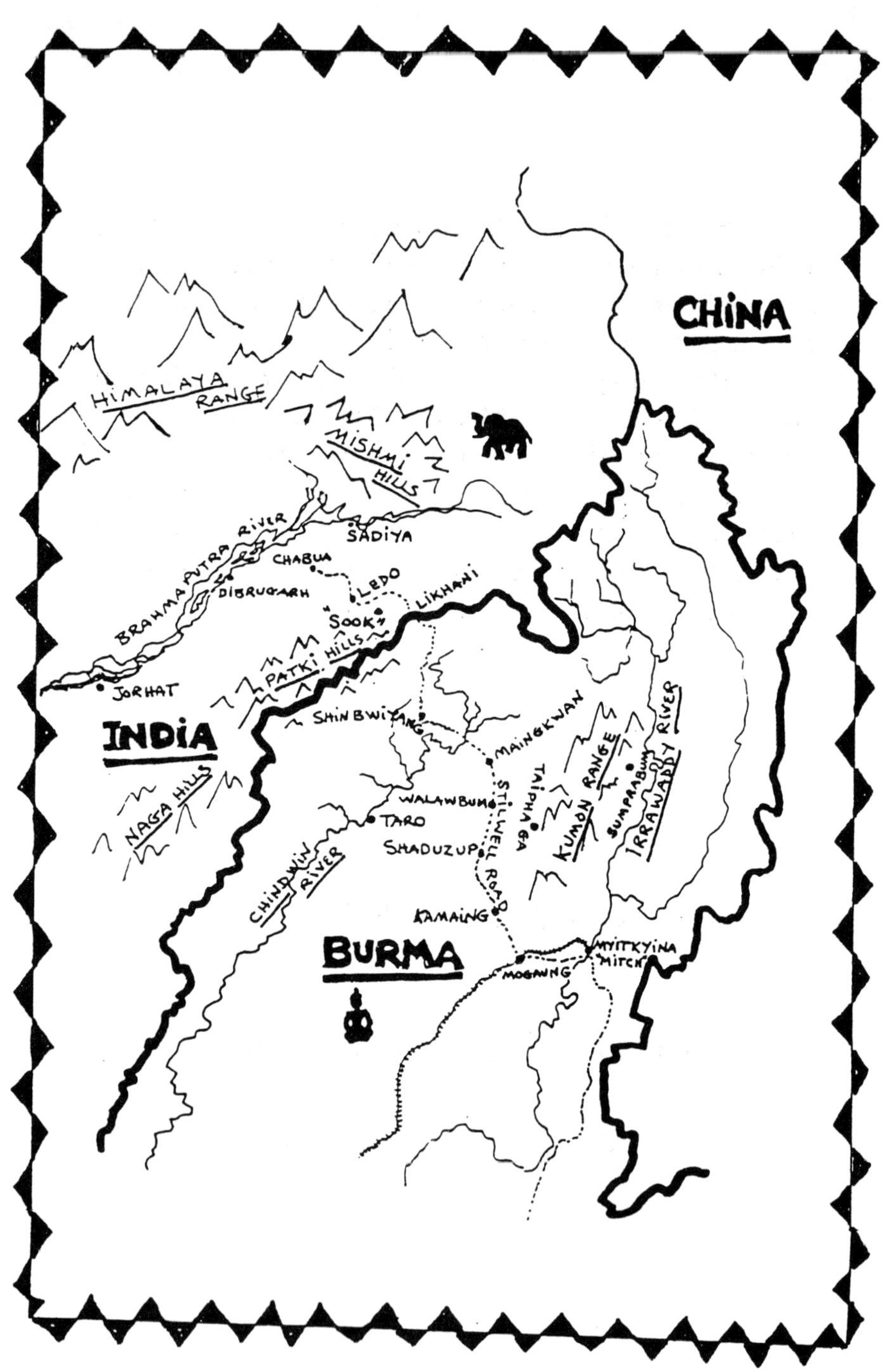

CHINA
HIMALAYA RANGE
MISHMI HILLS
BRAHMAPUTRA RIVER
SADIYA
CHABUA
LEDO
DIBRUGARH
LIKHANI
SOOK
PATKI HILLS
JORHAT
INDIA
SHINBWIYANG
MAINGKWAN
NAGA HILLS
KUMON RANGE
TAIPHA GA
SUMPRABUM
IRRAWADDY RIVER
WALAWBUM
STILWELL ROAD
TARO
SHADUZUP
CHINDWIN RIVER
KAMAING
BURMA
MOGAUNG
MYITKYINA
MITCH

For Marian

Acknowledgments

The writing of *The Loyalties of Lieutenant Hawk* came decades after the American, British, and Chinese forces gained their "little patch of ground" in Burma. What profit in it, half a century later, is still difficult to assess, the loyalties engaged for the most part never visible, very often made manifest by a quart of rye whisky which could be chosen in place of an air medal. Most of all, we were grateful for those pilots who had taught us something about flying, the instructor in Texas who showed me why an unfastened safety belt is the quickest way to fall from a plane and a pilot in Burma who demonstrated the best way to stay alive with a Japanese Zero on my tail. I wish especially to thank Mary Ellen Therriault and my son Gordon M. Clark for their work in restoring the manuscript after a near printing disaster. I also wish to thank Margaret and Jack Neeson for their patience and skill in putting the book together as well as for Marian Clark's readings of these chapters to the point where she claimed illiteracy had its benefits. And for encouragement in my initial attempts much thanks to Hall Tennis in Florida and David Steingass in Wisconsin.

Hamlet: Goes it against the main of Poland, sir,
            Or some frontier?

Captain: Truly to speak and with no addition
             We go to gain a little patch of ground
             That hath no profit in it but the name.

HAMLET IV. Iv.

For this thing I know in my heart, and my mind knows it; there will come a day when sacred Ilium shall perish, and Priam, and the people of Priam of the strong ash spear. But it is not so much the pain to come to the Trojans that troubles me, not even of Priam the King nor Hekaba, nor the thought of my brothers who in their numbers amd valour shall drop in the dust under the hands of men who hate them, as troubles me the thought of you, when some bronze-armored Achaian leads you off, taking away your day of liberty.

Homer, *Iliad*
(Hector to Andromache)

1

ON the map thumbtacked to the rear wall of Operations, the airstrip Sookerating, Sook makes a brown slash in the jungle below the northern slopes of the Patkai Range, a dotted line tracing the border between northern Burma and India. The Brahmaputra River, fifty miles to the north, winds southwest past the village of Sadiya, its fingers snaking from the Mishmi Hills and the eastern Himalayas bordering China. On Lieutenant Hawk's flight map, already battered after only three days of flying, there is no mistaking their isolated airstrip and the Patkais lifting five thousand feet or more to where the war is.

"Not that I've really got a look at it," he remarked to Major Jedd Butler, Intelligence, working over his littered desk in the corner. "Bet if I could get up beyond the Mishmi Hills I could get some good shots of the Himalayas. I promised to send some home."

"The Mishmis!" Major Butler frowned over a clutter of photographic equipment. "You out of your fucking mind, Hawk!" He leaned back, burying his hands in sweat-soaked armpits.

"Well, Major, nobody here has briefed us on that area. Who knows, the Chinese troops they're moving in here may be headed for Russia's soft underbelly."

Butler gives him a disgusted look, snaps his head as if bothered by a fly, runs his hands through his thinning hair and turns to glare up at the wall map.

"Unfortunately, although I doubt if few in this squadron know it, the Russians switched to our side over a year ago. All we're left with is a bunch of 'slopes' who'll end up running off and hiding in the jungle until we wipe out the 'slant-eyes'." He stood up, red-faced and fumbling at his loosely pinned insignia on his frayed collar and gave Hawk one of his weird looks. "But just you make sure you keep your ass out of the Mishmis Lieutenant. Understand?" Adding enigmatically "There ain't no elephants up there."

That night Hawk dreamed again of where the war is. . .

Two days of squadron briefings and by the end of that second afternoon, all fifteen planes of the squadron had made at least one supply drop -- food and ammo just over the Patkais just below Shinbwiyan on the Sitwell Road. He saw the Asian dawn slide up over Burma in green waves that could have come riding in on his Maine coast, then leaning forward in the cockpit of his C-47, the "gooney," he felt its lift on an updraft. Schultz, his co-pilot, turned on the radio to a Lili Marlene broadcast, leaned back and closed his eyes, probably dreaming of Florida; then as a news flash, no bombs on London that night.

Hawk came awake. So this is the way we go to war -- off to save India from the Japanese or British, or maybe save it for ourselves. How many times, he wondered, has the world been saved? Was Genghis Khan the first? A sigh of rain swept their compound, ground fog wrapping their tents. If the rain holds they will not fly, as scheduled, at dawn. Maybe give him time to get rid of Schultz as co-pilot. He draped an arm from the cot, feeling for his beautiful boots of camel leather he'd bought in Alexandria for six packs of cigarettes. Already they gathered mold every night. Barpa, their tent boy, had said they must be kept clean. He sat up abruptly as a high sharp cry severed the night. He raised his arm, shoved his wrist close. The luminous blur resolved to minutes after one. The jackals again.

They had come already during the squadron's first night on the compound. Manchu, their cook, who had supervised setting up the mess tent before their arrival, had told McCabe he must have protection for his supplies. Hawk listened. No sound except the steady whisper of rain and the heavy breathing from the other three cots. The darkness seemed fluid, flowing in between their tent flaps. Then for some reason he recalled that his boots were not just for cigarettes but a waterproof wristwatch that had leaked badly. Barpa, he reflected, already had his eyes on the boots. He stiffened as something moved outside the tent, rustled into silence. Yes, Barpa definitely had his eye on the boots. Each morning when he arrives to clean the tent, his first glance is toward the boots. lifts them from under the cot and wipes off the night's mold, almost caressing them as he aligns them back under the cot. Barpa told him everybody knew the squadron was coming, even before the advance Americans arrived. They even hired Barpa to get a crew for raising the tents. He is twelve and darkly handsome. Intelligent. His English limited but direct and clean. Eventually, Hawk thinks, Barpa will steal his boots. He said to Hawk on his second day, "When you leaves you may leave your boots behind."

"It will depend," Hawk shrugged, "on the nature of one's leave-taking."

Barpa had frowned, studied Hawk, nodded and smiled. His teeth were very white. "You will fly into the war beyond the Patkais."

"Yes, Barpa. My plane might fall from the sky or the Naga tribesmen of the hills might eat me."

Barpa's eyes held wide for a moment then smiled. "It is only talk, Lieutenant. It is they who believe you will eat them." He bent and adjusted a boot. "If some day I am allowed to fly with you, I would not be afraid."

"You have been beyond the Patkais, Barpa?"

"Yes, before the trouble. In the valleys there the hunting is good. The Nagas know where." He turned and took down Hawk's shoulder holster hanging from the over-crowded tent pole. He wiped off a trace of mold, slid one finger over the shiny metal of the .45 automatic. "You are sometimes afraid, Lieutenant?"

"Yes."

Barpa stared from the automatic to Hawk.

"The Japs have bigger guns, Barpa."

Alan Hawk turns on his side. Now vaguely awake he inspects the formless tree of weapons, clothing, bags, a green bunch of bananas that is their tent pole. The last, Barpa gift to the tent on his first morning. Water glistens faintly in oily bubbles on the canvas. Lieutenant Robb coughs in his sleep. Lieutenant Schultz mutters unintelligently and snores. Fitzgerald is silent. Hawk closes his eyes, tries and finds a kind of sleep.

He drifts with his plane, the gooney, sliding on high above Sook toward the Mishmi Hills. Whats with Butler and the Mishmis? Is that where the snow leopards are he wants to photo? Hawk banks over the Brahmaputra's sleek brown flow. Ahead, down-river, the port of Dibrugarh and beyond it Tinsukia, a distant blur of white angles and a minaret. He banks toward Sook, angling for his downwind leg. Schultz, flying co-pilot, calls the tower.

"Clear and number one to land" Captain McCabe snaps from the tower. "Where the hell you been, Lieutenant -- doing some sightseeing?" McCabe, Operations, is pissed off because one of his enlisted men on tower duty is sick and no replacement available.

Hawk slides in on his downwind leg, glimpsing below him the long white house of the tea plantation and azure swimming pool where the day before he had glimpsed the woman.

"Oranges!" Schultz exclaims in his sleep. Schultz is from Florida, from which he perceives the rest of the world as an inferior extension. New to the squadron, he'd been Hawk's co-pilot all the way from Sicily. Of German descent, he confided to Hawk in his foul-mouthed manner, that he was positive he'd been sent along with the squadron because they thought he was probably a German spy and didn't trust him on the Italian front.

On their last leg east from Karachi he'd roughed in Hawk with an account of his past. "Was about to buy me a fucking nice little grove near Lake Placid. Four years crop dusting. More single engine time than all the asshole instructors in my flight training. I breeze through Fighter pilot! P 51's! So do they give me one? Shit no! I end up a fucking Troop Carrier chasing Japs out of a goddamn jungle in a gooney bird!"

"Correct, Lieutenant." Hawk tells him -- this as they were passing east over Agra through a circling of vultures -- "and as a co-pilot all you have to do is raise and lower the wheels when I signal and try to hold us on course and level whenever I feel in need of a bit of sleep. Maybe after we get to Sook, if the airstrip is level enough, I'll let you try a landing."

"Fuck you, Hawk! If they'd have given me a chance I'd have signed off and flown for the fucking Nazis!"

"Spoken like a true American!"

Hawk dreams back into the squadron's first day of missions into Burma, finds himself at fifteen hundred feet over Sook, returning from his first "drop" to some unit called Merrill's Marauders in the jungle north of a place called Walawbum. No problems. As he begins his descent he sees the distant Mishmi Hills folding into a cloudless horizon, the jagged mass of the Himalayas serrating its western reaches. Schultz listening to BBC, a recording of Lili Marlene. *They drop toward the airstrip. He motions Schultz for wheels-down, reaches up and switches to tower frequency. The gooney shudders slightly as the wheels drop. He throttles back. Flaps down a half. Below them, on their downward leg, the Indian men and women working on widening the airstrip move in a kind of sinuous ballet, baskets of rock and earth on their turbaned heads. Abruptly the air becomes a barnyard of sound -- a Jap transmitter in the hills trying feebly to jam reception, everybody in the air visiting, McCabe blasting from the tower* ". . . a goddamn flock of crows coming in to roost! Shut up!"

"Why Captain," *somebody calls,* "that's not a nice way to talk to us. You've hurt our feelings."

"Sounds like wise-ass Bierman," *Shultz observes.*

Another voice -- "Where is that whiskey you've been promising, McCabe?"

Suddenly the high distant cries of jackals shatter Hawk's dream. He sits up, wide awake in the heavy odors of vegetation, animals, a drone of rain on the canvas, glances at his watch. The luminous numbers read toward four. Abruptly the night splits apart in a bedlam of jackals.

Schultz curses in his sleep. Hawk wonders if the new cook, Manchu, is awake and waiting with his borrowed carbine. A stiletto of scream from the surrounding jungle. Robb thrashes free from his sheet. Fitzgerald sleeps on. Hawk leans back on his elbows as the howling penetrates. The jackals close in.

Manchu's quarters and kitchen are two ancient, mud bricked buildings adjoining the long high-roofed bamboo house, the squadron mess and bar. Newly re-roofed, an overlay of metal over thatch. Attached to this Manchu is in the process of erecting various wire enclosures where he will keep his constantly changing wild supplies -- a pig-wallow, a chambered habitat for rabbits, a long screened chicken-run, several penned goats and a couple of tethered dogs. The dogs, Manchu has assured all, are not to eat but scare away the jackals. But in the first raid, the dogs, magically, had become silent, flattened extensions of the earth, only rising to bark fretfully after the jackals had vanished.

"You awake, Hawk?" Robby whispers.

Hawk swings his legs from under the sheet. Sweat beads his shoulders. A drop ices down his spine.

"Beats the hell out of me," Robb says. "How they're going to get at the chickens this time. Manchu got new wire."

The jackals do not raid every night. Sometimes, Manchu had explained, they merely come to circle and intimidate. The dogs know this and are cocky loud. And in spite of his borrowed carbine it is not the loss of chickens that Manchu bemoans. The squadron mess is well-funded. Rather he speaks brokenly of evil spirits, malignant creatures who have tracked him from his distant homeland. McCabe asked him why he didn't summon his bloody dragons for their protection.

"No, it is not possible!" Manchu had waved an admonishing hand before McCabe. "Chinese dragons do not walk on foreign soil."

But this night the jackals come on, a clamorous surge between the tents to assault the wire barricades. The feathered bedlam is cut by a tearing of wood and metal and Manchu's high scream of rage. Then as quickly as they came, the jackals are gone on a sibilant rush of paws, pursued only by the dogs fretful barking. Manchu's keening slides through a rush of rain. Hawk sleeps again, awakes as the light of dawn is filtering through the canvas, the rain still solid. Is this the beginning of the monsoon? In April? Maybe they'll be out by late June. Hawk becomes aware of a rich, familiar stench rising about him. He rolls and stares down at a pancake of steaming fecal matter, then up into the red-lipped anus of a Brahma cow taking shelter from the rain. He reaches, punches its side. The animal barely moves.

"That god-damned cow," Hawk announces, keeping his voice level, "is in our tent again."

"O.K. this time I'll kill the sonofabitch!" Schultz's cot crashes over as he dives for the tent pole.

"No!" Robby and Fitz cry out.

In the damp confines of the tent the sound of the .45 is a physical blow. The cow jerks, shambles from the tent in a swirl of flying urine. Schultz stands motionless staring down at the .45 in his shaking hands. "Next time," he mutters, "next time, by the Jesus, sacred or not, the fucker dies!"

From the distant mess comes a faint clatter of crockery and metal. Manchu's voice trembles in one of its higher octaves, screaming at his mess boys. From the airstrip rolls a low blend of thunder as the flight mechanics check out their goonies, just in case the weather lifts.

"Good morning, Lieutenants." Barpa smiles into the tent, turns and draws the flaps wide aside and secures them. "Rain is now soon over. How everything go?" He wears a spotless white shirt loose over dark shorts, his black hair parted and combed flat. He glances down at Hawk's boots beneath the cot and smiles again.

2

MAJOR Butler's typed notice thumbtacked to the bulletin board outside the thatch-roofed officer's mess and given authority by Lt. Colonel Tyrone's flourish of a signature: APRIL 24TH- - - SQUADRON MEETING IMMEDIATELY FOLLOWING BREAKFAST. 8:30 SHARP. NO EXCUSES. PER ORDER, MAJOR BUTLER.

Hawk returns to the tent. Barpa has already cleaned out the cow shit and raked the dark soil into neat swirls except beneath where Schultz still lies entangled in a twisted sheet. He moans, sits up abruptly and glares beyond Hawk at Barpa, perched on Hawk's cot, polishing the boots. Hawk mentions the meeting to Schultz. No, he tells Schultz, he doesn't know what the meeting is about. Yes, the airstrip is still socked in. No, he will not give Schultz's regrets to the colonel.

Barpa follows Hawk outside, glancing back at the tent. "Sahib, the lieutenant is very angry. He believe I let the cow in. He say he think maybe he kill me."

"Mornings are not a good time for the lieutenant, Barpa. Don't worry. Bring him a cup of tea and see he comes to the meeting."

One of the long mess tables has been placed across the farther end of the mess. Manchu has spread a white cloth over it. He steps back, beckons toward the kitchen entrance. Three mess boys, white-trousered acolytes, glide in, each bearing a polished brass salver of fruit and three carafes. Manchu smoothes the white cloth and steps back, motioning the boys forward and folding his great arms atop his paunch. Wrapped in a sarong-like girdling of bright cloth, he appears to Hawk as some potentate arrived from an ancient eastern city, some Xanadu which he proclaims the high and shining center of the earth. He would bring some sense of ceremony to this sweltering outpost where ignorant armies clash by day and night.

Major Butler, Intelligence, and Captain McCabe, Operations, come forward from their tables to stand behind the bamboo chairs Manchu has produced. They leave the center one for Colonel Tyrone. Butler sits, leans forward to lift his carafe. There is a sharp clap of hands. One of the boys comes trotting as Manchu hisses a command. He is followed by the other two bearing trays shimmering with glasses. The first boy glides before Butler, takes his carafe, a glass, and pours.

Colonel Tyrone arrives, removes and places his pith helmet before him on the table, tugs his bush jacket straight, stares out over the tables until the mess is silent. Thin-faced, lean, stiff-lipped, the Colonel reminds Hawk of a modern Major-General out of the *Pirates of Penzance*. He bends and adjusts his carafe, straightens and nods to Butler who rises, fumbling a sheaf of papers.

Jedd Butler is wearing regulation dress, pressed khakis and tie. Perhaps it's his age, Hawk reflects, that gives him the appearance of having stepped out of W.W.I.

"Now, first things first," Butler says briskly in his mid-western accent which only shrills when he is taxed with the unpleasant. He had been an early air-mail pilot, survived a few crashes, resigned to become an early airline pilot, then joined the Air Corps after the Japs visited Pearl Harbor. Now he flies only occasionally, just enough to give him his flight pay. Mostly checking out new pilots. His consuming hobby is photography, especially animals. He looks the squadron over, his disapproval of their assorted, brief, non-regulation attire quite apparent in his lined, regulation face. "So, gentlemen, which of you cowboys has been buzzing elephants out beyond Sumprabum on your way back from your 'drops'?"

Outside a bird on their roof sings off-key to their silence.

"That means -- " Butler's tone rises a pitch. "That means the Colonel's orders to maintain designated altitudes have been violated." He makes it sound like an accusation of rape.

The bird continues its melodic discord. Butler fingers his tie, tries a conspiratorial smile. "Now look, you all know we haven't got even one extra plane anymore. Anyone wrecking another gooney will spend the rest of his life paying for it. Hard cash. That is if you don't die with an elephant tusk up your ass. O.K.?"

They remain silent. A few glance at Lieutenant Week who had, the day after they arrived, wiped out a gooney while shooting landings. Butler's tone slides to a plea for accord. "It's not that I don't understand how it feels, coming in low over the animals, the bulls raising up their tusks, but after all, we've got a job to do here." His glance finds Hawk. Both know Hawk will not mention Butler's request the day before to co-pilot with Hawk some day. Butler had managed a little side trip up into the Mishmis where a big elephant herd was reported.

"So, Major," Hank Romano calls. "How much you planning on soaking us for wrecking a gooney-bird?"

"Fellas, now come on!" The lines on his face warp into a smile. "This Burma thing aint no R & R party. As Terry McCabe has told you, we've intelligence there's considerable Jap Infiltration everywhere, the Katchin Hills, the Patkais, the

Hukawng and Mogaung valleys. They're not going to drive us out but they could stop us from taking 'Mitch' which is why we are here. Furthermore there's no way of stopping them from setting up along your 'drop' routes and giving you an ass full of lead. We're short of first pilots, short of gooneys. So let's do our job and get the hell back to Sicily."

Abruptly Butler sat down, wiped at his forehead and nodded to Captain McCabe, who rose, leaned down and muttered to Al Tyrone, who nodded. McCabe straightened.

"First item." McCabe jabbed one hand through his sandy hair, dug a slip of paper from his shorts with the other, his red face already prickled with perspiration. His accent is all Boston. "Word is we've started a big push somewhere below Maingkwan. With some luck, the monsoon holding off, the nice way we're supplying Merrill's Marauders, we'll take 'Mitch' in no time. That is, if you jokers don't spend your time buzzing elephant herds. O.K.?"

"Now, second item." McCabe consulted his paper. "Combat missions. As you know, a combat mission is any time you fly south of Shinbwiyan, just over the Patkais. Group Headquarters at Jorhat has that more or less straightened out. On our clear days most of you will be getting three, four combat missions. Of course our flights will get longer as the troops move south out of the Hukawng into the Mogaung Valley. It may be that soon all you'll get for flying beyond Shin is an ice cream cone. But anyway, my point is, your missions are starting to add up. So Group HQ has decided that starting today, every ten combat missions gets you an air medal. O.K.?"

"Can we take the option of ice cream cones, Captain?" Romano yelled.

"Sir." Lieutenant Gimbel stood up. "What about the combat missions we've already flown?"

"They're on the house." McCabe grinned. "Think of them as your contribution to the war effort."

"What about our crew chiefs, Terry?" Lieutenant Ericson, tall, blond and frowning, rose. From Minnesota. An excellent and cautious pilot. "Seeing we're running out of co-pilots, they've all been getting some right seat time."

"And the enlisted men, Terry?" Lieutenant Paul was from Mississippi. "The ones kicking our 'drops' out the back door. Helping with the unloading. That's no picnic. On my last 'drop' I went back to help out and almost fell out!"

"Keep at it, Sam," Lieutenant Cordner yelled. "We may luck out!" A wave of applause.

Hawk leaned back, closing his eyes as McCabe took over, his thoughts turning to the squadron take-off from Comiso days before, images unreeling, Sicily fading, the Mediterranean shelving up against the dark bulk of Africa.

Pantelleria, the small round island off to the west, which the by-passed German garrison still held after the German retreat from Africa. No threat but still recognized as a combat zone. It was where, while based near Tunis, they had flown out the visiting brass from Washington. A circle of the island and return to Tunis (worth an air medal for the brass when they returned to Washington), refueling at war-ravaged Benghasi, then on along the desolate coast, the shambles of Tobruk and out over Homer's wine-dark sea, the coast and desert approaching Alexandria, the shattered carapaces of tanks. He wondering aloud to Schultz how many armies had moved in defeat and victory along that forsaken coast. Schultz's response an obscene rendering of a verse from *Lili Marlene,* Alexandria and the hotel elevator, a missing door and the elevator a floor below but rising as he pitched out, hands clamping at the grease-covered cable just enough to slow his fall. Cairo from the air, the pyramids like old sand castles, camels and people staring up. Tourists beyond Jerusalem. He let Schultz go back and sack out, with Chavez, their crew chief, taking over the right seat while he propped a clipboard in his lap, tried and failed to write a letter home. The Arabian desert, *Arabia Deserta*, T. E.. Lawrence's *The Seven Pillars of Wisdom.* But that was an old war and most of them were dead. Refueling at the oasis of Habbaniya. Had Alexander stopped there? He'd leaned back, slept until Chavez awakened him and

Schultz for the Sharja approach, the long gulfs of Persia and Oman, bare mountains above azure seas where Sinbad had sailed, courtesy of illustrations by N. C. Wyeth. Karachi, temperature 120° India, a tattered oriental carpet, Agra, a glimpse of the Taj Mahal, the sky alive with circling vultures. (Avoid -- can take out the wind-shield of a gooney-bird.) The Brahmaputra winding south out of Assam to the Indian Ocean. Sookerating, a jungle village, tea plantation, raw swath of earth and their airstrip still building.

Someone gave him a jab in the back "applies to all personnel," Terry McCabe was saying, "that means all personnel on any combat mission."

"Sir?" Lieutenant Rogers, sitting ahead of Hawk, rose. A sailor from Connecticut. Yachts. Racing. "Captain," Rogers said, "most of us have, as you said, hauled in a few missions. Any kind of decent weather, we could average four a day. In a month we'll have enough air medals for a fruit salad hanging below our balls!"

McCabe grinned, waved his arms on high to silence their applause. "The higher-up gentlemen, have in their infinite wisdom, foreseen that possibility. Which brings me to item three." Again he glanced at his paper, squinted, turned to Colonel Tyrone. "Al?"

Al Tyrone nodded, rose tall and slim, smoothed at his bush jacket, leaned forward and aligned his pith helmet beside his carafe, carefully unfolded a paper from a jacket pocket, studied it, smiled and began reading in his slow Texas drawl which, according to Fitzgerald, contained the rhythm of Scott Joplin's ragtime. Tyrone had also been born in Texarkana and carted a prized old phonograph wherever he was posted in order to play his collection of Joplin 78's.

"From Group HQ," Al Tyrone read. "In consultation with the commanding officers of all four squadrons of the 64th Troop Carrier Group, now on detached service from Sicily to Upper Assam, India, the following amendment to air medal awards for combat missions will be observed. Each combat mission flown may be credited by the personnel involved either toward an air medal or a two ounce liquor ration." Tyrone paused and smiled benignly as the mess hall came cheering to its collective feet. He raised an admonishing hand and waited until they subsided.

"Officers," he read on, "will accumulate their rations by means of one bottle at a time. Enlisted personnel will exchange mission credits on a daily basis, to be consumed on day earned." Tyrone paused again, looked up, smiled. "Major Butler is working out the details. Questions?"

"How many ounces in a bottle, Colonel?" someone called.

"That depends on the size of the bottle. Major Butler, what size bottle will Headquarters be sending on?"

"Fifths."

"And how many ounces in a fifth, Major?"

"I don't drink." Butler paused. "Sixteen or maybe thirty-two."

Schultz gave a snort and stood up. "A fifth is one fifth of a gallon, for god's sake. A fifth is four fifths of a quart."

"So, Lieutenant," Butler said sharply, "how many ounces in a quart?"

"Jesus!" Schultz exploded. "Thirty-two!"

"So, gentlemen," Butler said grimly, "sixteen combat missions will get you a fifth."

"Beg pardon, Major," Lieutenant Roden said, "but that should get us more than a fifth. Four fifths of a quart is about twenty-five ounces."

Butler's lips twisted crookedly. "I stand corrected by our lead navigator. Let's hope he's as accurate with his charts!"

Al Tyrone rose, a hand waving. "I'm sure we can work out all minor details, gentlemen. Yes, Lieutenant Paul?"

"We get a fifth of what, sir?"

Tyrone looked at Butler who shrugged and looked away. "Rye, I suppose," Tyrone said. "Or maybe bourbon. Isn't that what everybody drinks?"

"We've got a few," Schultz called, "who drink Scotch." He glanced back at Hawk. "*La de da!*"

"We can only wait and see," Tyrone said. "Anything else?" Sam Paul rose again. "I've just figured out that even with three or four missions to a day it will take us a week to get a jug. The enlisted men will be able to start sipping the day the juice rolls in."

"I guess you'll just have to suffer through," Al said.

"I understand," Romano offered, "that Manchu is acquiring access to a line of gin."

"If you like flamingo piss," Murphy added. "He gave me a test run."

Colonel Tyrone tapped firmly on his carafe. "Gentlemen, this has been an interesting discussion. I suggest we do not get bogged down in details. Maybe they'll only send us pints. I'm sure the Major can work things out for us. Now I'd like to get to our last item." He pulled a small white envelope from his pocket, removed a small folded sheet of note-paper. "Gentlemen, we have received an invitation from Major and Lady Greystaff, over whose adjoining tea plantation we take off or land each day. I have, naturally, accepted with great pleasure. Jedd will handle the details of our attendance in accordance with the Greystaffs' wishes. That is all. Captain McCabe."

Terry McCabe rose. "Early noon mess today. All crews report to Operations by twelve sharp. Let's start working on those jugs."

Back at the tents, the rain ending, Barpa had rolled up the tent sides. The women had come and taken away their laundry. Heat hung in the dissolving clouds. Hawk slipped on sneakers and shorts. An old shirt for ground wear in case he had to hang around too long while unloading at Shinbwiyan where the horseflies were as big as sparrows.

"If you think I'm going to waste my time at a goddamn tea party, " Schultz said.

3

*A*PRIL 26*TH* AND THE *L*IKHANI INCIDENT, Hawk writes, though having no intention of writing an account of the disaster. What's Hecuba or Lieutenant Weed to him or he to. . . .He leans forward on his cot so his sweat misses the clipboard propped against his knees. He writes - *IT HAPPENED THREE DAYS AGO. THE THING TO DO IS TO GET IT DOWN AND AWAY.*

The tent is empty. For him a morning off. He stares out between the drawn tent flaps into the heat which is an almost perceptible coiling between the tents. A week at Sook and the airstrip at Likhani hadn't even been mentioned during their first days of indoctrination. Only what waited beyond the Patkai hills, the jungle terrain, valleys and mountains, the Zeros that hung like hornets behind the clouds, how to find and drop to the Chinese and American troops moving south through the jungle. Pilots had been issued heavy, twelve-inch knives, the hilts capped with vicious brass knuckles. Fritz refused his, claiming as a co-pilot he was supposed to be protected by his first pilot. Hawk dropped his in his flight bag hanging on their tent pole.

The Likhani incident. It helped thinking of it as an incident. The kind of thing that was bound to happen. Orders that morning: two planes to Likhani, a small strip in the Patkais beyond Ledo. Being phased out. He and Lieutenant Gimbel were assigned to fly in. Not over the Patkais, it wasn't even worth a combat mission. On top of that, Butler had assigned Schultz to him as co-pilot, putting Weed with Gimbel, even though he'd told Butler he'd had enough of Schultz, was tired of listening to Schultz's cursing and his complaints that he should have been a fighter pilot. Schultz's lack of imagination in cursing was appalling. Hawk told Butler to check out Schultz as first pilot. Schultz was a fine pilot, only needing to be cautioned that the gooney has two engines, should not be used to keep in practice for crop dusting, and should not be looped.

So when Schultz appeared that morning Hawk told him it was a mistake. Schultz was supposed to co-pilot for Gimbel. Schultz muttered something about Gimbel being too much of a hot-shot and slid into the right seat. Besides, he said, Gimbel had never flown in to Likhani. No thanks. Let Weed fly with Gimbel.

"Likhani is narrow and all set about with fever trees," Hawk said. He'd set things straight with Butler.

Hawk did not look forward to Likhani. It was a very short strip, the jungle cleared only at one end so it was a one-way approach, ground soggy, the only way in with a three-point landing at the cleared end. Otherwise a good chance of taking a trek into the high jungle at the farther end. It had only been useful at the start of the push into Burma.

The tower held them on the ground until the planes on missions below the Patkais were off. Then finally, the tower clearing them for take-off and while they taxi down the line, McCabe comes on the air. Hawk was to get rid of his small load of supplies for Likhani and fly on to Shinbwiyan and pick up VIPs and take them on to Taro. Gimbel would return to Sook and another flight to Likhani. Over the radio Gimbel breaks in complaining why does he get all the crappy flights. McCabe tells him to shut up and mind the Likhani airstrip, reported to be a bit wet.

Schultz asked McCabe where Taro was.

"Maps!" McCabe bellows. *"You know, those rolled up pieces of paper behind the cockpit with funny little lines and numbers all over them."*

"Shit, Captain," Schultz said, *"I thought that was our toilet paper."*

Taro, Hawk remembered, was somewhere southwest of Shin, an old, abandoned airstrip used by the Japs in '42 during their push toward India and Imphal.

By then Gimbel, who had taken off first, was a couple of miles ahead and climbing hard. Hawk called him, saying he'd already landed at Likhani and why not let him go in first. Which was obviously not the way to talk to Gimbel, who in his New York way, suggested Hawk 'spin in.'

Fifteen minutes later and the Patkai hills lifting under and ahead of them, Gimbel was higher and maybe ten miles ahead. Shortly the Likhani airstrip became visible, a gash in the jungle atop a long, jungle-covered ridge. Hawk throttled back, deciding to come in low across the strip for a check. He was close in when Schultz pointed ahead and up. Gimbel, already with wheels down, in a steep approach. At the same moment Hawk spotted the dark pools of water lacing the strip.

"Jesus H. Christ!" Schultz yelled.

Gimbel began calling the Likhani control for permission to land, control answering with permission to land, only which plane was landing? Hawk came in low across the strip, banking hard right to see Gimbel coming in too high, nosing down sharply, leveling, then realizing he couldn't make it about the time his wheels hit in a pool of water. The gooney skidded. Gimbel corrected, plunged straight on down the strip and off.. Hawk held in his turn long enough to see the plane's wings fold neatly back as it bored into the jungle.

Hawk dragged on out over the jungle and into a long, low approach, dropping the gooney in with a three-point landing on the end of the strip, then taxiing on toward the torn gash in the jungle. No smoke. GIs and Naga tribesmen were running forward on both sides. The gooney's tail still stood straight. By the time Hawk cut their engines a quick-witted sergeant already had some of his men blocking the way. When Hawk and Schultz came running up he gave them a flick of a salute, yelling at his men to let them through. Things didn't look too bad, he had men in there with fire extinguishers. The air stunk of heat and gasoline.

They clambered over a tangle of smashed limbs. Three GIs were clustered just forward of the tail section, the left wing, folded back, enclosed them. They were motionless, staring up at the hole where the cargo doors had been ripped out. Gimbel sat in the ragged opening, legs dangling, looking nowhere. The acrid stench of gasoline thickened. One of the men turned to them.

"It's going to blow!" he yelled. "And the crazy sonofabitch just keeps sitting there! Tell him to jump!"

Hawk crashed forward, yelling up at Gimbel. He didn't look down, remained motionless.

"Where's Weed?" Schultz bellowed.

Gimbel kept staring nowhere. Hawk nodded to Schultz. They jumped at the same time, each grabbing a foot, yanking Gimbel out and down. He began thrashing about, still silent. The GIs helped get him under control and out to the strip, warning Hawk again to get out. It could explode.

Hawk and Schultz stared back up at the opening where Gimbel had roosted.

"Give me a hand up," Hawk said to Schultz.

Schultz boosted him. He grabbed the edge and pulled himself in, turned and gave Schultz a hand up. Looking up the plane's interior they saw the nose half-torn away, the fuselage twisted. No sign of Weed.

"He probably got out the front," Schultz said. "I'll go tell the men to look out front. Probably lying there."

Hawk edged his way forward. The smell of gas made it hard to breath. He clambered over the smashed bracing behind the navigator's compartment and froze. Weed was looking at him -- that part of him that wasn't in the cockpit. Slightly in profile, Weed's head hung impaled on the shattered end of a massive branch that had slammed high through the nose, leaving Weed's body in the cockpit while carrying his head back into the navigator's compartment. Weed looked better in profile. Half his head was missing.

Back on the ground Hawk sent Schultz off to have the tower report back to Sook, explain and have them send a plane up for Weed's body.

"What about us?" Schultz demanded, his voice uneven.

"We'll unload and go on to Shin and Taro as ordered."

Schultz gave him a weird look, then took off mumbling. The Sergeant already had men up with a stretcher. They emerged immediately looking sick. The Sergeant said he'd make sure they got all the pieces.

Hawk found Schultz sitting below the control tower dragging on a cigarette. "Sook is sending up a small plane. You still planning to fly on to Taro?" Schultz said flatly.

Hawk nodded.

"It's a goddamn shame!" Schultz bursts out. "We should take the body back ourselves. What if it had been one of us!"

Hawk told Schultz to see their plane was unloaded immediately. "No sense you sitting around getting hysterical."

"The hell I am!" Schultz snapped. "What about you. Look at the way your fucking hands are shaking!"

The take-off from Likhani bothered Hawk less than Schultz. He taxied back down the airstrip toward the hole in the jungle, the tail section of the gooney poking from the jungle edge. On take-off Schultz held himself tense, motionless. Hawk lifted from the splatter of muddy pools at full throttle. They roared up over the jungle. Less than half an hour would bring them to Shin. Hawk climbed at a steep low angle, feeling better when he'd put a ridge of the Patkais between him and Likhani. Topping the mountain ridges, they eased down over the green jungle falling away to the Hukawng

Valley. On their right the Ledo Road, a copper snake scaled by truck convoys winding toward the front, miles beyond Shin at Walawbum.

There, word was, the Japs were giving the combined Chinese and American drive a hard time.

Hawk glanced at Schultz who still held himself motionless. He sat stiffly upright, staring ahead. Hawk reached up and switched the radio to alert. Just in case. Even this far north the Japs still raided, hunting gooney-birds, sitting ducks for their Zeros. What you do when an alert comes, Al Tyrone had said, is to get down on the tree tops or hide in a cloud. Hawk thought of faking an alert to jar Schultz back to normal. Better not. Schultz's reactions tended to be unpredictable.

When he spoke to Schultz they were a few minutes from Shin. Hawk told Schultz to get the tower. The tower reported two planes on the ground, one just taking off, the other off the south end with a flat tire.

"You're clear to land straight in. Your cargo is waiting."

"Want to take the landing, Schultz?" It might, Hawk thought, take his mind off Weed.

"Fuck you!" Schultz stared grimly ahead.

Hawk reached down and dropped the landing gear. The departing gooney, from another squadron based at Chabua, lifted off and up past them with a tilt of its wings.

Shinbwiyan had been taken in fierce fighting, most of it destroyed. A few thatched-roof long-houses on the strip's perimeter, an alignment of new troop tents back in the torn jungle, the charred wreckage of two gooneys and some small tanks. Hawk dropped flaps, eased down, managed a stop halfway down the strip, wheeled and taxied up before the tower, a screen-enclosed cabin set on high posts.

"Might as well drive right in," the tower called, *"if you can manage without knocking us down. Bad accident at Likhani?"*

"Whatever you heard," Hawk replied. He glanced at Schultz as he edged forward into the space before the tower. "Get the steps down. Our cargo is probably in a hurry."

"So am I," Schultz said flatly. "I was counting on getting off and taking a piss."

"If you can make it," Hawk said grinning. "Or try from the door."

"Fuck you!" Schultz unsnapped his seat-belt and stamped off down the plane.

Hawk eased the plane about and cut the engines. Three men appeared from a building set some way back from the tower, one tall and in jungle dress that faintly suggested a uniform, the two shorter, darker men in civilian slacks and shirts. All three wore side arms. The three paused and surveyed the plane. Then the tall one said something to the other two. They nodded, thin smiles creasing their dark faces.

"What the shit we got here?" Schultz yelled as Hawk came down the plane to the cargo bay opening, under which Schultz stood zipping up.

Hawk jumped to the ground and walked up to the men.

"Nice of you to come on so quickly," the tall one said. His accent was very English. "We've got our gear back in the shed if you chaps would care to give us a hand." He was older than the other two, a slight graying of sideburns, no insignia, the build of an athlete. "What's the report on Taro, Lieutenant?"

"I've never landed there," Hawk said. "We got a quick briefing -- there's a few old bomb craters messing up one end. Probably a lot of water."

The tall Brit glanced at the other two. "Sounds like the old place, doesn't it."

They nodded. Both were young, lean to the point of wasted, one with the dark face and eyes of an Indian, the other with an oriental cast to his rounder face. They nodded without smiling.

"Come on," Hawk called back to Schultz who had remained by the gooney. "They need a hand." He followed the three, Schultz trailing, back to the shed and a pile of smallish boxes wrapped tightly in waterproof. Schultz immediately grabbed one and heaved it to his shoulder.

"Careful, chum," the Brit said. "Probably wouldn't go off but one can't be sure."

Schultz gave him a glare and stalked off to the plane. They followed. A number of trips and they had everything on board and lashed down. Without a word Schultz went forward into the cockpit. Each of the men had a light, waterproof roll of blankets. They piled them forward against the bulkhead of the navigator's compartment, sat down and lit up.

"Thanks, chums," the Brit called as Hawk went on into the cockpit.

"Chums!" Schultz exploded as Hawk started the engines. "Fucking limey!"

"Ah, your gift for words," Hawk said, calling the tower.

"Up yours, Hawk," Schultz snapped. "Looks like we got a limey, a Hindu and maybe even a Jap spy!" He slouched down in his seat.

The tower cleared them for take-off. Hawk taxied part way down the airstrip, did a one-eighty and jammed the throttles forward, letting the tail lift, then holding the gooney close to the ground, then pulling up hard with a sharp bank to the left. Anger flooded over him. Why the hell hadn't he told Schultz to go fly with Gimbel! He leveled off at 2500, the Chindwin river glinting ahead.

"Get on the goddamn map and give me a heading," he told Schultz. Schultz took his time unfolding it.

"Two hundred and twenty," Schultz finally said, frigging around with a thumb and finger. He let the map drop. "Actually all you got to do is follow the Chindwin river. After a while we'll probably find one of their lousy villages and a bombed-up airstrip. The map says it will be Taro."

"Spoken like an old Florida crop-duster." Maybe Schultz was snapping out of his depression. "Or is it crap-duster?"

"Fuck off, Hawk!"

The Brit came forward, bending between their seats, peering ahead where clouds were rolling in from the southwest. "Monsoon clouds," he said, "but still bloody nice here now. Not so the first time. Japs were chasing us out of Burma, your General Stilwell and all. But that was two years ago, like being in another country. A lot of them are dead."

Schultz glared up at him. Hawk held his breath. Schultz remained silent.

The big Jap push of '42 into India?" Hawk said.

The Brit nodded. "They almost took Imphal, mate. A bloody mess. We got out over the Chin hills." He pointed off to the west. "A flanking attack got us rather chewed up. You chaps think you'll take Mitch?"

Hawk shrugged his shoulders. "All we do is fly the gooneys. Nobody tells us anything. Got a prediction for us?"

The Brit clapped a hand on Hawk's shoulder. "Dare say you'll do it, chum. We're going back in to see if we can, in our way, give you a hand." He straightened. "Guess I'll go back and join my chaps. Don't suppose there's any tea you could break out?"

Hawk shook his head. The Brit waved and disappeared. Schultz jerked forward abruptly, shaking his head.

"Something bothering you, chum?" Hawk grinned at Schultz. "Don't Florida pilots take a break for tea?"

"Up your ass, chum! Tea! Why don't you go back there and make them a cup!" Schultz turned away, staring out his side window.

Their course carried them along the winding Chindwin. The dark forms of water buffalo specked its sand spits. A long canoe, hugging the shore, disappeared abruptly as they passed over. A long stretch of green plain but no elephants. Schultz remained staring grimly nowhere. Far ahead beyond a jungle stand Hawk glimpsed an area of ravaged trees, a ragged plain, a faint, raw strip of earth which had to be the Taro airstrip. Hawk slanted down, crossing the river a few miles upstream, coming in low for a look. No sign of life, only the usual waste of brush, the dark posts of burned buildings already draped in vines. They came over the strip at 200 feet. Not too many bomb craters and those mostly grouped at the eastern end. Beyond the opposite end, the shattered remains of a small temple poked from a clump of trees. Hawk banked, circling to make his approach in over the river and ruin, gesturing to Schultz to drop the wheels. Schultz did, then glanced back down the plane. "Jesus H. Christ!"

Hawk looked back. The three men were now up, strapping on shoulder holsters. Lugers? The oriental-looking one was handing out long, thick-handled knives. Machetes? They looked like an army in the making.

"Maybe we'll have to fight our way out of here," Hawk said, his mind actually on their landing. A wheel landing, he decided. Easier to avoid the craters or get a quick lift-off if things went awry. The Brit should have told them there might be trouble. He held the plane off over a soggy spot, touched down. A slight angle past the first crater, a slight skid and straight on, braking gently, dropping the tail and coming to a stop with a mild lurch into a shallow, water-filled crater.

"If you can manage again, chaps." The Brit was between them again. "A little farther on and a hand with our gear." He checked his watch. "They should be picking us up in minutes."

Hawk gunned the engines, eased on, picking his way around craters. Just before he reached the end of the strip two helmeted soldiers in camouflage appeared ahead from the brush, leading a pack train of three mules, followed by two more men, rifles at ready. Hawk cut the engines.

"Come on, let's give them a hand," Hawk said.

"I'll give them five minutes," Schultz said, following Hawk down the plane where the three were freeing their gear. "It looks like they're expecting a fucking ambush!"

Working together they got the gear out, loaded, and lashed down on the mules while the riflemen kept a constant circling of the plane. Then they headed off into the brush.

"Thanks for the lift," the Brit called from the head of the pack train. "Good show!"

Hawk watched the pack train vanish into the jungle brush, then turned to the plane where Schultz waited impatiently to pull up the steps. "I wonder where they're headed?"

"Who gives a shit," Schultz said. "Let's haul ass!"

Hawk started the engines, worked the gooney around and taxied slowly down toward the smoother end. The ruined temple poking from the trees caught a transient ray of sunlight. He went on, turned, cut the engines.

"What the fuck!" Schultz said.

"Come on," Hawk said. "I've never seen a Burmese temple."

"You crazy? Them guys didn't have all them guns for a sight-seeing trip. I'm staying here. Anything happens, I'm off!"

Hawk went back to the cargo opening, studied the terrain for moments. It looked clear. He jumped down, headed in through the brush, losing sight of the temple behind a screen of thorny trees from which a whirring of pigeon-like green birds screeched off. He pushed on through a tangle of jungle and into a clearing. The remains of the battered temple, a still live palm slanting out beside the remains of smashed limestone steps and broken columns. Uncovered in its center, a headless statue. Buddha? He climbed the steps. Golden traces on the shattered torso. Suddenly the sound of Schultz calling, more impatient than alarmed. He knelt and picked up a stucco fragment, a wash of gold on its reddish surface. Schultz's shouting increased. Clutching the fragment, Hawk ran.

When he reached the plane, Schultz was kneeling at the cargo opening, his .45 at the ready, glaring out toward the jungle. He did not offer Hawk a hand up, rising and stamping up the plane. When Hawk came forward Schultz was slouched in the right seat.

"No," Hawk said. "You're flying us back."

"Is that an order?"

Hawk remained standing, waiting. Above all else Schultz liked to fly. It was time to take his mind off Weed and whatever else was eating at him. Schultz looked up with a disgusted look then yanked himself across into the left seat, started the engines and brought them cleanly off, leveling at 2500 feet.

Hawk relaxed, leaned back, checked the alert channel. Silent. North over the river clouds were breaking over a green and blue world. Somewhere below them a war? He pulled the fragment from his pocket. How many years had the temple been there? How many Burmese had come to kneel? Is being human, he thought, inseparable from suffering? Certainly Weed had no time to suffer. The only thing certain in his own case - flying with Schultz had become insufferable.

Schultz gave him a glare. "What's so goddamn funny?"

Had he been smiling? Hawk leaned forward, checking Schultz's heading. "We can save a few miles by cutting back over Likhani."

"No way!" Schultz jerked so hard on the wheel he momentarily veered from his heading and dropped a couple of hundred feet.

"Look, Schultz, I'm as bothered as you about Weed being killed. But things like that happen. So why don't you calm down. I'm tired of your mouth."

Schultz's stare was accusing. His eyes turned into red-rimmed slits. "Who the fuck was it wanted me to fly with Gimbel this morning? What if I had? Where the hell would I be!"

Hawk leaned back, closed his eyes. Had he heard correctly? He smiled. When the idea came he began laughing. "But of course, Schultz," he said softly, "you're never going to be able to prove I wanted to kill you. I'll deny everything."

Schultz's heavy-lidded eyes came wide open. "I didn't mean that! But just tell me this, where would I be now if I'd agreed to fly with Gimbel?"

"Only one direction that seems suitable, chum. And if you'll bother to look ahead you'll notice you might make it. You're running into the Patkais."

Schultz gave a startled look and pulled up steeply as the land lifted under them. They climbed until the sky opened clearly beyond the hills. Hawk switched from alert to the Sook range. The air was noisy with planes. Everybody all chattering.

Hawk waited until they passed west of Likhani before diverting Schultz's attention from the cockpit, then dropping his arm, he switched off the gas line feeding the right engine. In seconds the engine responded, missing. Schultz gave him an alarmed look. The right engine went dead. They began to lose altitude. Schultz fought to keep them level, throttled the left engine hard forward.

"What the fuck's the matter!"

Hawk shrugged. "I don't intend to go out there for an inspection, chum. How about getting us to Sook?"

Schultz feathered the still spinning right prop, checked and adjusted his controls and worked them into a steady, even descent. Hawk waited until they were only a few miles out before tapping Schultz on the shoulder and pointing down at the closed valve.

"Might as well turn it on and take us in," he said. "You've done a perfect job on single engine."

Schultz gave him a long look, reached down to open the valve, then stopped.

"Fuck you, jack! I'm taking it in the way it is! Call the goddamn tower!"

Hawk called the tower. *Coming in on single engine*. Which Schultz did, bringing them down and in on a long, curving approach to land smoothly. Trailed by the squadron's combination fire truck and ambulance, they taxied from the strip and down the line. Schultz turned in and cut the engine.

"So O.K.," Hawk said. "We'll just forget how this happened to happen. You've done a first-class job. Consider yourself checked out as a first pilot. I'm sure Butler will be glad to sign the necessary documents. We're through!"

Schultz looked stunned. "Well, gee, Hawk. Thanks. Sorry I got a bit out of hand."

"Forget it." Hawk unbuckled his safety belt and rose. "Just thinking of myself. This way I won't have to fly with you again. I'll make new arrangements to have Gimbel kill you!"

4

CAST in the green light of the late afternoon sun, the Greystaff's tea plantation seemed to Hawk an entrance into another world. The white gate barrier rose between royal palms. A lean, turbaned Indian smiled their jeep through. Major Butler slowed, the drive winding in between flowering shrubs, a variety of palms and a sweep of tailored lawn, a brief vista of the plantation beyond the long white house. Butler let the jeep roll to a stop before wide wooden steps descending from a wide columned verandah. Everything, Hawk thought, except a tapestry of peacocks.

A young, dark-skinned boy in white hurried down to them. Above, an elderly, heavy-set man of florid complexion limped to the porch edge. Adjusting his bush jacket he glowered down at them.

"Leave your machine running, Major," he called gruffly. "Masoud will see to it."

"That's Major Greystaff," Butler said softly to Hawk.

As Cordner, Fitz and Ericson climbed from the rear seat Butler lifted his heavy camera case from between his legs. "I was thinking of bringing it in," he muttered. "The old boy has some absolutely incredible heads. Think he'd mind?"

"I think he might," Hawk said. "Better ask."

"No need to worry about your gear," Greystaff called down. "Just leave it in the machine."

Butler led them up the steps as a pleasantly smiling woman in a light, flowered frock joined Major Greystaff.

"Jolly good of you to come," Greystaff said as Butler made the introductions. "Molly has so wanted to meet some Americans." They all glanced up as a gooney roared overhead, its shadow slapping the palms.

They were the first group of five from the squadron chosen for the Greystaff's afternoon teas.

Colonel Tyrone, concerned with protocol, had gone with Butler the previous day for a brief call on the Greystaffs. It was essential, Tyrone informed them, that they were to set a proper tone. Dress khakis, of course. No sandals or sneakers. Bush jackets were out because they had not been tailored and looked like potato sacking.

Ties not required but only the top button of the shirt to be left undone. They would arrive at four thirty and leave promptly at six. Major Greystaff, though not in the best of shape, would give them a short tour of his plantation and be delighted to show them his famous trophy collection. Tea would be served on the patio beside the pool. No, Major Greystaff had made no mention of swimming.

Hawk was surprised that not all the officers were interested in attending a tea. Al Tyrone announced they would all be expected to attend, Major Butler in charge of groupings. Schultz immediately put in a plea that he be allowed to join the first group. Butler said he was sorry, he'd already made up the first list, which included Hawk and Fitz. Two from one tent was enough.

Back in the tent Schultz had turned on them. "Why the hell should it be you and Fitz?" he snapped.

"Because," Fitz replied, "we are suave, dashing and from New England. What does a Florida 'cracker' do at a tea party?"

"Fuck 'em!" Schultz snarled.

"Exactly," Fitz said.

Major Greystaff led the way in through a long, paneled foyer past a mounted pair of elephant tusks facing a slender-necked gazelle, a delicate lyre-like curve to its horns. Centered over the arched entrance to a light-filled room, a massive shaggy head with ox-like horns hooked down at them. Hawk and Fitz, walking beside Lady Greystaff, paused.

"A gaur or seladang, Lieutenants," she said. "Quite rare now. John bagged it many years ago when we first came to the plantation. That was after the first great war. John had been with Allenby in Arabia. When this war came they told him he was too old to serve. John was very upset but we chose to stay on. After all, they still must have their tea back home." She paused and gave them a girlish smile. "It's so nice for you Americans to come way out here to give us a hand."

"Thank you, Lady Greystaff." Hawk smiled.

"We'll do what we can," Fitz said.

"And please call me Molly, young men. I haven't had many opportunities for that in a long time."

They joined the others gathered in the living room about a sideboard set with glasses, a punch bowl and a tall vase of roses. The lemonade had been laced with bright slivers of some scarlet fruit that hung like goldfish in the translucent liquid. A young, slim girl in a white sari, her large brown eyes curious but circumspect, served them from a gleaming silver ladle.

They sipped. Lady Greystaff moved to her husband's side and nodded gently, clasping her hands in a girlish gesture. Major Greystaff cleared his throat and gave them a challenging smile.

"Dare say you have a nice little war going on beyond the Patkais. Close call. We need you chaps. Course it's not like the old days when you slogged through the desert by foot and camel. But you've got the Nips on the run. When we first came out here there was splendid shooting in the Hukawng valley and along the Chindwin. Have you taken Maingkwan yet?"

Greystaff blinked around at them. They waited for Butler to reply. Colonel Tyrone had been emphatic there was to be no talk of their activities.

Well -- " Butler hesitated. "Everything is fluid. Command doesn't keep us up on how things are going."

"You've got planes, Major," Greystaff said emphatically. "See more from them than astride a camel. BBC claimed last night you'd taken Maingkwan." Greystaff frowned.

"Actually, sir," Hawk offered, "we don't take anything. We haul supplies, kick food out our cargo doors to various units and buzz elephant herds on our way home."

It eased things.

"Got one of my best buffalo along the Chindwin below Taro," Greystaff said. "That was years ago. Caught me on a spit. Edge of the river. Biggest buff I'd ever faced. Not more than ten feet from me before I dropped him. Got to shoot for the nose in cases like that. Great horns. Fifty-one-inch spread. Like to have a look at him?"

"I think, dear," Molly Greystaff said softly, "we must do our little plantation tour first. Then, afterwards, tea and your trophy room."

"Of course, my dear." Greystaff blinked and led the way from the room through a pair of open glass doors and along a vine-roofed patio, low palms shielding the pool beyond. They came to a garden-like planting of shrub-like trees fragrantly in flower.

"Bergamot," Molly Greystaff said, pausing docent-like in their midst. "A sort of wild lime. The skins' aromatic oil is used in perfume."

When they approached a wide, louvered door in a white-washed brick wall it opened silently outward, managed by a small, white-clad boy who stood aside smiling as they filed out into rows of ordered, clipped tea shrubs folding into the distance. Molly Greystaff led them a short distance between the tea shrubs, then paused and turned, waiting for an overhead plane to drone past.

"From these shrubs we get our black tea, souchong," she said, still the docent. "We maintain our quality, picking only the two terminal buds for fermenting. However the war has made it difficult for us to get enough pickers. You have lured many away to work on your airstrip. But fortunately now is not one of our flush or growing periods. The next will come with the monsoon. Are there any questions?"

"If you don't mind, my dear?" Major Greystaff had trailed them and stood red-faced and perspiring, wiping at his neck. "I'll go back and wait by the gate. The boy has let the hinges get in terrible shape. Must speak to him."

Lady Greystaff nodded and led them on along a maze of paths between the dark-green pruned shrubs. After a while, deep in a labyrinth, she stopped and gestured about her. "Now these, you'll notice are a different variety." No one had but they all smiled and nodded. "From these we get our gunpowder tea, a green tea, which is not fermented. Not widely grown in Assam but doing nicely."

They went on past a white screened gazebo and, sooner than expected, emerged abruptly from the shrubs from a different angle to see Major Greystaff propped on a low bench beside the gate, still wiping at his face and neck. The boy stood patiently beside the open entrance.

"Warrant Molly's shown you more than you bargained for," he boomed, heaving himself erect. "No place to be, out in this heat." He led them back through the bergamot and along the patio.

Hawk trailed, admiring the long pool partially shielded from the house by small palms and a twining curve of scarlet bougainvillea. Yes, he thought, obviously too much having a bunch of Americans crashing about in the water. Would they miss him if he slipped gently in? Abruptly he stopped. Beyond the bougainvillea, by the pool, he made out the lovely profile of a woman. She reclined in a deck chair, reading. A sheen of shadowy sunlight gilded a bare arm and shoulder. As he looked she turned a page. Was she aware of him?

"This time of day," Lady Greystaff said, magically beside him, "the pool is unpleasantly warm. Evening or toward morning is best."

"Yes, of course," Hawk replied, finding it difficult to give her his complete attention. The woman, a young woman, had glanced their way. Lady Greystaff smiled and waved a hand.

"It would not be improper if I were to introduce you, Lieutenant, but helpful if I knew your name."

"Alan, Alan Hawk."

"Her name is Jamila and she is very dear to us. Please, come with me."

She led him from the patio between the palms. At their approach the young woman laid aside her book, shading her eyes with a slim hand. As she looked at him Hawk felt his breath catch. A shimmer of white cloth partly covered her jet-black hair. Sloe-eyed. Her sari traced the curves of her body.

"Jamila, may I present Lieutenant Alan Hawk." Molly Greystaff's voice carried a hint of command. "He is one of the American flyers who wakes us each morning. Alan, this is my daughter, Jamila Rahma."

Hawk made a small bow. She sat up, extending her hand. Hawk stepped forward, finding her grip very firm. Below her high cheekbones her skin held a faint cosmetic blush. Her look was searching, as if regarding him from a great distance. He found himself unable to release her hand.

"Forgive my staring," he said. "Something about the way you were sitting. An illustration from a book when I was young. There was an azure sea and pirates. Maybe they were stealing you or maybe you were a pirate queen. I forget." He released her hand.

"Why not both, Lieutenant?" Her fine brows arched as she glanced past him to Lady Greystaff, nodding as if in confirmation of something. She gave him a faint smile.

"So, you are one of the selected ones, Lieutenant." It was not a question. Her accent quite English.

"Well actually -" He paused. "I mean, what I should say -" Hawk heard his words stumble into silence.

"I'll leave you, Alan Hawk," Lady Greystaff said, "to extricate yourself as best you can. But briefly. The others will be coming soon from the trophy room and you must join us for tea."

"Thank you, Lady Greystaff." Hawk smiled after her, then down at Jamila, who had raised her book as if to continue reading.

"I've never been much good at extricating myself from anything," Hawk said. "This is one of the occasions when I welcome whatever handicaps I bring." He smiled down at her. She studied him for a moment; then laid her book aside. Her dark eyes contained a soft, yellow light.

"Americans;' Jamila said. "That was Molly having fun. She believes I dislike all Americans, even though I've insisted one cannot logically eliminate a whole nationality."

"I doubt we humans do very much on a strictly logical basis, Jamila." He paused. "Forgive me. May I call you Jamila? It has a nice sound."

She shrugged. "Seeing you've already begun, why not?"

He wondered then about her age. Surely as old as he. She leaned forward, gesturing to a wooden stool behind her bamboo chair, indicating he place it before her. Drawing it up and sitting down he noticed the flecks of mud which had destroyed Barpa's immaculate polish.

"Naturally I don't dislike all Americans," Jarmila said softly. "But I've lived quite a bit in England, Lieutenant. In fact was there when you Americans decided to join our war. It's just that so often they tend to irritate me."

"Wake you up too early every morning?" He smiled.

She gave him a long glance, dark eyes serious, but her lips curving. "I'm serious Lieutenant. It's just that Americans never seem to have any loyalties."

"Please," he said, "I'd prefer it if you called me Alan. First names. An American habit. We do have our loyalties or else would we know who we are? But they are not words"

"I'm not sure I understand."

"Loyalties are the things we do, not what we say."

She studied him again.

"We have been told, Jamila, that Americans have an exuberant insensitivity. Will that do?"

She smiled, glanced down at her book, bent over an illustration. "It's a start. Pirates are always exuberant, aren't they?"

"With their treasure. And yours?"

"Oh these are not pirates. Gods." Her eyes lighted. "And they are never exuberant. They sit in solitude, some by an azure sea, others above mountains, Some -- " She held up her open book. Tendrils of a rainbow encircled an embracing couple. It's in Hindi."

Above them two jade-green birds, breasts iridescent, beaks of coral, commenced a soft muttering. He glanced up. Should he suggest some kind of omen? He said, "They sound like mourning doves from my own country."

"Green pigeons," Jamila said. "Rather messy things. Do you like wild creatures?"

"I grew up in a country of wild creatures. So far I've seen a few birds, a glimpse of jackals at night. Down in Burma we sometimes see a herd of elephants."

"You like to hunt?"

"Not really."

"But you must see the Major's trophy room. He is very proud of it."

Hawk shrugged. "Right now I much prefer two green parrots and a swimming pool, even though we were cautioned not even to think about swimming."

Jamila smiled. "I believe the Major let it be known he didn't want a bunch of American yelling and thrashing about."

"Which we do exuberantly." Hawk watched Jamila's eyes shade from grave to luminous. She sat up, her sari slipping from her shoulders, revealing a black swim suit, as she placed her book to one side.

"And what is this country where you grew up, Lieutenant?"

"Please, my name is Alan. My country is called Maine, a state on the Atlantic, the farthest northeast corner. Lots of deer, moose and bear."

Jamila smiled. There were spaces between her beautifully white teeth. She adjusted the strap of her swim suit. "There are many animals here. They don't interest me much. I am more concerned about the many people everywhere whose world has changed or about to change. I listen and read about the war, actually the many wars. For instance, your war south over the mountains in Burma.

"They say your squadron came from the Mediterranean. And we hear of the great air battles over Europe and the coming invasion to destroy the Nazis. Tell me, did you fly all the way here just to see Burmese elephants?"

"Yes. But first there were the pyramids of Egypt. Most of all I wanted to see the Taj Mahal. Unfortunately we were in a hurry and I only saw it from the air. No one tells us what we are here for. Some say to save India from the Japanese, others to save India from the English. Or is it to save China?" Hawk paused, smiled up at the pigeons and took a chance. "Maybe I flew all the way here just to meet you."

Jamila laughed softly "And when Americans are not bobbing about in swimming pools they are making passes at every woman they meet?" Her glance was accusing.

"Exactly," Hawk said. "But so far not much luck. I can't even get you to call me Alan. Perhaps that's because you must have spent a lot of time in England." She frowned, puzzled.

"Your accent, Jamila, is very English."

"It probably goes deeper than that, Lieutenant. I suspect if the war hadn't happened, I'd still be there."

"But you were born here?"

"In Sadiya, a small river town east on the Brahmaputra near the Mishmi hills. I doubt you ever fly in that direction."

"We fly where we are ordered, Jamila. Against the main of Poland, if necessary."

She frowned, studied him, then abruptly smiled. "I'll take a chance. Against the main of Poland. I had several courses in Shakespeare." She stared up at the pigeons, shook her head in frustration. "I give up."

"Close enough," he said. "From Hamlet. As Shakespeare suggests, whoever tells soldiers the real reason they go to war? You've studied then in England. How did you get here?"

She closed her eyes, was silent for a moment. "I came to the Greystaffs when I was very young. Brought down here on a river barge, certain I had been sold into slavery. At first I was nothing but the youngest of the Greystaffs' servants." She smiled. "Now I'm their daughter and I help the Major manage his tea business."

"When were you last in England?"

"In forty-one. My school got bombed. We had already been moved outside London, toward Coventry. Then the Major, in India, had a heart attack. Molly needed me to help out. Strings got pulled. I ended up on a RAF transport manifest as miscellaneous cargo to Casablanca, the rest of the way here by lorry, camel, boat and train. Since then I've taken care of the bookkeeping. Molly handles the plantation, the Major does what he can and Molly and I take turns at Dibrugarh out on the river. That's where we ship out our tea while keeping an eye on our not altogether trustworthy agent. I shall return to England as soon as the war ends."

"Soon, Jamila? Three months into forty-four and we're only a hundred miles into Burma."

"I know. Only as far as Maingkwan."

"How do you know? I mean - " He stopped for she was smiling and he knew what he'd done.

"You see, if I was a spy, I'd be a very good one, Lieutenant. That's why they told you not to talk about your war."

She'd nettled him, and he said with a touch of impatience, "Then you must know when the war will end."

Jamila shrugged, then smiled. "A year, Lieutenant. It's what the Major claims. He has an excellent short-wave, and also friends on Mountbatten's staff at Kandy. Yes, the talk is, a year from when you move into Europe your war will be over."

"My war? Not your war, too?"

She studied him. "My war is the one that frees India, forces England to leave India. Is that why you're here?"

Though her voice remained soft, even warm, Hawk suddenly felt the space between them widen. Not so much a drawing back as a deepening of the silence between them. "I'm here, Jamila, because this is where I was told to come. A patch of ground."

"And your war over the hills in Burma brings freedom for whom?"

"I don't know." He shrugged, annoyed, not at his inability to answer her question but that he'd lost control of the direction of' their conversation. He shrugged again and tried a gambit. "I assume your Mr. Gandhi is handling that department for you. I've read of him and admire him."

"Perhaps you should have some choices, Lieutenant. The Japanese have attacked India to free us from the English, or they attack us merely to gain India. Or is it the Chinese troops have been brought here to drive the Japanese from China? Or to aid your country so they can continue to supply Chiang Kai-Shek in his struggle to free his people from Mao Tse-Tung's Communist forces -- or vice versa? Then, of course, we have the Indian troops fighting with the Japanese to drive both Americans and British back where they came from." Jamila paused, adjusted her sari. "So tell me, Lieutenant - which way do your loyalties lie?"

"They still need sorting out, Jamila. But tell me, as a spy, how long will it be before I'll be free to leave India?"

Her eyes darkened, flashed angrily. "If you don't keep on losing planes like you did at Likhani, you will go when you capture Mytikyina, the place you call 'Mitch'."

He stared at her. She leaned back. "I'm sorry, I shouldn't have mentioned it. It's just that word about everything spreads so quickly. Everyone talks." She stared upward. He noticed the pigeons were gone. "You must believe I did not mean to cause you pain."

"I'll believe you if you'll call me Alan."

They looked toward the house when Molly called. "Please, Jamila. They are beginning to come from the trophy room."

"Coming, Molly." Jamila rose, wrapping her sari carefully.

"If we could talk again, Jamila."

"I'm sorry, Alan." She extended her hand. "It has been interesting talking with you. But there is so little time between wars."

He followed her between the palms to where Lady Greystaff stood talking to Fitz in the wide open doorway. Fitz's appraisal took in Jamila, a raised eyebrow for him.

"Lieutenant Hawk," Lady Greystaff said, "your Major Butler and John are still in the trophy room. John will be extremely disappointed if you do not look in."

Down a hallway lined with photographs, mezzotints and prints of hunting scenes. Hawk entered the trophy room beneath an arch of gleaming tusks. The room itself was quite dim. Electric spotlights. A musty, animal odor hung heavily between the walls festooned with heads that gave off a dark sense of a not entirely peaceful or subdued jungle kingdom. The Major and Butler were in a far corner staring up at a rhino head. They turned and waited as Hawk paused to stare up where an immense boa constrictor, looking as if it had only recently fed, slid across the high white ceiling above the press of horned and fanged beasts.

"Come here, Hawk," Butler said. "Something I want to show you." He moved impatiently as if needing to find a bathroom.

"It must have taken a long time, sir," Hawk said to Major Greystaff, glancing about the room. "Really impressive."

"Thank you, Lieutenant. From every continent. Take the big cat up there. From your own continent. A jaguar from British Honduras. I was just a lad when I dropped him."

"And this, Hawk," Butler said, voice rising, grabbing Hawk's sleeve and pulling him toward the far wall. "You've got to see it. Absolutely incredible!"

It was only an enlarged and slightly faded photograph, wreathed in a frame of golden vines.

"So, it's an elephant," Hawk said.

"Jesus!" Butler muttered. "Look! Not just an elephant. It's an albino elephant! Practically a mammoth. The Major says it may still be alive in the Mishmi hills. Correct, Major?"

Greystaff nodded. "Snapped it a little over ten years ago. 'Course I'd had to give up hunting by then. Not that they'd have let me, anyway. Wouldn't have been cricket. Absolutely magnificent beast. They took me to see the elephant after I promised not to spread the word. Wouldn't even let me have a gun bearer." He edged toward the door.

Hawk studied the photograph. The albino stood in a clearing, ears flared, head raised, enormous tusks that must have glinted in that long ago sunlight.

"Didn't have real decent film," the Major said. "Developing damn poor. Intended to return. No luck. Bloody heart started acting up. We'd better go now and join the others."

At the tables the talk turned to flying as incoming flights droned over them. There was a choice of black or green gunpowder tea and small sweet biscuits. Hawk looked about but Jamila did not appear. Molly Greystaff caught his eye and smiled. Then it was time to leave.

On the verandah, shaking hands with the Major and Molly Greystaff, Fitz came up to Hawk.

"Trust you to manage something like that," he breathed. "She's really beautiful."

"She was very pleasant," Hawk replied casually. "Probably no chance to see her again."

They descended the steps as their jeep was brought up by Masoud. Butler got behind the wheel. The others piled in the rear. Hawk slid in beside Butler, found some rupees in a pocket and handed them to Masoud.

"In fact," Fitz said, leaning forward to Hawk, "she's up there now at the curve in the porch, looking at me." He gave Hawk a shoulder punch and leaned back.

Butler raced the engine, leaned toward Hawk, eyes excited. "Look, no talk about that albino elephant. I've got this really great idea. I've been thinking and just maybe we could turn this into something big."

5

COLONEL Al Tyrone arrived early next evening for the meeting of all flight personnel. Another bad flying day had held them to under ten missions. Three missions canceled.. Captain McCabe, Intelligence, had spent the afternoon piecing together blown-up copies of section maps covering the squadron's area of operations and thumbtacked them to a side wall over an assortment of pin-up posters.

"Where's Butler?" Tyrone demanded. "I wanted to talk to him about easing off on his time snapping shots of family life here in the compound and get more action shots."

"He was checking out Schultz," McCabe said. "They went up about three, came in about five. Butler mentioned he wanted a closer look into the Mishmi hills."

"What for?"

McCabe shrugged. Colonel Tyrone stared at the maps, focusing on the rumored objective of their war, the rail town of Myitkyina below the Kumon range. "Nice job with the maps, Terry."

"Thanks. There may be some rioting about my covering the pin-ups."

Major Butler, followed by a cluster of flight personnel, pushed in carrying a small burlap sack. It rattled of glass when he placed it on the table below McCabe's maps. He untied the sack and with a flourish withdrew three bottles, pulled an opener from a pocket and pried off a cap. "Ale, gentlemen. Sorry I'm late, Colonel. My conference with Manchu required some diplomatic pressure. Give us an official testing, Al." He proffered the bottle. "Still even a bit cool. Real British ale. Manchu claims it's fresh in."

Al sipped, took a longer sip, passed the bottle to McCabe. The enlisted flight personnel crowded forward.

"Manchu says he can tap into a regular supply from Dibrugarh, back on the river. Only payment must be in American dollars."

"The source?" Tyrone asked.

"Manchu said he could not reveal that. But he said absolutely no problem and price firm at thirty dollars a case, which includes middlemen and transportation."

"And Manchu," McCabe added. He paused and looked at Colonel Tyrone.

"I believe a sampling by all personnel present is the fair and democratic way to handle this, Captain."

"How'd the check-ride with Schultz go, Jedd?", Tyrone inquired.

"We've got another first pilot." Butler took a pull of his ale. He thought of where he and Schultz had flown, the lovely Mishmi hills lifting east into China. How from the right seat he'd directed Schultz in long patterns over the jungle, scattered villages and clearings. Somewhere below them the great white elephant still wandered.

"Which leaves us with only three co-pilots -- Christopher, Fitzgerald, and Murphy," Al Tyrone said. "We'd better get everybody checked out, use the navigators and crew chiefs for co-pilots and hope for replacements."

He glanced over the now crowded room. He wanted everyone in the squadron to have a real sense of where they were, their major objectives and the possible length of time they'd be in the CBI theater. Not that morale was low. On the contrary, he'd remarked to Butler, in spite of the heat and humidity, the jackals and a reported snake in one of the enlisted men's tents, everyone appeared to be surviving. He'd caught McCabe's lifted eyebrow and said that fortunately he was able to get off a wire to Lieutenant Weed's family.

"Who's Officer-of-the-Day?" Col. Tyrone asked Butler.

"Romano," Butler said, sipping his beer. "He's going to do a thorough check of the airstrip patrol and a perimeter check of quarters. Manchu claims not all his livestock is being ripped off by the jackals."

"I wouldn't give a rat's ass what Manchu tells us," McCabe said. He chug-a-lugged his bottle and banged it down on the table. "You've gotta watch the gooks!"

"He's a damn good cook," Butler said. "I hired him. My responsibility if he starts selling our planes."

Colonel Tyrone smiled. "It looks like we're all about here. Terry, if you'll call the meeting to order."

McCabe rose, grabbed his bottle and thumped it steadily on the table until the room quieted. "Gentlemen," he called, pausing to wonder about his salutation, seeing this was a general squadron meeting of both officers and enlisted men. Hell, why not! "Gentlemen," he called again. Also, having been an enlisted man once himself, he didn't care what Colonel Al Tyrone might think.

"Hey, Captain," someone yelled. "When you passing out beer to the rest of the troops?"

"After you all shut up and listen to what the Colonel has to say. O.K.? Now Colonel Tyrone has called the meeting to give you some answers on why we're here, our major objectives, and when we might be leaving the CBI"

"And also where you latched on to the beer!" Romano yelled.

"The reason you find us here at the table with bottles," McCabe replied, "is that we felt duty-bound to sample our new stock to make sure it meets the high standards of jungle juice you're used to guzzling." McCabe waited for the applause to subside. "I'll now turn the meeting over to Colonel Tyrone."

McCabe sat down and Tyrone rose, wishing he had the easy style that was McCabe's hallmark. This evening he had chosen the cool elegance of loose white slacks and shirt, a dash of blue from a silk scarf folded under his shirt collar. He wore only his lieutenant colonel's insignia and pilot's wings. Rising, he stepped forward, waited until his audience mumbled into silence. He smiled. Not really a forced smile, Hawk thought. More a real smile worn away by his many years of military service. Had Tyrone, Hawk wondered, now accepted the fact of being, after so many years, no more than the Commander of a Troop Carrier Squadron stuck away in an unimportant corner of the war? Tyrone tried but never seemed quite able to bridge the distance between himself and his men. Certainly he was incapable of the rough arrogance of McCabe or the chameleon-like ability of Butler to blend with all. Still, Hawk doubted anyone in the squadron disliked Al Tyrone.

"On April 10th," Tyrone began, "we flew in. On the following day we flew our first missions. It's now April 25th. In spite of poor weather we've flown nearly fifty combat missions over enemy terrain. I'm proud of our squadron!"

Tyrone paused and waited. The squadron waited.

"So tomorrow, men, we'll fly again, our drops a little farther south along the Stilwell Road. We'll be dropping to General Stilwell's men, our Chinese allies and Merrill's Marauders. Keeping them moving forward is our mission. As to when we'll be leaving the CBI depends on the overall situation here and how things go in Europe."

Again Tyrone paused, waited, shrugged inwardly. Hell, his speeches never did excite anybody. He slid a small notebook from his hip pocket, flipped it open and glanced down over his neatly entered list of items. For the first time he smiled, sure his first entry would amuse. He hesitated. Might it not be judged inappropriate? A revelation of his questionable judgment? The item, one of several he'd picked up at Group Headquarters Command in Jorhat the previous day. He reread it silently.

"General Joseph Stilwell, Commander of the Allied Forces on northern Burma has trouble dealing with Chiang Kai-shek and often refers to him as 'Peanut'."

He wondered now why he'd jotted it down? Admiration for a man who was known for his courage in saying what he thought? Tyrone pulled a slim pencil from his pocket and drew a line through the Stilwell entry.

"Gentlemen, as most of you probably know, General Joseph Stilwell is our Commander here in the CBI He's a front-line general. That means that before we're through some of you may run into him. The Japs ran him out of Burma in May, forty-two. He's back now and things are moving the other way, down the Stilwell Road to eventually link up with the Burma Road south of Mitch which joins the Burma road into China. Any questions? Yes, Lieutenant Hawk?"

"What about the Chinese troops we're dropping to?"

"Well, they're on our side."

A cheap shot, Tyrone thought, but pleased at the ripple of laughter it evoked. He didn't want Hawk's question to get them into some kind of racial crap. "Seriously, gentlemen, the Chinese are turning into damn good fighters. Their units are training here and near the front. We've been dropping to them, you know. Anybody have a question? Yes, Lieutenant Schultz?"

"Why the hell aren't the limeys giving us a hand?"

"They are. Farther south, down around Mandalay, places like that." Actually he didn't know much about the British-American drive into south Burma. "Anyway, our job is here -- help take Mitch, get our road linked up with the Burma Road into Kunming. Yes, Lieutenant Hawk?"

"What about right here in India, sir? I mean, we hear some talk about tension between the Indians and the British, Gandhi, rumors the British will give up India."

"I wouldn't say that was any of our business." What the hell was Hawk trying to do, give him a hard time? "We're here to help fight a war. Let's stick to the subject, Lieutenant. Subscribe to your local newspaper for the rest of the news!"

That brought a few laughs, but Tyrone thought he'd better let McCabe take over after the one piece of information that always worked. He raised one arm. "I finish with the news that we should have a plane in tomorrow with our first mail from Sicily!" He waited while the cheers died down, nodded to McCabe and sat down.

Terry McCabe picked up a piece of bamboo lying on the table, turned and lifted a flak jacket on which he'd been sitting. Holding the metal-lined jacket over one arm he stepped to his map and jabbed with the bamboo.

"Actually I don't give a rat's ass whether or not you know the details of this war as long as you keep our planes flying and find our drop zones. But my first question is this -- why have I been sitting here on a flak jacket?"

"Maybe the ants are starting to snap at your ass, Captain." Isaacs, one of the crew chiefs, smiled around at his buddies.

"You got it, Sergeant. And what did I tell our dumb-ass pilots to do when flying over enemy terrain?"

"Sit on 'em."

"Why?"

"It's the only way to stop the Japs on the ground from giving you an ass-full of lead."

"Thank you, Isaacs. Yes, Sergeant Chavez."

Luis Chavez stood up. "I haven't had a chance to tell Lieutenant Hawk until now. But going over our plane after the last mission today I found we'd picked up two hits. One in the left wing tip, the other in the fuselage just back of where I was sitting in the right seat."

McCabe waited a moment. "Were you sitting on a flak suit, Sergeant?"

"No, sir."

McCabe looked them over. "Not that a snap or two in the ass might not wake you guys up, but we can't afford the possibility of losing planes. I'm sorry if some of your fat asses can't stand the chafing and if some of you are so short you can't reach the pedals while sitting on a flak jacket, but from now on that's where you sit. And that's an order! Understood?" He waited while the solid round of applause died away.

"I think, Terry," Colonel Tyrone said softly, yet not without a touch of envy, "you'd better get on to your maps."

McCabe flung the flak jacket back on his chair, jabbed again at his maps, ran the bamboo pointer north to south. "The river," he said, "our base, Sook, then Ledo and up in the Patkais. Then over them into the Tanai Valley and Shinbwiyan, where the gooks cleared off the Nips before we arrived. Notice I'm following the Stilwell Road. Taipha Ga and Yupbang which Merrill's Marauders and the gooks took before moving on to Maingkwan, where we've started hauling in supplies. Beyond there, where the road is are Walawbum, Shadazup and Kamaing. Then there's Mogaung where the railroad comes up from Mandalay and swings east to Mitch. None of this have we got yet. The hills and mountains are full of Nips. They're still sending Zeros over." McCabe paused. Tyrone had wanted him to give a sort of picture of how the whole Burma war looked. The hell with that. "Any questions?"

After a moment of silence, Colonel Tyrone rose. "Perhaps you could fill them in on the picture farther south, Major Butler."

McCabe handed Butler the pointer, rearranged his flak jacket on his chair and sat down. Butler ran the pointer along the base of the map from the Chinese border west through Mitch to the Indian border. "O.K., so think of what Terry has shown you as the small end of a wedge. The bottom half, where the limeys and Americans are driving the Japs back is the rest of the wedge. The strategy, our strategy, is to join up and drive the Japs southeast out of Asia." Butler glanced at Tyrone for approval.

"Actually," Tyrone said -- he didn't like Butler's use of the word strategy. True or not they had no business mentioning it here -- "we're just guessing. Was there anything else, Major? If not I suggest we adjourn to the mess and that ale everyone gets to sample."

Hawk walked back up to the mess with Fitz and Schultz. Schultz was feeling quite exuberant, McCabe having already scheduled him for his first mission as first pilot the next morning. His only concern was that he'd been given Robb, a navigator, for co-pilot.

"You should be pleased McCabe feels he can trust you with one. Got your flak jacket ready?"

The mess was full when they arrived. Everyone in a good mood. Surmises as to when the mail would arrive tomorrow. They'd already been told there'd be no direct mail to them while in the CBI And new rumors -- their promised whiskey had arrived but had been taken over by the brass at Tinsukia and Jorhat for the ATC crews ferrying supplies over the Hump to China. Chavez joined Hawk, Fitz and Schultz. Had they heard that at the first showing of a movie down at Maingkwan -- Betty Grable flick -- three Japs had sneaked in and watched the whole film and got away?

"Glad you found the bullet holes, Luis," Hawk said to Chavez.

Chavez shrugged. "Easy enough to patch. Biggest problem could be if they hit a gas tank."

"I can think of an even bigger problem," Fitz said, rising, holding up his empty. "I'm going to go see if I can talk Manchu out of another round."

"I've heard," Schultz said, "they're flying in a lot of nurses for the hospital at Chabua. And I'm scheduled for the next tea, day after tomorrow. Barpa was telling me this morning, before I left for my check with Butler, there's a real hot broad who lives there." He winked at Hawk.

"Incidentally," Hawk said, "what did Butler have you do on your check?"

"Not a goddamn thing, naturally. He knew you'd checked me out." Schultz frowned, finished off his beer. "You know what we did for two fucking hours? We dragged ass over the Mishmi hills!"

"The Mishmi hills? What for?"

"Pissed if I know. Butler said we weren't supposed to be flying there. I'm not supposed to mention where we flew. Butler just said he wanted to fly over some new country. Looked just like all the rest, jungle and more jungle."

"What altitude did you hold?"

"You'd think to fuck we were on a strafing expedition. Every piece of open land we were down on it. But nothing, just a few buffalo and elephants."

Fitz appeared above them, two bottles clutched in each hand. "Manchu was holed up in his kitchen, my friends. I cashed in a few of my fortune cookies."

6

THIS time another troubled dream.

Hawk was flying over an endless expanse of jungle under a low, dawn-streaked sky, a distant horizon pierced by jagged peaks. He could not figure out where he was and banked sharply

He awakened, kicking free of a tangle of sheet , letting his feet hit the earth.

"The Mishmis," he said aloud, then "Jamila."

"Shut up!" Robb hissed from across the tent. "We've still got half an hour!"

From the airstrip came the first gutturals of engine testing. Overhead something, maybe a palm rat, clawed among leaves. What sounded like a cicada began to rasp.

Hawk stood up, fumbled into his flight bag hanging from the tent pole, yanked out his briefcase, sat down on his cot and groped inside, working out a small envelope, a single sheet of paper and his pen.

Naturally, when he tried out his flashlight from under his pillow he forgot to cover it. The light stabbed across at Robb who gaped, moaned and turned away. Hawk swung his legs up and over the cot to face the side of the tent. It stank of mold. He propped and shaded the light with the sheet. Using his briefcase as support he paused, then wrote swiftly..

DEAR JAMILA,

MAYBE IT WAS MY DREAM OF THE MISHMI HILLS. I AWOKE REMEMBERING YOU TELLING ME YOU CAME FROM SADIYA AT THE EDGE OF THE MISHMIS. IS THIS EXCUSE ENOUGH TO BREAK SOCIAL CUSTOMS UNKNOWN TO ME AND ASK IF I COULD SEE YOU? WE ARE SUPPOSED TO HAVE EVERY FIFTH DAY OFF FROM FLYING. IF I CAN MANAGE A JEEP PERHAPS WE COULD FIND A PLACE TO LUNCH SOME DAY IN CHABUA?

Hawk dressed quickly, shorts and a clean shirt, kicked into his sandals and found mess just opening. Returning from there, he found Barpa at his morning adoration of the boots. He took the note from his briefcase, read it over and folded it into its envelope, addressing it to *MISS JAMILA RAHMA, CARE OF MAJOR AND LADY GREYSTAFF.*

"Barpa, could you deliver this note to the tea plantation this morning? Either Major or Lady Greystaff."

Barpa lowered a boot and his polishing cloth. "I go right now, Lieutenant. Masoud will be up."

"No, it's too early. Later this morning. Do you have to give it to Masoud?"

"Masoud is my friend. He would be unhappy if he did not deliver it to the Greystaffs."

"I understand, Barpa. Thank you."

Not that I really do, Hawk thought, switching from sandals to sneakers. Down by Butler's quarters the first transport truck began honking.

A clear morning, the air only lightly dusted as the gooneys, loaded for the first drops, were being taxied up the flight line by the crew chiefs. An arrival of trucks grinding heavily in along the farther side of the airstrip where the daily line of women, baskets of crushed stone on their turbaned heads, wound in from the ragged edge of jungle.

Operations a blaze of lights, McCabe standing over his desk, assignment sheets in hand, glaring down, finger-jabbing his typewriter. Hawk paused, watched Butler lean back from his desk, listening to Corporal Inglis, in charge of 'kicker' assignments, explain he was a man short. He wanted no more of Private Peavey. Inglis paused and stared down at Major Butler, whose phone started ringing.

"O.K., Corporal," Butler said softly. "Tell Peavey to come see me."

"Yes sir, Major!"

"Hawk, get your ass over here," McCabe yelled.

Butler reached for his phone.

McCabe pawed among a stack of flight orders, yanked out one and held it out to Hawk. "Here, take a look." He turned to the wall behind him, jabbed one finger at the Jaino hills separating Walawbum and Shadazup on the Stilwell Road.

"Where I'm pointing is a valley, runs through the Jainos south-east of Taipha Ga. The Marauders are in there. Japs giving the Chinese a hard time. They want to take Walawbum. There's some talk the Marauders may go over the mountains in a try for the airstrip at Mitch. Word is Stilwell wants Mitch by May 12th. Anyway, here are your coordinates. Marauders may be fifteen or fifty miles up this valley, about twenty miles east of the Stilwell Road. Drop zone laid out last night. A narrow valley but no cul-de-sac. But Jap patrols on both sides of the hills. You're dropping chutes. Ammo. Three passes should do it. I've given you three good men."

Hawk glanced at his orders. "And Chavez for co-pilot again?"

"You complaining?"

"No way. Just didn't want Murphy loaded off on me."

"He'll be a good lad soon enough," McCabe said defensively

"If he stays alive."

Murphy and Christopher had arrived from the States just in time to fly to India with the squadron. Didn't seem to take to flying. Complained a lot about a bad stomach.

"Here, take your orders and get going." McCabe slammed back to his desk. "Schultz!" he yelled. "Where the hell is Schultz!"

Schultz pushed in through the door, shoving a torn shirt down inside his shorts. He came up to Hawk, grabbing his arm. "Hey, why didn't you give me the real skinny on that Indian broad at the tea party, friend? Or do I know the answer?"

"Fill in whatever blanks become your nature," Hawk snapped. Ignore him, Hawk told himself. Then, "Was she at the tea?"

"Couldn't get near her." Schultz leered. "Out by the pool. Wow! When I went looking she disappeared."

"How was the tea?" Hawk felt relieved.

"Flamingo piss."

"Talk about lack of discipline!" Butler said to McCabe.

Hawk went out the door and down the line to his plane. Chavez sat in the open cargo doorway smoking a cigarette. Inside the three 'chute men were working on the release lines.

"All checked and ready to go, Lieutenant."

"Thanks." Hawk watched McCabe hurry along the line, reach their improvised tower and haul himself up its ladder. "Make sure they have the first chute lines free. No time for tangled lines this trip."

Hawk went in under the plane, checking the tail, wing ailerons. Chavez had done a neat job patching the two bullet holes. Chavez was the best crew chief in the squadron. A bonus -- he could fly well enough to get the plane down in one piece if something happened. Chavez, an illegal, had come to L.A. from Mexico, dodging across the border as a young kid. Maybe some day they'd find out and send him back. Now he said O.K. with him if they sent him home. A little hill town below a place called Palenque. Mayan ruins. After the war Hawk could visit him and they'd ride up to *las ruinas* on horse-back from the ranch of his family. The caudillo was trying to steal it. Always someone trying to grab the Indians' land. It was nice land. Maybe after the war Hawk should come, stay with him. There were many pretty girls.

As Hawk climbed into the plane one of the 'chute men pointed to the lines securing the 'chutes stacked on the far side. Six to a stack. Last time Hawk had made a rough turn and almost lost a stack out the cargo opening.

"Thanks, nice job. I'll try and be more careful this time."

This was only their second ammo drop. He'd managed to get the first in the drop zone -- all but one, which he heard had to be chopped out of a tree.

"Rice to the gooks is one thing," McCabe had cautioned him. "But ammo and medical supplies are something else."

"I heard the Chinese don't even eat the rice we do drop," Hawk replied. "Probably sell it to the Japs."

"The trouble with you, Hawk," McCabe snapped, "is you don't like the Irish."

"Au contraire, Captain," Hawk said. "I had the pleasure of growing up in a neighborhood lousy with micks.''

McCabe's jaw tightened. Then he grinned.

Chavez dropped into the right seat, slid on his earphones and called the tower. Hawk pulled on his earphones and started the engines. "Clear and number one for takeoff," McCabe yelled. Hawk eased off the brakes, taxied out and down the line to the far end of the airstrip, swung out without pausing and pushed the throttles forward.

"Adelante!" Chavez yelled.

They were down the strip, lifting quickly up through dissolving mists, climbing up over the Ledo road that beyond the Patkai hills became the Stilwell Road. Heading: south -- 175°.

Hawk cracked back his side window and lit a cigarette. He didn't smoke much but that first one on a flight, with the slip of cool air, sort of put things together. The gooney was lifting easily. A light load. He banked a couple of times, passed over Ledo at 2500' and the Likhani airstrip where Weed had died. Practically abandoned now. No sign of the smashed plane. Covered by new growth? Or had the Naga tribesmen hacked it up for their own uses?

Chavez tapped his shoulder, then his earphones. Chavez was on alert range. Hawk heard a series of mumbles and squawks, a distant voice,

English accent. *Near Mandalay, flight of six Zeros moving northwest at 1500.* Hawk shrugged. Not their war. The sky clear except for two gooneys, headed diagonally and descending. From one of the other squadrons. Probably headed for Shinbwiyan.

Past the Patkais, holding now at 6000', Hawk altered course to bring them out over the wide reach of the Hukawng Valley, 'where the buffs and the elephants play'. He smiled. Chavez again tapped his earphone. Hawk switched again to alert.

Still the clear English voice, measured, dispassionate, which would announce the end of the world with the same impersonal tone it would proclaim free beer at a local canteen. The Jap fighters had split, three heading north-north-east, the other three south.

Hawk began a slow descent to 3500', heading for the western thrust of the Kumon Range that stretched south from the Indian border to Mogaung and Mitch. Once there he'd turn south toward the Jaino hills and the valley McCabe had described. Chavez removed his headphones, picked up their map and studied it.

"We're taking the scenic route, Lieutenant?"

"I'm hanging the edge of the Kumons, just in case." Hawk searched the sky ahead. "Once to the Jainos --" he pointed ahead to the distant loom of lower hills -- "we'll head west until we spot the valley where the Marauders are waiting. I'd say about thirty miles."

Chavez ran a finger back and forth over his map. "Nearer forty."

A slight haze hung in the low valleys of the Kumon Range. Hawk turned south. Ahead, above the still distant Jainos, a wedge of high cirrus had shelved in from the southwest. Signs of the coming monsoon? New rumor now circulating -- It was too late for Stilwell to take Mitch before the monsoon closed down operations.

Hawk checked his altimeter, held at 200' above the jungle. Open stretches flicked past. A few elephants. The Jaino hills rose before them. He waited until they were close in, then banked west, glancing back down the plane. The three chute men sat easily, backs against the stacked chutes. One threw something out the cargo doorway.

"Go back and give them a briefing, Luis. We'll be going up the valley at 200 feet, air speed 140. We dump the first cluster of chutes on the first pass. On your signal from me. They'll have maybe five minutes to get the next batch ready if I can find a place wide enough to bring the gooney around. If I have to go all the way through before I can make a 180 we'll let them know. O.K.?" Chavez nodded, slid from his seat.

Hawk glanced at his watch. Thirty to forty miles. No wind drift. Fine. What he didn't want was a wind funneling up the valley. He glanced at his watch. Air speed now 140. An open stretch, a small herd of elephants breaking into a run as he flashed past. He checked flaps. No wind meant he could drag in over the drop site between 90-100 mph. He glanced at Chavez's seat. Bastard hadn't been sitting on his flak jacket. Another open stretch, a small stream, two or three buffalo wallowing. Five minutes gone. Chavez returned, dropped into his seat and snapped on his safety belt.

"You'd be safer sitting on your flak jacket," Hawk yelled.

"So would you!" Chavez shouted.

"I'm the pilot. Don't have to." Hawk grinned. "The men all set?"

Chavez nodded. Hawk edged in closer to the hills on their left. His left foot caught momentarily on something. He glanced down. Sneaker lacing had come untied. He kicked it off. The pedal cool against his bare foot.

"McCabe didn't know how far in for the drop zone," Hawk said. "Maybe halfway. Hope to hell they've picked a wide spot"

Chavez pointed. A gap in the hills. But only a narrow opening. Hawk held his course. A rough headland loomed ahead. Hawk lifted over it. Chavez raised both legs in mock alarm.

"And here we are!" Hawk yelled, banking sharply left, heading across maybe three miles of heavy jungle into a valley that twisted out of sight into the solid green rise of the Jaino hills. "Alert the men. Remember, I yell O.K., you signal to let chutes go. O.K.?"

Chavez gave him a thumbs up, turned sideways in his seat, staring back down the plane. Hawk leveled, holding to the valley center that narrowed. It damned well better open up. Unless it wasn't the valley! He pulled back on the wheel, lifting a bit, an instinctive reaction. Then ahead he glimpsed a trail, blasted trees, a muddy swath, felt his chest loosen. A couple of close hills. The valley widened, a five mile spread of flat land before it disappeared into a higher mass of hills.

"Men all set, Lieutenant." Chavez glanced ahead. "Where's the drop zone?"

"How the hell would I know." No break in the jungle, no clearing, *nada*! Then suddenly a muddy streak, an orange streak of cloth diagonal where the chutes should land. Narrow. The encroaching trees could neatly slice off the gooney's wing tips. He was over and past it too late to signal a drop. Some GIs appeared at the clearing's edge. Waving? Or giving them the finger?

Hawk banked sharply right, leveled, banked left. Straight on, banked left and held it, leveling, slanting back, drop zone dead ahead. He eased the flaps down, gunned the engines. "O.K., Chavez!"

Chavez's arm jabbed down. The drop zone flashed beneath them. Another bank right, then left. Hawk glimpsed the six chutes falling gently, the last one drifting off zone. It would snag up in the jungle edge. Rest on target. Hawk banked and leveled for the second pass. "O.K., Chavez!"

Again Chavez's arm jabbed down. On over the drop zone. This time Hawk circled wider. The second batch were falling better. "We've got it!" Chavez yelled. A faint cheer from the chute men.

Hawk felt moisture on his palms and the wheel. Four more passes to go. Damn the gooney was a fine plane! Banking, he let its power soak into him. He banked tightly around and came low over the drop zone on his way out. Now the Marauders were out, a ragged looking bunch, dragging the ammo and chutes into the jungle. The orange diagonal marker already vanished. "The men O.K.?"

Chavez looked back. "O.K." He swung around in his seat.

Chavez slipped on his earphones. They came out of the valley. Hawk commenced an easy climb. Ahead and high up a returning gooney. The sky was clear, the day unchanged. In the narrow valley there had been neither time nor geography. Chavez poked him in the arm, gestured at his earphones. Hawk slid on his. That English accent again... *repeat over Kamaing at twelve thousand, three Nips heading north-north-east. . .* (voice fading, then returning) *immediate cover advised . . . Mustangs . . . Mandalay . . . repeat, take cover.*

Chavez picked up the map. Hawk grabbed it, motioning Chavez to take the wheel. Kamaing, close, maybe fifty miles south. Too close. Sky clear. The lone gooney vanished. He took the wheel, pushed the nose down. Get down on the trees, get over to the edge of the Kumons, Hawk thought, work his way north up the Hukawng. Could a fighter spot a camouflaged gooney hugging the trees ten thousand feet below?

"Maybe I should tell the men," Chavez said.

Hawk shook his head. "What you want them to do, bail out?"

Now on top of the jungle Hawk looked up. The sky was clear. Behind him? He had a cinematic flash of three Zeros barreling down behind them. His earphones came to life in a smash of static . . . *canceled, enemy has turned southeast . . .Mustang got one over Mandalay . . . alert canceled . . . all.*

"Mandalay," Hawk sang, "On the road to Mandalay where the flying fishes play!" He began climbing again.

"You gone foolish in the head, Lieutenant?"

"Been and gone, Luis." Now planes appeared above them, like insects after a summer storm. They passed west of Maingkwan and Taipha Ga, the Shin tower advising all clear. They were skimming the Patkais and home to Sook. McCabe still holding forth from the tower. Clear and number one to land. The tea plantation, a brief glimpse of the pool. Was she there, under the palms?

"You've got maybe ten minutes," McCabe advised from the tower. *"Taxi down to the loading zone. Rice for the gooks this time. Just above Walawbum a mile off the road."*

"Thanks," Hawk said. "Any beer in Operations?"

"The clerks probably drank it all."

Mud matted the airstrip, churned by the planes landing and taking off. Hawk and Chavez walked to Operations past the long line of workers. Major Butler, stripped to the waist, bent sweating over his desk, trying to clean a camera lens. No beer. He pointed to a wooden container of water and bottles of Indian lemonade. Butler hadn't heard about the alert. He muttered something about moisture ruining his cameras.

Hawk took a pull at his lemonade. "Hear you gave Schultz a ride over the Mishmis, Major."

Butler gave him a hard stare. Chavez sat down on the floor, back against the wall. Ericson and Murphy came in from their first flight. Ericson explained they'd have to delay their next mission. He rolled his eyes ceiling-ward.

"I let Murphy try landing at Shin. They're checking the landing gear."

"I didn't hit that hard," Murphy said.

Ericson grabbed a bottle of lemonade and headed for the door. Murphy grabbed a bottle, gave Butler a sullen look and followed Ericson.

"Hawk," Butler said loudly. "Schultz gave me a ride over the Mishmis. We've got us a damn good pilot." He stared at Hawk. Hawk could see the wheels going around. "Tell you what, Hawk." Butler gave Chavez a glance. Chavez was lost in a cloud of cigarette smoke. "This idea I've got. You really might be interested."

"We'll see." Hawk turned to the wall map.

"What was that all about?" Chavez asked as they returned down the line.

Hawk shrugged. "He hasn't told me yet, Luis."

The gooney was loaded. A half-assed job, Hawk saw immediately. Chavez knelt on the plane's floor and gave the lines securing the eighty pound bags of rice an irritable jerk. Stacked too high. One rough turn could break them loose. Their three kickers sat forward near the cockpit door, absorbed in cleaning their .45 automatics. Orders had come from somewhere that the 'kickers' were to be issued .45's for every drop. A theory that if the plane crashed they could fight their way out of the jungle?

"O.K., let's get this load untied and lashed down properly!" Chavez bawled. "And put away your popguns. One might go off and hurt somebody!"

Hawk went forward to check the map. Chavez stood over the three men who looked pissed off. Chavez gave a jerk at their lashing. "And stay back from the cargo opening. I'll give you the signal when I want you to jump out."

"*Vete al cuerno,* Sergeant!" the small one said.

"Only a goddamn Pole could fuck up Spanish that bad," Chavez yelled. "Now sit down and hold on!" He strode forward, grabbed his flak jacket and slammed it on his seat. "Put your flak jacket where it belongs, Lieutenant!"

"Something bothering you, Sergeant?"

"Wise ass told me to piss off," Chavez jerked his head backward. *"Hijo de perra"*

"One war at a time, Luis. McCabe is screaming at us to move. Two more gooneys with us on this drop, Schultz and Gimbel, Cordner and Fitz. Let's go!"

Cordner was already out, taxiing down for take-off. Schultz wheeled out in front of Hawk. Two incoming planes. *"Move it!"* McCabe yelled.

Cordner churned off through the mud, then Schultz. Hawk moved into the mud. Sky clear, planes over the Patkais like a straggle of crows. Cordner climbing hard, Schultz holding lower and fast. They took off.

"No need to rush, friends," Hawk announced in his mike. "We'll get one more drop after this, maybe two. Beaucoup ounces for the ledger." He motioned Chavez to take over, leaned back and checked the map again. Over the Patkais again.

Walawbum. Now a Chinese Division base, spread out around the beaten-up village. A big drop zone, north-south. He'd give the other two plenty of time, try a slow approach, hold at fifty feet for the drop. Maybe it would save a few sacks from breaking open.

He took over halfway through their descent into the Hukawng. Chavez leaned back and closed his eyes. Hawk turned the radio dial. BBC. Same music as back on Sicily . . ."if you wish upon a star, makes no difference where you are". . .. Not much different than driving a truck. Like Schultz, his flight training had been for fighters before the brass decided what they really needed was cargo pilots. Like Schultz, he'd been transferred to the gooneys the day he got his wings.

Walawbum, the sprawling division tents, the wide drop zone and a wind sock hanging limply from its pole. A small explosion of earth as Cordner, dropping too high, made his first pass. One sack disintegrated in a splotch of rice.

Chavez swung about in his seat. Hawk glanced back. First bunch of sacks lined up before the door, kickers sitting, ready to kick at Chavez's signal.

Now Schultz was going over, lower than Cordner, a little off center, a few men bursting from the trees, arms waving. Maybe they were going to try and catch the sacks. Several fell at the edge of the jungle.

"Come on, Schultz," Hawk radioed, "you can do better than that."

Then they were coming in, half flaps, real low. Chavez a bit tense. He held steady. "O.K.!" Chavez's arm jabbing down, a slight lifting of the plane as the first sacks tumbled clear. Flaps up and dragging along. Four times and they lifted empty.

"No problems," Chavez said. "Real hot shots. Take a look." He motioned back down the gooney.

Hawk's glance caught two of the kickers, backs against the inside fuselage, polishing their

.45's. One sat in the cargo opening, arm wrapped around a line, staring out.

Forty five minutes back to base. A northwest wind had pushed into the Hukawng, jostling the gooney. Hawk glanced at his watch. They'd probably get in only one more drop. Still, six ounces of whiskey for the day's work. And through by four. Would Jamila have answered his note?

The next mission two hours later, a facsimile of the previous except for the rough air over the Patkais. Heavy cumulus to the south, an afternoon slant of light. High above them he spotted a vapor trail. One of the big ATC jobs heading east over the Hump to China. Again Schultz and Cordner ahead of them, slanting down over the Hukawng. A truck convoy like a brown earthworm winding south along the Stilwell Road out of Shin. A quiet afternoon over northern Burma, except, in the tumbled sweep of jungle-covered mountains, hills, and valleys ahead, a war was going on. Men were dying. Hawk grabbed his mike and called Schultz, a few miles ahead.

"How's everything look, cracker?"

"Not a fucking orange tree in sight, Yankee."

"Just make sure you don't start planting any."

"Up yours, Buster!"

A couple of gooneys in loose formation came over them, returning from Walawbum. A dip of wings.

Again the long slant down. Chavez leaned back in his seat and dreamed out his window. No flak jacket under him. The jungle of trees, mahogany, teak, palms. Frangipani? Schultz went in first this time, his first pass off to one side, sacks just missing the trees. Big smash of rice. Cordner didn't do much better. By the time Hawk roared over a surge of Chinese troops had appeared. They looked pissed off, fisting the air. A lot of broken sacks.

Schultz's voice over the intercom: "Next run I get one of them fuckers!"

"Unless they get you first," Chavez yelled into his mike.

Three passes and they were done, lifting up over the Hukawng. No one interested in buzzing a buffalo ambling across a clearing.

Hawk climbed to 5000' and leveled off. He decided to just clear the Patkais, slide in under and ahead of Cordner and Schultz. He was adjusting his trim tabs, about to let Chavez take the wheel when the first explosion slammed through the plane.

Even as he twisted into a dive he thought: Is this what it sounds like when a Zero blows you out of the sky? Chavez turned, snapping his safety belt loose, diving back down the plane. Three more explosions ripped through the plane, a couple of hoarse cries. Controls still working. The gooney began to vibrate from his dive. Did Chavez intend to bail out? A quick glance. Chavez was on the floor by the cargo opening, he and the other two kickers holding the third who hung halfway out in space. No sign of damage. Hawk eased out of his dive, jungle flashing past only feet below. Chavez came back up the plane carrying three .45's, and slid them on the floor.

"Hijos de perras! They said all they were doing was taking a little target practice!"

At Operations everyone was happy. Mail finally in. Whiskey in from Group Command. Distribution that evening. Hawk and McCabe sat down with the three kickers. McCabe wanted to ground them for good. How simple shit-headed could they get?

"If it hadn't been for Chavez we might be dead," the youngest of the three said, tears in his eyes.

"Which is a goddamn shame!" McCabe snapped.

"My wife's got three kids," the oldest one said. "We need the extra money I get for flight pay."

Hawk glanced at McCabe. Being a kicker, in spite of the flight pay, was not one of the popular career ladders. They were short of men. They were short of kickers.

McCabe stood up. "They're yours, Hawk. If you want to, take 'em up and throw them out on your next run."

Somebody had left Hawk's mail on his cot. Two letters, the usual V-mail from his mother. The other stamped, the return address smudged. He opened the V-mail first. Why in hell couldn't his father take a minute off from hammering his bloody piano to write!

His mother complained of a very cold spring and the government always slow sending his allotment check to them. She had knitted him a sweater and hoped it would arrive safely

DEAR ALAN HAWK, the other letter began. *PROBABLY YOU'VE FORGOTTEN ALL ABOUT ME BY NOW. I CALLED YOUR MOTHER AND SHE GAVE MY YOUR APO. I AM HOPING YOU CAN HELP ME OUT -- .*

No, he hadn't actually forgotten Alma Worth. A high school cheerleader. It was with her he'd discovered the pleasures of non-coital back-seat intercourse. They'd soon parted. She'd married Fred Jilbert right after graduation. Alma had sent him an invitation but he'd gone off to college.

Fred, Corporal Fred Jilbert, Alma had printed, was somewhere in Asia. She'd seen something in the paper about Hawk being over there. Congratulations on his air medal. Anyway, here was Fred's APO. He was with the 988th Signal Operations. Maybe he could get in touch with Fred and tell him it was a boy. After the two girls that ought to please him. She'd be waiting to hear from him.

Hawk tossed her note aside. Time to go collect his whiskey ration, even if he didn't like rye. Somewhere there must be someone with a bottle of Scotch to trade.

Back in Sicily they had a decent Officer's Bar. Here it was the mess tent. Tyrone had put McCabe in charge of distribution., Manchu handling the pouring. Chavez had already taken care of his day's ration. He looked appealingly up at Hawk. Hawk uncapped his bottle.

"O.K., a bonus two ounces for action above and beyond the call of duty. But next time let 'em fall out. Two ounces. I want you flying tomorrow, not tonight."

Colonel Tyrone appeared briefly, praising the squadron for its work. He toasted them with a bottle of Indian lemonade.

The evening went well. Back in the tent Schultz already passed out, Fitz and Robb threshing into an Indian wrestle. A new letter had been added. A small parchment-like envelope with a Hindi inscription, his name in swirling script.

Fitz and Robb lurched over onto his cot. Fitz looked up. "Barpa brought it, about an hour ago."

DEAR ALAN HAWK,

IT WOULD BE DELIGHTFUL TO HAVE LUNCH IN CHABUA SOME DAY. IF YOU CAN'T MANAGE A JEEP PERHAPS A TONGA WILL DO. MOLLY IS NOW WONDERING ABOUT OUR INTRODUCTION BUT SEEMS RESIGNED.

JAMILA RAHMA

7

OVER several days the air thickened, closed against them, heavy in their lungs. They flew through skies unclouded but opaque, an undulating mass without boundaries spotted by a pale sun. Their props pulsed through a labored range as if searching for the proper speed to stir a thickening liquid.

APRIL 23RD, ELEVEN LANDINGS -- Hawk wrote, hunched on his cot below a circling of bat-winged insects. Early morning sweat beaded his forehead. A V-mail letter home. . . . *ELEVEN MISSIONS. AT TWO OUNCES OF WHISKEY A MISSION. IT ADDS UP BUT I STILL PREFER MANCHU'S RUM.*

Schultz rolls heavily up on one elbow, squints at Hawk's letter. "Trying to hold down the other end too? Give her my love. Be glad to take over here. Florida gave me a taste for dark skin."

Hawk wrote . . . Our *SQUADRON REALLY BEING PUSHED. SCUTTLEBUTT RAMPANT. YOUNG CHINESE BOYS*

TRAINING HERE THINK THEY'RE GOING TO INVADE INDIA. MUST GET WORD TO GANDHI. THE BATTERED MARAUDERS HAVE DECLARED SHADAZUP THEIR CAPITAL AND ARE CLAMORING FOR EVENING TEA DANCES. AT OUR IMPROVISED CINEMA AT TAIPHA GA THE JAPS HAVE BEGUN SNEAKING IN FOR THE NEW BETTY GRABLE FLICK. FITZ AND ROBY ARE SUGGESTING A PICNIC UP IN THE KUMON HILLS. RUMOR HAS IT CHIANG KAI-SHEK ("PEANUT") IS OFF TO HAWAII WITH OUR GENERAL FOR SOME GOLF. FREE TRAIN TRIPS FROM MOGAUNG TO SINGAPORE FOR EVERYBODY WITH A GOOD CONDUCT MEDAL.

"Want me to censor that letter for you?" Schultz said. "Looks like you're giving away our positions."

Hawk wrote . . . *CHECK IN OUR OLD ATLAS FOR THE KEY TO THIS.*

Sweat ran down Hawk's arm smearing his letter. An insect dove. Hawk swatted. The bug crash-landed on Roby, nakedly asleep on his sack. He came upright, glaring at Schultz.

"Hawk just shot down a cockroach, Roby," Schultz said. "It crawled up your ass and died."

I've three bottles of rye, Hawk thought, scribbling in the last few lines. Should be bribe enough to loose a jeep from the motor pool. If not I'll ask Barpa about a tonga. Just make sure Butler doesn't pull his trick of switching assignments. Nothing is going to ruin my day with Jamila.

Hark wrote. . . *TOO BAD I CAN'T BE THERE SHOVELING SNOW FOR YOU. HEY DAD, HOW ABOUT A LETTER FROM YOU? HOPE YOU ARE WELL. LOVE*

He folded the letter, looked at Schultz and scribbled across the right-hand top . . . *CENSORED BY LT. ALAN HAWK.*

"Lousy rotten spy," Schultz said.

Stripping, Hawk kicked into his sandals, wrapped on a towel.

"Showers are jammed," Schultz said. "Drop your soap and it's sodomy hall." Even before they'd left Sicily, Hawk had ceased trying to figure out the range of Schultz's mind. From Schultz's cursing, the sexual connotations of his remarks, the unexpected flashes of perception, no center was apparent. He left the tent and took the path to the showers, two chattering monkeys following him through the tall press of bamboo.

The shower talk was all of Colonel Tyrone's recent Solomonic handling of the latrine problem, seen as more noteworthy than Tyrone's decision that McCabe, Butler and himself were going to try and squeeze in a mission every day. To be expected with a pilot shortage. The latrine affair was something else. A team of brass from the Office of the Inspector General had appeared at Sook. Its minions, a lieutenant and a major, assuring Colonel Tyrone their concern was not with flight operations but rather with general military rules and regulations. A copy of their report duly arrived days later and was immediately posted. The squadron had received a satisfactory in all areas except a general tendency to ignore proper military dress. However, on the subject of the latrine the report did not mince words. The officers and enlisted men had been found sharing a common latrine. This matter should be immediately remedied, followed by a report of action taken.

As Al Tyrone confided to Butler and McCabe, he was nothing if not a man of action. The latrine, a reasonably long, palm-thatched structure, had a door at only one end and numerous window-like apertures which created a cool, shadowy retreat from the heat. A native carpenter was brought in, another door added to the opposite end, the appropriate signs of Officers and Enlisted Men hung over each door. Major Butler took photographs. The squadron report, signed by Colonel Tyrone, was sent off and the undisturbed interior left as before, a tranquil resort for discussion and meditation.

Butler didn't show up at noon mess, but had left word he'd like to see Hawk. After he'd finished Hawk walked down to Butler's tent, the place in its usual disarray of strewn photographic equipment, papers, a half-finished meal on top of a metal file cabinet into which Butler was probing with both hands. Both rattan chairs were heaped with folders. Hawk sat down on the end of the unmade cot.

"Glad you stopped by," Butler said. "Been meaning to see you. Suppose you'd like to know what's going on."

"I didn't know anything special was going on except the war, Jedd."

Butler backed from the file cabinet clutching a bunch of photos, cleared one chair, took the mess tray from the top of the cabinet and sat down.

"It's that other matter I mentioned, Hawk." He gave Hawk a calculating look, tried a forkful of food, rejected it, gave Hawk another look. "I've been over to the Greystaff's a couple of times."

"So I heard. Also about you checking out Schultz over the Mishmis. Is that the other matter?"

"The albino elephant," Butler said, giving him a long look. "The albino elephant."

"We've seen the photograph at the Greystaff's. So?"

Butler tried his food again, frowned and swallowed. "Actually this hash isn't bad.. Did you try it?"

"Wasn't that hungry Besides, the word going around is Manchu finally cornered some jackals the other night for us to try."

"Not funny, Hawk." Butler frowned, paused. "What if," he went on, spacing his words, "there is more than just a photograph?"

"Don't tell me the Major has the albino elephant hidden away, stuffed and rampant?"

"No, Hawk. What I'm telling you is that the albino elephant may still be alive in the Mishmi Hills!"

"Is that why you and Schultz took that flight over the Mishmis? You want to get some photographs of it?"

"No, what I mean is --" Butler stopped as McCabe pushed in through the tent flaps.

Rain tomorrow, McCabe announced. "We're going to try and squeeze in the morning. Word again that tough weather might be moving in early."

"Which reminds me," Hawk said, "day after tomorrow is my scheduled day off. Can I count on it, Jedd?"

"Absolutely, Alan." McCabe made no motion of leaving. Butler gave Hawk an odd wink. "We'll get together soon on that other business."

Back in his tent Hawk wrote a short note to Jamila. He'd call for her at noon on Friday.

The rumor of a weather change appeared without foundation. Next day the morning missions lifted off from Sook, ground up into an horizonless gray dome spotted by a rheumy sun. The Patkais were a green blur as Hawk climbed, leveled, then slanted down into a Hukawng Valley lacking form or substance.

"*¿Que es los que me mira con ojo vidrioso?*" Chavez pointed skyward at the sun, grinned at Hawk's blank stare. "A favorite line from a childhood story," Chavez said. "What stares at me with glassy eye?" He crossed himself.

Hawk shrugged. Their load was drums of gasoline for Walawbum, forty miles down Stilwell

Road. Chavez went back to sniff for fumes, reporting everything sealed tight. They'd be unloaded and back in Sook for a second easy run back to Walawbum. If with any luck the rains came, he'd have the afternoon to check the motor-pool for a jeep. If that failed Barpa had said he could procure a tonga. He spoke her name softly, testing it -- Jamila.

But their second mission was not another load of gasoline for Walawbum. Over the radio McCabe sounded excited: Food drop at a new location in the foothills beyond Taipha Ga. With poor visibility it was no fun frigging around in the hills. Yet it turned out fine. A decent clearing, well-marked, their 'chute' men worked smoothly, the orange chutes well on target. The ragged crew of Marauders gave them a thumbs up as they roared over after their last pass.

Not until noon on their return, as they lifted up over the hills east of Walawbum that Chavez nudged Hawk, pointed off to the south-west. A mass of heavy clouds, dark edges sharply defined against a band of blue sky were shouldering raggedly upward. Ahead the Hukawng Valley came almost magically into focus as if cleaned by the sweep of a giant suction.

"Something's moving up," Chavez said. He crossed himself. "Is this the way the monsoon comes?"

"Who knows?" Hawk said. "If so we're out of luck. We'll be in the air all afternoon." McCabe brought them in, his voice sharp as they turned from the strip and taxied down the line. *"Lieutentants Hawk, Ericson and Rogers report immediately to Operations"*.

"I suspect our afternoon recess is off, Luis. Give the gooney a check and fuel up. I'll go see where the picnic takes place."

Ericson and Rogers were in Operations when Hawk arrived. A clerk was typing rapidly in one corner. Butler and Colonel Tyrone were bent over a spread of maps on a table. Hawk noticed Tyrone had on a regular issue, zippered flight suit.

"A little afternoon excursion," Tyrone explained.

"The weather could build up down there," Ericson said, running a hand through his blond hair. Rogers shrugged. The clerk rose and handed Tyrone a typed sheet.

"Special orders from Stilwell's Headquarters at Shinbwiyan," Tyrone said. "Ammo and medical supplies for Merrill's Marauders. Must reach them today. I've assigned three gooneys so we'll be light. Three passes each and we're out. The new drop is in the foothills. We'll follow the road to Shadazup, then southeast to the hills to the drop zone, which incidentally is on a dead end." His fingers traced the map. "So we go in one at a time, drop, do a one eighty and out." He waved the paper at them. "Any questions?"

"We?" Ericson said.

Tyrone nodded. "I'll co-pilot for Hawk." He smiled. "McCabe and I flipped for it. Both of us are low on whiskey. He lost. Schultz will co-pilot for Ericson, Fitzgerald with Rogers. Time I had a good look at things down there."

"Any ceiling left?" Rogers asked.

"Shadazup reporting 500 feet and holding."

"Chavez will be expecting to fly with me, Colonel," Hawk said.

"Then you'd better tell him he isn't." Tyrone paused and glanced at his paper. "Now, they'll be using red flares to bring us in. Orange markers for the drop zone."

"Great," Ericson said softly. "That way the Japs in the surrounding hills will think we're celebrating the Fourth early!"

Again Tyrone glanced at his paper. "Marauders report no contact with enemy." He turned and jabbed a finger at the wall map. "My guess is the Japs pulled out yesterday when the Chinese started a push down the road on Kamaing. If so the Marauders can go in over the Kumons and take the airstrip at Mitch while the Japs think our real plan is to take Kamaing and the railhead at Mogaung, the Marauders making just a feint."

Hawk peered at the map. "From where the Marauders are now it's maybe fifty miles to Mitch over 6000' mountains. You mean they're going to charge over the mountains and capture Mitch all by themselves?"

Tyrone grinned. "Not unless we drop our strategy session and get them their supplies. Jedd, call and see what's holding up the loading."

Butler cranked up the phone. Planes were still droning in. Butler spoke and nodded to Tyrone, then held the phone out to Hawk. "Sergeant Chavez wants to know if he can come along as crew chief. He's willing to help out the 'chute' men."

"Request refused," Tyrone said sharply "Sorry, Hawk. I understand his feelings. Tell him we don't need unnecessary weight."

Sorry, Luis," Hawk said. "Matter of weight. You're too fat." He paused, receiver still at his ear, then said, "Luis, if you really meant what I think you said in Spanish, it's a court martial." He handed the phone back to Butler.

"Our little phone visit being over," Tyrone said, "*vamos!*"

Chavez had brought Hawk's plane out first. He came down the cargo steps as Hawk and Tyrone arrived, waited while Tyrone and Hawk climbed aboard, then released the steps. The first drop of chutes already on the release wire. Hawk went on up to the cockpit and paused.

"You going to take it Colonel?"

"No thanks." Al slid down into the right seat. "You're the expert, Alan. I'll handle the gadgets." He picked up his mike, shoved on his earphones. *"Tower from Tyrone. Let's move out."*

"Clear and number one for take-off, sir."

The sky had taken on a jaundiced cast as Hawk swung on to the airstrip, though no clouds loomed above the Patkais. He let the gooney ease forward. Beside them the airstrip workers moved through a light veil of dust. Throttles hard forward. Now the sudden sense of being completely contained in the present, a time that already held what ever lay south of the Patkais. Lift-off!

"What in hell are you smiling about, Hawk?" Tyrone's look was puzzled as Hawk gestured for wheels-up.

"Reflexive action, I guess, sir." His momentary glimpse of the Greystaff's pool had come and gone. He set into a steep climb. Now a dark roll of cumulus was lifting above the Patkais.

"See if you can get through to Shin, Colonel. What ceiling they're reading."

Tyrone lifted his mike, unzipping his flight suit. His T-shirt revealed a diving P-40 Tiger logo. Al Tyrone never talked about his fighter-pilot days with Chennault in China. Shot down twice, wounded once. Back in the States the vagaries of military logic had brought him to multi-engines and a high level command with Troop Carrier involved in the Allied invasion of North Africa. All this according to Major Butler. All Hawk knew as fact was Al's skill as a pilot and how, just weeks before their departure from Sicily, Al had been ordered to return his French mistress, Jeanne, to Tunis. They had met in Casablanca. She had come on with him as the Allies drove eastward along the North

African coast - Oran, Algiers, Bone, El Djem, Tunis and finally Sicily, where fate or the law of averages (widely debated in the squadron) caught up with him in the form of a military dictate. Lieutenant Colonel Alfred Tyrone was given the choice of returning his lovely dark-haired Jeanne to Tunis or being shipped back to the States to his wife and five children living on an airbase in Midland, Texas. No one ever mentioned the affair in the presence of the Colonel.

Shinbwiyan burst loud and clear from a racket of radio noise: ceiling holding at 500 feet. Yupbang and Maingkwan reporting a 500 foot ceiling with increasing rain.

"Best thing," Hawk said, "is to slide over the top here and get down in the Hukawng. Go all the way at 500'." Tyrone nodded.

Ahead the clouds appeared to lift, then spill down over the Patkais. Suddenly they were on instruments. Hawk kept his steady climb. No turbulence. He leveled at 6500' checked his watch. Twenty minutes and they'd be well clear of the crests. The descent would bring them out over the upper Hukawng. Smooth air meant little or no wind-drift -- that is unless the whole of northern Burma was being torn away by a monsoon ambush.

Tyrone contacted Ericson and then Rogers. They both came in loud and clear. They'd hold for fifteen minutes before beginning descent.

"I'm right behind you," Rogers called. *"Practically got your tail in sight."*

You've always been good at keeping tail in sight," Hawk replied. *"Make sure you hold your airspeed at one seventy I don't want our tail chewed off."*

"State I'm in," Rogers cracked, *"sounds O.K."*

"Listen," Ericson broke in. His voice had an accusing edge. *"I think the whole idea of radio silence over enemy territory is for the birds. Anybody know any word games?"*

"Starting my descent in ten minutes," Hawk said. *"Over and out."*

The air remained unusually calm, gray, soup-like, still without form or substance. Altimeter reading 6000 feet. Mist beading the windshield, slapped aside by the wipers. 5000 feet. A slight shudder as if something lurking in the void had reached out and touched them. 4000 feet. Al had turned, was staring down from his side window. 2500 feet. Another gentle shudder. Hawk glanced back down the plane. The three 'chute' men sat huddled together, heads down, against the chutes. 1500 feet. The little light they had faded abruptly with a slash of rain drumming against them. Hawk resisted the impulse to quicken their descent, tensing for a jolt that never came. 1000 feet -- 900 -- 800- an increase in light and a ragged twist of cloud into which they plunged -- 600 -- abruptly they emerged -- 450 feet. Hawk leveled over into a dark world of green light.

"Stilwell Road about three miles off on our right," Tyrone said. "I'd say we're a few miles north of Shin. Nice job, Hawk. We keep radio silence. I'll keep an eye out for Rogers and Ericson."

A few minutes later Tyrone spotted the two planes off to their right over the road. Shin was trying to reach them. No one broke radio silence. Under the slate-dark roof of cloud the green light sharply defined the jungle.

Hawk figured forty miles to Shadazup. Around fifteen minutes. They'd turn east to Taipha Ga, then slant into the Kumon Range. Only an east-west line of hills between Walawbum and Shadazup. The ceiling holding. The road thick with transport. A wide gap where it wound through the hills. Hawk swung left, angling toward Taipha Ga. It would save them a few miles. The rain increasing.

Taipha Ga, a sprawl of beaten-up buildings and small clearings. A scurry of troops at their sudden low passing. Five miles ahead the first lift of land into the Kumon Range. Hawk decided to hold a little to the north and swing down along the foothills until they spotted the Marauder's flares.

Rogers and Ericson had closed in, trailing a hundred yards, one off each wing. Once the flares were spotted they'd swing off in circling patterns, giving each of them time to go in for a drop and get out.

Now Hawk sensed the solid upthrust of the Kumon's dead ahead. A sudden lifting of the first hills. Goddamn the lousy rain! He banked sharply right along the foothills. One minute. Two. Three. Where in hell were the flares! Then abruptly the first one fountained directly ahead in a dirty-red arc. Then a second farther on into the hills. Hawk banked left. Tyrone signaled back to the 'chute' men. Ahead a third red flare slashed up. The land held level ahead but closing in on both sides, narrowing into what appeared to be a solid mass of jungle. Two orange flares! Drop zone coming up! Hawk felt his breath catch. A clear slash in the jungle, the white-crossed mat of the drop zone! Ten seconds. "O.K. Al -- drop!" Tyrone's arm flashed down.

They came over the clearing at 300 feet. Enough room on his left for a tight one-eighty. Banking hard he glimpsed the fall of their orange chutes. Then he was back down the gap. The red flares continued to rise. Where the hell were Rogers and Ericson? He broke radio silence.

"Whoever's next, get in there. Two orange flares and you're there. Be ready. They're not giving us much time. A one-eighty to the left and you're out!"

Directly ahead, seeming to come right at him, Roger's plane came slanting down, flashed past them and in. Farther out over the valley they spotted Ericson in a wide waiting turn. The rain came heavier but the ceiling held. Hawk trailed Ericson. Rogers emerged. Ericson banked hard and went in. They each went in twice more. Done! They lined out for Talpha Ga.

"I always loved merry-go-rounds," came Roger's voice.

"Anybody get the brass ring?" Hawk called.

"Shut up," Ericson snapped. *"We're not home yet!"*

"You know," Al said to Hawk as they flashed over Taipha Ga, "you chaps do a fairly decent job when I'm around to keep an eye on you." He turned and glanced back down the plane, giving the 'chute' men a thumbs-up.

They got through the hill gap above Shadazup before they lost their ceiling. First a few downward tangles of cloud, then the world disappeared. Hawk began a slow climb. Tyrone tried Maingkwan and Shin. Both socked in. They were at 3500' over Shin when Sook came in, a faint almost garble of words. McCabe's voice " . . . *socked in here . . . visibility . . . rain . . . grounded . . . suggest Jorhat . . . alternate . . . breaking . . . visibility . . . shit . . . "*

"Jorhat," Tyrone said. He unfolded the map another fold. "We should bear off west about twenty degrees."

"And an extra hundred miles," Hawk said. "Let's see how Ericson and Rogers are reacting."

Ericson came in finally. *"Shifting course to Jorhat. Rogers following. Will climb and hold at 7000' until we get a cloud break. Over and out."*

"I suggest we try for Sook, Colonel. If they're getting heavy rain it may be things will break, give us enough of a ceiling to get in. If Sook stays socked in we can head down the river, find something nearer."

Tyrone gave him a look, then shrugged. "You're the Captain."

Yes, Hawk thought. I'm also the one who has tomorrow off and a date with Jamila for lunch. Chances are if we can't make Sook we'll be hung up somewhere down the river tomorrow. No way of getting back in time for Jamila.

At 6500' Hawk leveled off. The air remained stable, only an occasional shudder to suggest something prowled their impenetrable gray world. Once or twice a curious slipping motion seemed to propel them sideways.

Tyrone gave him a look. "Feel like anything to you, Hawk?"

"A bit of wind trying to nudge us about. Try a fix on the Sook range."

Tyrone tried the range. Their direction finder drifted. An easterly drift. Hawk corrected course and held it for twenty minutes. Tyrone tried and finally raised Sook. McCabe was screaming for someone to pull up and head for Jorhat. *A hell of a lot of lightning over the Patkais. Airstrip awash. Anyone wanting to land will need a submarine.*

"We must be over the Patkais now," Tyrone said.

"Might as well keep on," Hawk said. He peered ahead. A glow from the late afternoon sun could be hinting that things were breaking up. Or were there fifty thousand feet of thunderheads piled up over them?

Hawk caught himself trying to see ahead, his eyes lifting from the instrument, as if he might be able to fathom the hidden intensity of the storm, guess its strength, the reluctance of the gooney to respond. He tried a quick bank left and right, straightened. Then the lightning came.

Abruptly they were caught in what seemed the center of violence, a blue implosion of light which for seconds illuminated a vast churning of clouds. The gooney lurched. Then absolute blackness as they slammed into turbulence, the gooney caught up, flung aside, seized and shaken. Hawk felt his controls go loose, wheel and pedals without resistance. They plummeted then jerked upward. His shout for wheels down came even as Tyrone dropped them. Again a feeling of falling, a battering sideways. Left wing wouldn't come up. Altimeter -- 4500 feet. Time enough to have cleared the Patkais? He held his breath, fought the gooney level. Lightning wrapped them again, a sudden blue halo of St. Elmo's fire ringing both props.

"Maybe we can hold it here," Hawk yelled. Now it felt as if someone outside was beating on them. Drumming a last tattoo? Their altitude slipped below 4000'.

"So," Tyrone said softly in a brief lull of thunder, "if the Patkais don't get us we can try for the Himalayas." His hand went up to an earphone. He gave Hawk a quick glance. Hawk's earphones had fallen off. He crammed them back on. McCabe was blasting loud and clear, a voice out of the whirlwind.

" . . .*that crazy sonofabitch wandering around up there, hold a northerly course . . . weather . . . breaking beyond the Brahmaputra . . . let down . . . one- eighty . . . come on in . . . ceiling 300 feet and lifting . . . but strap on your water skies . . . .*"

The airstrip showed little islands of earth above the water. Hawk dropped the gooney three point, managed to catch their skid in time, slid just off the strip halfway down. It wasn't until then that it occurred to them to look back. Aside from the dangling chute release cords the plane was empty. Hawk became empty. A vision of the 'chute' men hurled from the cargo opening somewhere over the hills flashed before him. This in order to keep a date? He was out of his seat and down the plane, already past the cockpit bulkhead and navigators' compartment before he glimpsed the three men still sitting motionless against the bulkhead in a tangle of lines hooked to cleats. The center one, a sergeant, his customary bronze skin a graveyard pallor, stared up at him.

"Chavez!

"I traded places, Lieutenant. It cost me a week's whiskey ration." Chavez glanced back at the Colonel behind Hawk.

"Sergeant Chavez," Tyrone snapped. "See that our plane is towed away. I want a thorough inspection. Furthermore, your little excursion into Burma is going to cost you another week's whiskey ration."

"Yes sir, Colonel." Chavez tried to salute but his arm got caught in one of the cords wrapping the three men.

Colonel Tyrone didn't speak again until he and Hawk were slogging their way up the line to Operations. "Your decision, Hawk, to try for Sook is the dumbest thing I've seen a pilot do in this war."

"Yes sir," Hawk said. "I realize that." But his breathing was easy now.

Returning to his empty tent he found Barpa sitting on his cot polishing his boots. Barpa smiled up at him. "Thunderstorms made great booms, Lieutenant."

Hawk smiled. "Yes, Barpa. Big booms."

"You be pleased," Barpa said, "I arrange for my cousin, Kalim, to come for you here at the hour of eleven tomorrow morning with his tonga."

"No Barpa." Suddenly Hawk felt exhaustion hit him. He sat on the cot, tilted sideways on the pillow. Would the squadron appreciate his being taxied off in a man-pulled tonga on a mid-day date?

"I think it is better you tell your cousin, Kalim, to meet me at the Greystaffs."

8

HAWK clung to the jeep as the driver cornered hard through the mud of a thatched-roofed settlement. He thought of the one brief time with Jamila by the pool. Maybe he wouldn't have another chance. The jeep slid sideways through a feathering of chickens, snapped straight and plowed on under a still-soggy tunnel of palms. The scent of bergamot had stayed with him, the singing birds in the tree, the blue glint of the pool he sought each day as he lifted from the airstrip. Would she be waiting for him on the broad verandah? Was all of this feeling merely the framing of a desire to take her to bed?

The driver hit his horn, blasting a scattering of ducks from a puddle before a thatched, open-sided basha. Beautiful wide-eyed children came smiling at their passing.

"Take it easy, soldier," Hawk said. "There's no fire."

"Under my ass, sir, if the motor pool finds out I'm running a taxi."

The driver eased up a bit on the last stretch to the Greystaffs'. Clouds still hung wet and heavy. No sound of planes. Maybe the whole squadron would get the day off. They came to a stop before the plantation gate where Masoud, with a hawk-faced man, stood leaning against a worn two-wheeled tonga. A small donkey cropped a tuft of grass from between its shafts.

"Thanks," Hawk said, leaping free. The motor-pool driver managed a casual salute, wheeled about and was off.

Masoud smiled and gestured. "This is Kalim, who says to tell you it's a very long ride to Chabua."

"Tell him I shall remember that when we return."

Kalim gave the shadow of a bow, motioning Hawk to the rear-facing padded seat, and sprung nimbly to his high driver's perch. The wooden wheels creaked lightly as they proceeded on up the winding drive, a smiling Masoud running along behind.

Hawk again tried to visualize Jamila. The dark shape of her eyes came to him, the way her sari had wound around her lithe body. Had she been swimming? A long luster of jet-black hair. Again, the remembered scent of bergamot.

Immediately, it seemed, the tonga was before the house, Masoud trotting up the verandah steps, the front door opening. Jamila stepped out as Hawk reached the verandah.

She was smiling. She wore a light khaki skirt, a white shirt open at the neck, leather sandals. He had expected a sari. If her toes had not shown bright coral she could have been a member of some women's auxiliary.

"It's good to see you again, Jamila."

She took his hand. Maybe she was made of sugar and spice. "Yes, Alan," her voice soft as if until that moment she had not been sure what her reaction would be. "Molly and the Major are looking forward to seeing you again. Come in."

"Thought at first your Major Butler's interest was all in my trophies," Major Greystaff said. He and Hawk stood staring up at his prize buffalo head in the trophy room, where Molly had shooed them while she and Jamila saw to some tea and cookies in preparation for the trek to Chabua. "But mostly he's been asking about the albino elephant. Can't make the chap out, if you follow me." Greystaff tapped the side of his head. "He'd study the photograph, then ask me about lines of fire as if I'd been to war against the beast."

"Jedd Butler does give us pause at times," Hawk said. They turned to the picture. "A real shutter-bug. Thinks about photography as much as the war."

"Don't suppose any of you chaps really have much idea what's been going on here in India, what?"

Hawk smiled. "Sorry. I read a brief history of India a long time ago. Something lately about your Mahatma Gandhi."

"Not mine, Lieutenant." Major Greystaff's eyes narrow, his color warming slightly. "Do you realize the man's intent is to clear us out of India?" He glared fiercely up at the great white elephant, gave a tug at his bush-jacket lapels. "Major Butler wanted to know if I still had the negative," Greystaff went on, evidently deciding against further political observation. "Of course not," I told him. "Poor film. Rotted away. So I let him take a shot of the print." He gestured at the photograph. "He took it down, rigged lights. Must have taken a couple of dozen shots. Different angles. I told him he'd better go off up there, find the bugger and get some live shots."

"You think the albino is still alive?"

"Could be. Took my photo over twenty years ago. He was forty or fifty then, according to my guide. That would put him at sixty or seventy now. Suppose one could find out. Told your Major Butler as much. Told him to go up river to Sadiya. That's where Jamila is from, you know. Look up my old guide. Bound to know. Now, let me tell you about these two tusks."

Enormous they were, crossed above the doorway.

"An African bull. Measure over ten feet. We were camped out in Kenya. During the elephant must period. Charged me. I used a Mauser and -- "

"Alan and John, if you'd care to join us," came Molly's voice.

They followed her out to the patio. The pool was aquamarine between the palms where a bird, maybe the same one, sang. Molly told about the last formal dance at the plantation. Jamila poured tea as amber as the color of her eyes. English cookies were served from a tin decorated with scenes from Mother Goose. Then it was time to leave.

Once past the still-quiet airstrip, Kalim's way toward Chabua revealed a countryside that unreeled from where they sat, backwards on their padded seat. Heavy clouds hung low over tall stands of huge trees clinging spider-like to the earth. From beneath these came children, trailing after, dodging puddles.

"Almost as if we were trolling," Hawk said.

Jamila laughed and turned to him. It was not a wide seat but their bodies had not touched. Now her shoulder brushed against his. "Yes, it is so!" Her eyes were wide and he saw now they were green, like grass against warm earth. "And do you realize those are the first words we have spoken since we began this journey?"

"Yes, it is so," Hawk said.

They both laughed, so loudly Kalim turned, his glance at them quick, as if making sure he had come the correct way. "Memsahib," his voice apologetic, "it is a poor road but makes the shortest way to Chabua." He turned, slapping a rein without effect on the donkey's pace.

"Thank you, Kalim," Jamila said.

"My first ride in a tonga," Hawk said. "My first ride anywhere since we arrived. I do not count the flying."

"Not count, Alan?"

"It's all the same. Hills and mountains and jungle. Somewhere south of us men are fighting and dying in a war I do not see. Only here in Assam, a sense of many people, the rivers, villages. On a clear day, to the northwest, I have glimpsed the beginning of the Himalayas. But all I know so far of India is an Indian boy, Barpa, who takes care of our tent and covets the beautiful boots I bought in Alexandria. It is as if today is my first day in India. I am riding with you in a tonga on a country road where people have homes and children and surely worry about the same things people worry about in every country. So far that's all, plus Barpa."

"Well," Jamila smiled, "it is a beginning."

"I know nothing about the restaurants in Chabua. I just assumed there would be some."

"Molly was a bit concerned but she had it from Masoud a new one has opened on the outskirts." Jamila spoke briefly to Kalim in

Assamese. He nodded, gave a light cry and slapped at the donkey. "Though certainly she wouldn't let me go alone to Chabua with all the unrest, though I have done so a few times. Now there are so many soldiers -- the English, Indians, Chinese, even some Chin and Naga recruits from the hills. And of course. . . " Jamila paused and smiled.

"And of course the Americans," Hawk said.

"Certainly they are the noisiest," Jamila said. "I mean your planes, even the high ones at night, flying on to China over what you call the 'Hump.' The Major is getting very impatient that you win the war and fly away. He dreams of the old days returning. But even Molly knows better. This war will change many things forever, don't you think so?"

"I don't think about the war, Jamila."

"But you think you will win? Yes? 'Bluebirds again over the white cliffs of Dover?'" She gave a sad smile. "Last time I was there that's what people were singing."

"My only theory about war," Hawk said, "is that no country has ever won a war. It merely loses fewer lives than its enemy and celebrates with monuments to its dead. This war's like a play that's had too many rehearsals."

Jamila studied the road unfolding under them. "Perhaps, Alan." A long silence, a tilt of her head. "A theory I suggest you do not propose to Major Greystaff. Underneath he is a very kind man to whom I owe much."

They rode for some time in silence, her shoulder warm against his. The clouds were lifting, their heaviness filtered with a yellow light. Distantly came the sound of planes. The land opened around them to rice paddies, men appearing to walk on water behind their white Brahma cattle, more people on the road, and always the children, especially when they passed through groves of trees, magically appearing in the dark interstices of trunks and branches.

"A rupee for your reveries, Alan."

"Oddly, it reminds me of Maine," he answered. Wrinkles appeared between her eyes. "Maine, the place where I grew up. I lived in the country and believed that night did not come from the sky but hid in the forest that covered the long hill behind our house. Night was darkness that in daytime hid in the trees, making deep secret caves from which creatures watched."

"Terrible creatures?"

"Not at all. Just those who lived in the night."

Jamila studied him, smiling, quoted, "'Tiger, tiger, burning bright, in the forests of the night'." She leaned forward, looking off at a distant grove of banyan trees. For a moment one hand rested lightly on his arm. "I think I understand."

"Yes, one of Blake's magical lines, Jamila. In England you were a literature student?"

"Even before then. Molly has quite a fine library. Her one escape from the Major. Much poetry. She taught me to read almost from the time I first came to them. That's where I read Blake and also your Walt Whitman."

"You were in college in England?"

"Until the war began. At Girton, Cambridge. I was planning to teach. I was changing to nursing when the raids began. Then the Greystaffs insisted I return with them."

Again they rode on in silence. Now there were more houses, many built of mud-brick, some with fences and gardens. Lanes threaded off from the widening road. Small pastures held black-faced sheep. Goats were staked out along the road. More tongas, the wallahs shouting at one another as they passed. The last mists had vanished and as they came up a small crest Kalim cried out, pointing ahead, his curved nose in profile, a smile of triumph. "Chabua, Chabua, Chabua!" he cried.

Far off, a pattern of wooden buildings emerged, low ones seeming to gather about higher ones with balconies. Now a trace of dust in the air, a sense of sunlight flooding behind the clouds, and from beyond these, the sounds of planes going to war.

"Before half-hour," Kalim cried, still pointing. "The memsahib forgive if I must now make search."

They had indeed some trouble in finding the newly opened restaurant that Molly had mentioned. Unfortunately, it did not yet have a name or the name was not yet posted, the location incorrectly given, which Jamila said was to be expected. But Kalim, following the lead of constant inquiries, brought them circuitously through Chabua's outskirts to a long, low building half-hidden by trees and surrounded by a high, yellow brick wall with an open iron gate. Inside they followed a drive, through the remains of what had been formal gardens gone thickly to bamboo, blue-flowering jacaranda trees, and papayas. They came to a wide, cleared area where several tongas were parked, their wallahs sitting on the ground playing cards. Beyond them was a ragged line of jeeps bearing a variety of military insignia.

Kalim called to the wallahs. They nodded, pointing to an entrance buried in the many-tendrilled embrace of blazing bougainvillea gone berserk.

"A bit early for tiffin," Jamila said. She gave the establishment a cautious glance. The wallahs had stopped their play and were watching. She shrugged. "But it does seem to be open. I believe this was once the residence of an Indian regional official, then for a while the British club."

From inside the building came an arpeggio from a stringed instrument. Kalim brought the tonga to a stop before the entrance. Hawk climbed down and held his hand up to Jamila. She hesitated, studying the flagstoned pathway into the bougainvillea.

"I am wondering, too. It looks repectable," Hawk said, as a large figure moved out from the entrance.

"Welcome, Lieutenant Hawk. I am most honored that you and your beautiful friend have chosen my Most Celestial Dining."

Manchu, round, opulent in a shimmer of silk and dark locks gleaming, smiled out at them. "I believe you will find my menu better fragrant, Lieutenant, than the Sookerating mess. Not only of oriental cooking but also of European. Please to follow me."

Before this time Hawk had held little more than the briefest of conversations with Manchu. Because of the flying, there was at noon only an informal mess, handled by Manchu's Indian boys while Manchu himself was off on what Butler called "squadron business." But his appearance as a restaurant proprietor came as no surprise to Hawk. Manchu had already revealed his talent by acquiring control of the Dibrugarh gin traffic, and there were rumors of other dealings pleasing to the military mind. Before now, the local restaurants had tested the squadron's intestinal fortitude and found it wanting. What more logical for the troops of Upper Assam than a clean and quiet place?

"I suppose his real name is listed in the squadron records," Hawk said to Jamila as Manchu turned from their window table, leaving them with a broad smile and two menus, hand-written on carefully torn sheets of rice paper. Script in English, Hindi, and Chinese -- Most Celestial Dining.

"Why do you call him Manchu, Alan?"

"After an evil world conqueror in the Saturday Evening Post stories of my American youth," Hawk said. "However it's not considered good form among us to address him as Manchu and so mostly he is not." He studied the menu. "May I ask for guidance? Something with curry? Chutney?"

Jamila's eyes sparkled behind long lashes. "It depends."

"Depends?"

"On what we choose. Curry dishes are best when the spices are freshly ground. Shall we test your Manchu by trying his East India Chicken Curry? It might be rather hot. The Chinese tend to do that, so as a safety precaution we might order his unidentified cold beer."

"You are beautiful and you cook."

"No. In England, at Girton, I worked as a waitress in an Indian restaurant. A very good restaurant." She glanced out through partially restored wooden shutters onto what must once have been a flower garden. Lilies arched from a moulder of palm fronds. Her profile took his breath away.

"O.K. You are only beautiful."

They were alone in a small room of four tables. When Jamila continued looking away, remaining silent, he realized he'd come on too strong, made a dumb remark.

"Sorry, Jamila. I know what you're thinking. Just like London. Typical American. It's just that I really did want to indicate how I feel."

"It came through quite clearly." Jamila faced him again, smiling. Her teeth were very white. Was she wearing lipstick? "And I thank you. But I like to feel my appearance alone is not enough. For instance, I speak several languages, one of which I shall use on our young waiter now approaching."

A slim Indian boy, skin golden against his white tunic, came cautiously up to their table, paper and pencil in one hand. "Namaste," Jamila said.

The boy gave a nervous bow. "I, also, say 'good day' to you, lady and gentleman," he said, a bit sternly. "I am Kumar. I speak English for you." He glanced back over his shoulder to the doorway where Manchu hovered.

"We were wondering about your curry," Jamila said. "Also the cold beer. Is it British?"

His eyes widened in panic. Jamila then spoke quickly in Hindi. Kumar breathed deeply. They spoke again and he went smiling from the room.

"The curry was made today," Jamila said. "He believes the chicken has not been too long on this earth. The ale is British, though unlabelled because of the international situation. I'm not sure what he meant by that."

"I'm sure Manchu's explanation would be interesting. Tell me about your coming to live with the Greystaffs."

Part of him was listening to her telling of the village of Sadiya where she was born, the arranged marriage when she was nine, never to be consummated because both her mother and father died in an epidemic, her dowry money gone and she of no use any more. Beads of moisture grew on her upper lip as sunlight broke through the shutters. She wiped childishly at her mouth with a fist. Her glance caught his.

How does love begin? Who looks first from the forest? For this, Hawk suddenly knew, had become more than tiffin with an attractive woman whom you'd met briefly by a swimming pool and for a little while dreamed only of taking to bed. Jamila looked away and went on with her story.

Her mother's brother had tried to help but he could do little because, though he did have a position, a kind of sub-inspector at the fringe of the jungle northeast of Sadiya, he had a wife and seven children and they lived very near to poverty.

What use did the world have for a nine-year-old girl? How many rupees was one worth?

Jamila could not remember all the details of that time before she came to live with the Greystaffs. Only that there was this strange fierce Englishman who appeared in Sadiya during the months her uncle tried to keep her. Major Greystaff was with a hunting party. He had gone on up into the jungle and when he returned there was more talk between her uncle and aunt about the extra mouth they had to feed. That's when she first heard talk of the albino elephant. Then her uncle told her she would be leaving with Major John Greystaff to live in some distant place and she must do everything she was told to do, for indeed it was certain that Lakshmi-Shri, the Hindu goddess of fortune and prosperity, had nodded in her direction. But mostly Jamila remembered peering out through the rain on the ferry carrying her far off down the Brahmaputra River to a strange place where tea was grown, and all she could feel was that this was how one died.

It was Molly that brought her back to life, a life a nine-year-old girl could not believe in, a great house filled with many things, things she could touch and clean, the softness of a pallet in her tiny room and cloth seeming to be made from rainbows for her to sew, first for herself, and then for all the house. Molly taught her how to read, took her to the school in Chabua where at first the other children made fun of her country ways and accent. It came as a surprise to her when she discovered she learned faster than the others, was moved ahead, caught up with children her own age and then left them behind. She was twelve when the Greystaffs took her for the first time to England.

"Again I am here." Kumar materialized beside them, now that they had finished the chicken. "Suggestion cooling fruits in fine liqueur; Very good."

"It sounds fine, Kumar," Hawk said. "Thank you."

Jamila smiled after the retreating Kumar. "Your Manchu is working hard to train him."

"I'd guess Manchu works hard at everything, Jamila."

From the parking lot came the sound of jeeps arriving. Above them the hard murmur of the gooneys. A parrot on the blue-flowering jacaranda stared in at them. Jamila reached across and touched him lightly on one finger, eyes questioning. "And now about you?"

"Very well," Hawk said. "The true story of Alan Hawk, who was found in a basket at the mouth of the Sheepscot River in the State of Maine where his father, whom he really never got to know, sat playing at his grand piano in the surf while his mother stood on a rock singing lieder."

For a moment Jamila simply stared, then buried her face in her hands, the laughter coming softly, her shoulders shaking. She dropped her hands. "And then, Alan?"

"They put me to sea in a pea-green boat. Years later, I flew away to India."

She wiped at her eyes with both fists. "And what about in between?"

Kumar came with a silver tray and dishes of sliced melon adorned with sliced limes and oranges. His gestures in pouring the liqueur over their fruit from a slender flagon were dramatic. Manchu observed from the doorway.

"In the middle part of my true story," Hawk went on, "there came in my country while I was in high school what they called the Great Depression. Upon finishing at school I decided to be a newspaper reporter and hitch-hiked around our country and down into Mexico. I wrote a few stories about the people I met, poor people, and sent them back to a newspaper in Maine. The editor had told me he would be glad to read them. Even printed one or two but never sent me any money. I was in California, a place called Yosemite, when my mother wrote telling me my father's music school had failed. They were poor and I should come home. There was work in the shipyards, building ships for the coming war that had been playing previews in Africa and Spain and China. I was working when Japan bombed Pearl Harbor. We called it a sneak attack. I wonder what we expected? A formal announcement? Anyway, working in college.But then I heard the Sirens singing."

Jamila studied him, eyes serious. "And you went off to war."

"No, not really. I mean, I didn't see it that way. It was a Greek historian, Thucydides, who wrote of young men who did not think of war but merely longed to see far places and couldn't believe they might die. That's how I came to North Africa, to Sicily, and then -- " He paused. He wanted to say "to you."

Jamila smiled. "To India. You wanted to fly?"

"It was a new challenge. Perhaps I was merely deluded by a desire for motion, to escape into the excitement of all the foreign lands I had read about."

"Then you are not really here to save India?"

"An early war joke -- " he said. "A British merchant ship is under attack by a German U-boat. News is flashed to its Captain that the Americans have entered the war, which he announces from the bridge. Comes a query from the crew, 'On which side?'"

"Yes, I understand," Jamila smiled. "My country of India is really many countries and there are many sides." She gave him a troubled look. "But this is a pleasant day."

"And a marvelous meal." Hawk finished his fruit and Kumar again materialized, smiling.

"We have fine coffee."

"Thank you, Kumar," Jamila said. "But we must leave."

Kumar disappeared, came back immediately followed by Manchu, who nodded, smiling. "Now that you find Most Celestial Dining I hope to see you more times. Please to tell your many friends of Most Celestial Dining. Also, most sorry, but there is no charge." He gave a small bow and motioned Kumar before him from the room. Hawk left some rupees on the table.

In the parking lot the dust and heat hung heavily. Two squadron mechanics arrived in a jeep, gave Jamila admiring glances and a wave to Hawk. Kalim awoke and stood by his tonga.

Late that afternoon, Major Greystaff came with an ancient pair of grayish swimming trunks for Hawk and showed him to the changing room off the pool. The trunks were a bit large and the draw-string broke when Hawk tightened it about his waist. After Hawk and Jamila have cooled off with a swim, the Major told them, they are to join Molly and himself on the patio.

Jamila was a good swimmer. Hawk felt scarcely-used muscles tug at his back. Underwater he could not hold his breath as long as usual. The water was a fain't green and surprisingly cool. Jamila churned past him overhead, a nubile porpoise. He surfaced and on a second turn of the pool felt his crawl slide into place, sort of. He pulled himself up on the pool's edge beside Jamila.

"Our squadron had a beach in Sicily, near Agrigentum," he said. "Had to be careful. Much of it was mined."

Jamila curled her toes and skimmed the water with them. "Did you know there are Indian troops fighting with the Japanese in Burma against you? Many Indians believe the Japanese attacked because they are at war with England. If there were no English here they wouldn't bother us."

Hawk grinned. "So which side shall we fight on?"

"I refuse," Jamila said, "to conjure up an Asian conflagration on our day together. I am glad that we are here."

They swam again and afterwards sat with Molly and the Major on the patio. Masoud brought them cooling lime drinks. The late afternoon was filled with the sound of planes. Major Greystaff mentioned that Major Butler had come that morning to show him a map he'd marked, an area north of Sadiya, where Greystaff had photographed the albino elephant. Did Major Greystaff remember the name of his guide?

"Imagine the chap thinking I'd remember a name from twenty years ago!" Major Greystaff looked pleased with himself. "Of course I do, but the only reason is because the chap was Jamila's uncle. Remember, Jamila?"

"I remember my uncle Raju." Her words were low and strained.

Molly said quickly, very brightly, "And the restaurant, you found it satisfactory?"

Jamila looked away. Hawk watched Molly's glance move between him and Jamila. Jamila remained silent.

"We used to go there years ago for parties," Molly said brightly. "Remember, John?"

Now the Major did not remember. Jamila sat motionless, head down, hands in her lap.

"If you'll excuse me," Hawk said, "I must get back to the squadron." There were tears in Jamila's eyes when she looked up at him.

"There is no future for us," she said, as they walked to the tonga.

Kalim was waiting. Hawk shook hands awkwardly with Jamila. He watched her as the tonga wound down the drive, and imagined he saw a fain't smile when she waved. Kalim flicked the donkey into a trot. Yes: no future.

Hawk stepped down from the tonga at one of the squadron's make-shift, unguarded entrances to the compound. At first Colonel Tyrone had made an attempt at security but as he had observed, the jackals had no trouble getting in, nor the many natives looking for work, and he wouldn't be surprised if a hungry Jap soldier on the run might drop by for a snack. Given their limited personnel, securing the airstrip was enough of a problem.

As Hawk headed for his tent he saw Lee Ericson at a distance and waved. Ericson gave him a stare and went on into his tent without responding.

Robb, Fitz, and Schultz were all on their cots, Robb writing a letter, Fitz on his back, eyes closed. Schultz, cleaning his .45, gave Hawk a sullen look. A single letter lay on Hawk's pillow.

"Thanks, whoever," Hawk said, sitting, reaching for the letter. "Anyone want to hear about my day?" Schultz gave him another look. Hawk said, "Guess who's opened a restaurant in Chabua? Manchu. Chicken curry very good. A nice swim in the Greystaffs' pool. My first ride in a tonga."

"Too fucking bad Paul and Christopher couldn't have gone along with you!" Schultz said. "That way the Jap Zero wouldn't have nailed them. Shit, friend, they didn't even make it back for lunch. And not a goddamn river where they went down so they didn't get to go swimming. They just got burned up, leaving a bloody looking asshole in the jungle!"

Hawk had known Lieutenant Paul since Africa. Christopher was a co-pilot who'd joined them as they left Sicily. 'Anybody else?"

"They were alone," Fitz said, opening his eyes. "You know the place, Hawk. That gap in the hills east of Walawbum. An alert was on. They shouldn't have come out in the open. At 500 feet there wasn't a damn thing they could have done."

"Except take the fucking day off!" Schultz snapped.

9

BARPA found the still-unopened letter under Hawk's cot the next morning and put it on the pillow again, pointing to it when Hawk returned from mess. On this one, Alma Jilbert's name and address were printed in a childish hand, decorated by a V entwined with flowers. His name and AFO number were followed by Asia, The World. He shoved it aside. The letter was still there when Hawk returned late that afternoon from three routine missions hauling ammo to Maingkwan, which included a day-long argument with the Chinese battalion commander, who had refused each time to assist personally in the unloading of the mortar shells, even though Hawk and Chavez joined in with the commander's sweating crew of three, handing down the heavy crates. The commander had leaned against the tail section smoking a cigarette and issuing brief commands to his enlisted men. "I don't understand their insignia," Hawk said to Chavez.

"Maybe he's a general. Like in Mexico," Luis said loudly, eyeing the commander, *"Para los generales, trabajo es siempre deshonor."* The commander had nodded, smiled, spoke sharply to his sweating countrymen and lit another cigarette.

Hawk sat down on his cot and opened the letter.

DEAR ALAN, I HAVEN'T YET HEARD FROM YOU ABOUT MY FIRST LETTER BUT IT'S PROBABLY TOO SOON WITH YOU SO FAR OFF AND BUSY WITH THE WAR. ANYWAY, I CALLED YOUR MOTHER AGAIN WHO SAID I HAD THE RIGHT APO BUT YOU DIDN'T EVEN WRITE HER MUCH. ANYWAY, NOW I HAVE BETTER DIRECTIONS FOR YOU TO FIND FRED. HE IS A CORPORAL WITH THE 988TH SIGNAL OPERATIONS. HE'S WITH THE 3RD INFANTRY COMPANY NEAR A PLACE CALLED SHIDZUP OR SHADUZIP, SOME CRAZY NAME LIKE THAT. HE REPAIRS RADIOS. PLEASE TELL HIM MY ALLOTMENT HASN'T BEEN INCREASED LIKE HE SAID. YOU MIGHT AS WELL KNOW WE WERE HAVING TROUBLE BEFORE HE GOT SENT OVERSEAS. SO TELL HIM HE HAS A SON, WHO'S JUST DARLING AND LOOKS JUST LIKE HIM. SO I HOPE TO HEAR FROM YOU SOON SAYING YOU HAVE FOUND FRED AND TOLD HIM THE NEWS. MEANWHILE WE ARE ALL HOPING, LIKE THEY JOKE HERE, THAT YOU ARE CAREFUL AND FLY LOW AND SLOW. CONGRATULATIONS ON YOUR MEDAL, WHICH WAS IN THE NEWSPAPER.

YOUR FRIEND, ALMA WORTH JILBERT

"Here," Hawk said, handing the letter to Fitz, who had returned from the mess and announced that a squadron meeting was scheduled for that evening. Stretched out on his cot, Fitz read it over.

"Sort of tells you the real reason you're here," Fitz said, tossing the letter back. "It's these little personal touches that reminds us of what we're fighting for. When you plan on dropping in on Fred?"

Hawk lay back on his cot and stared up at the canvas where a scorpion was inching its way the tent pole. . . . .he smiled, remembering yesterday's squadron meeting.

No one had been excused except the necessary personnel at the airstrip. Manchu and his boys, after setting up the mess hall, had been dismissed. The squadron bar had not been opened.

As before, Colonel Tyrone, Major Butler and Captain McCabe sat at a long table facing the gathering. A thin stink of diesel fuel from the throbbing generator outside hung in the air. The light bulbs, hanging on their cords from bamboo poles, flickered rhythmically. Only Al Tyrone and Jedd Butler reflected some attention to military dress, Al in crisp khaki shorts, white dress shirt with blue epaulets, and a silver gleam of insignia on his open collar. He rose, adjusting his pith helmet on the table. He let his glance move across the room until silence reigned.

"Gentlemen, this is a sad occasion for us, and I'm beginning by turning the meeting over to Jedd Butler, who has a few words for us. Jedd?" Jedd, neat in khakis and insignia, cap folded over his belt, rose and stared wildly over them. His neatness contrasted oddly with his expression, his voice soft yet overlaid with a curious intensity. "*Esprit de corps*, gentlemen." Chin set, he looked them over. "*Esprit de corps*. Does anyone here understand that phrase?"

"Anybody here speak German?" Romano called. Silence. Butler waited a moment. "Does anyone here have *esprit de corps*?" Tyrone and McCabe exchanged puzzled glances. "I might have a few swallows left," Romano responded. "Drank up most of it." Restrained laughter. Again Butler waited a moment, then launched his tirade. "Devotion among humans for their group, is its purpose. It's something I became aware of in the air corps while you snot-noses were spinning in on your tricycles. *Esprit de corps*. It's what we ain't got. It's what I got thinking about when I was transmitting official notice of the deaths of Lieutenants Christopher and Paul to the War Department. It's what I was thinking about when I wrote personally to the men's families, telling them how much the two had contributed to our squadron spirit. Then it occurred to me -- what spirit? Do we really have any group spirit? Where is our *esprit de corps*?"

Robb found himself on his feet. "Major, I'm not sure what you're getting at, but I'll try and answer your question. Our *esprit de corps* is how we're delivering supplies to the troops in Burma. That's our job. We're doing it." He sat down.

"In my reform school," Romano yelled,"only the frogs drank *esprit de corp*."

"Maybe we should have a pep rally every evening," a flight mechanic yelled.

"In high school in L.A. I was a cheerleader," Luis Chavez offered. "I volunteer."

Butler's stoic demeanor abruptly dissolved. He ran a hand through his graying hair, shook his head in disgust and dropped into his chair. Terry McCabe was instantly on his feet, an uncommon solemnity of expression masking his features. "All I got to say about the Major's remarks is maybe he's right. I don't mean about that esprit business but about how we're running things here, this goddamn trucking service. We're delivering, as Robby says, supplies to the troops in Burma -- and doing a damn good job of it. We just don't go in singing songs and waving flags. So what I have to say is we're going to miss Christopher and Paul because they ain't going to get replaced. Group Headquarters has informed us we will get a replacement plane but no more pilots. And you all know what that means. We may end up having Manchu co-piloting for us!" McCabe paused, obviously hoping for laughter but settling for a scattering of smiles.

"Anyway we ain't here this evening for a memorial service or to talk about what to do when some Jap pilot gets a wild hair up his ass and decides to come out and raise a bit of hell. Alerts and open flat country don't go together, so even though, as Al will tell you, the Japs are pulling back, just barely holding on at Warazup, a few Zeros aren't worth bothering a rat's ass about. What does matter is that you all are going to be flying more. Only one day off in seven is all you get from here on. Now Al is going to brief us on the overall situation, and when we might be getting the hell out of here. Al?" Al Tyrone glanced across at Butler staring moodily nowhere, shrugged, adjusted his pith helmet again and rose.

"First off I'd like to take up Terry's reference on the overall situation, to what's going on in Europe right now. As we've all heard, there's going to be an invasion from England. It's just that nobody knows exactly when. But an educated guess would say it will be damn soon. That's why we're not being given any personnel replacements. O.K.? Now, as for Terry saying this isn't a memorial service for Lieutenants Christopher and Paul, he's correct. But I'd like to mention that I've written personal letters to their families. I know some of you have done the same. Which is as it should be." He paused and gave Butler another puzzled look. "As for the overall situation here: in a nutshell, General Stilwell seems set on taking Myitkyina, 'Mitch,' before the monsoon sets in. Whether he makes it or not depends on the weather and on the Marauders, up in the Kumons. The Japs are pulling back but not without a fight. They're giving the Chinese above Kamaing a hard time. I hope we can take Mitch. The Japs drove

General Stilwell out of Burma in '42. He's not going to let them do it again. Let's see -- what's the date?"

"Still 1944, Colonel," Romano said.

"Still April, Colonel," another added.

"The 30th, Colonel," Chavez put in. "And Colonel, sir, Lieutenant Hawk says he thinks all the enlisted personnel that are flying ought to be allowed their booze ration in bottles instead of our daily two-ounces-a-mission sips. I'm developing rye breath of the armpits."

Colonel Tyrone waited for the applause to subside, staring up where clouds of insects hovered around the naked bulbs. A bat made a hawk-like pass. "I'll see the committee takes the matter under consideration, Sergeant Chavez." He paused again. Two more bats swooped, banked and vanished. "As for how long we'll be here, gentlemen, the next month will be decisive. Either the troops take Mitch by then or the monsoon lowers the curtain on things. My best guess is that what with Europe coming up they'll be needing us back in Italy within a month." Again a long swooping of bats. Colonel Tyrone picked up his pith helmet. "I hereby declare the meeting closed and the bar open."

For several nights the jackals had been silent. Now their cries outside the compound rose in a high, sharp encirclement. Were they planning a night's foray? Hawk walked not in the direction of his tent but along the outer row of tents, away from the mess and bar and the worn lilt of an old Scott Joplin 78 Al Tyrone had brought with him from Texas. Claimed his mother had played it the day he was born -- "Cleopha." Low clouds reflected the jaundice-hued glow of the airstrip's security lights. Most of the tents were dark. Hawk thought that pacing the whole compound before hitting the sack might wear the cutting edge off of Manchu's gin. What he needed was one cool sharp breath of Maine air. How was Jamila sleeping in her bergamot-scented night? He turned up the next tent row. Darkness except where midway one tent pulsed with the white, hot glow of a Coleman lantern. Coming abreast the tent Hawk glimpsed Jedd Butler, through a curtain of mosquito netting, seated at his table and staring intently at something propped up before him. Butler had not remained long at the bar after the meeting. Hawk found himself, still slightly drunk, doing what he had no intention of doing. He turned abruptly and pushed through the flaps into the tent.

"Jedd," he said, "maybe you weren't looking in the right place for it."

"For what?" Butler didn't look up.

"*Esprit de corps*".

"You don't see *esprit de corps*, you feel it!"

Butler looked up, gestured.

"Come in, come in, Hawk. You're letting the scorpions in."

"You mean mosquitoes, Jedd."

"Those, too. Here, take a look. My best shot from the Greystaffs'."

An angle shot. Butler must have got down and focused from the floor. It gave the great albino elephant a sense of motion. "Looks as if he's about to charge," Hawk said, aware that Butler, red-eyed and haggard, was watching him intently. "So what do you intend to do, Jedd?"

"Go to Sadiya. Find the guide that led Greystaff to the albino. The old fool claimed he couldn't remember his name. Told me I shouldn't have much trouble finding the albino if it's still alive."

Hawk said nothing. Butler brought the photo close to his face. "*Esprit de corps* -- that's where you'll find it! Understand?"

"I'm not following you, Jedd."

"Schultz doesn't understand either. Did a co-pilot for him the other day. Coming back from a drop we saw a big herd crossing a clearing in the Hukawng Valley east of Shinbwiyan. We came down at them. Instantly the bulls took over, forming a line, the females and calves closing in behind them. The bulls reared up when we went over, tusks in the air! Absolutely magnificent. That's *esprit de corps*!"

"Jedd, don't tell me you were buzzing elephants again."

Butler gave him an angry glance. "I'm talking about *esprit de corps*, Hawk. The whole herd working together, not breaking apart. Females close over their calves. All those tusks raised up. Compare that to our squadron."

Hawk felt his drunkenness recede. He tried a smile. "I believe most of the squadron have all their teeth, Major."

"You're goddamn wrong there, Lieutenant. The whole military has become toothless. Back in the thirties we knew who we were. We worked together, officers and enlisted men. We knew where we were going, knew who we were, and we goddamn well didn't shit together!"

"It doesn't seem to have interfered with us doing what we're supposed to do, Major." Hawk stepped back toward the tent flaps.

Butler's eyes glittered. "Just like McCabe said. You're a bunch of truck drivers. How many of you would get caught out in the flat and stand up to a Zero like those elephants stand up to us?"

"I wouldn't bring Christopher and Paul into this, Major." Hawk felt his hand brush the edge of the canvas. "We're all feeling badly about it."

Butler picked up the photo of the albino, glared at it, slammed it down. "Who's talking about Christopher and Paul!" He slammed the photo onto the table. "You haven't asked me what my idea is about the elephant, Lieutenant. I thought you were interested!"

"Right now, Jedd," Hawk said softly, backing another step, "I'm interested in hitting the sack. Let's save it for tomorrow."

"Tomorrow! *Esprit de corps*! Shit, we can't even work together on little things. My idea is big!" A crooked smile worked out from the fury of Butler's lined face.

"O.K., Major. Go ahead. What's your idea?"

Butler's eyes narrowed, his smile vanished. "Promise you won't tell anyone?"

For a moment Hawk thought Butler was going to ask him to cross his heart. "My word, Major."

"I'm going up to Sadiya, to the Mishmi hills. I'm going up and find that albino. I know he's alive. What I'm going to do is -- buy him!" Butler's eyes lit up.

"Good idea, Jedd. And then what are you going to do with him?"

Butler leaned forward confidentially. "The question is, what are *we* going to do, Hawk? You and I. I'm going to need help. After the war we'll take the albino to the States. Do you see the possibilities?"

"Yes, Jedd. Several have now dawned." Hawk partly turned and pulled aside the tent flaps. "I'd like some time to put them in order."

Butler followed him out into a now rain-washed darkness. "But first we've got to get up to Sadiya, see? Nail the deal down, start making arrangements. My idea is we should start by working out of Texas. Big bucks! Here, come back in and let me show you my plans."

"Tomorrow, Major. Tomorrow. Good night."

Now all the tents were dark. It took Hawk some stumbling to find his tent. He stripped silently and slid onto his cot, hit his head on a hanging lamp. Schultz's flashlight gave him a flickering jab.

"So then, how were things at the tea house, lover boy?"

Hawk closed his eyes. He watched the albino elephant press massively on into an endless jungle, into his sleep.

Two evenings later Major Greystaff was commenting that, even escorted by Hawk, he didn't like the idea of Jamila going to Dibrugarh. He fumed that the business could wait until he finished his bloody hospital visit. Jamila pointed out that the business couldn't wait, this being the third time there had been trouble with their tea shipments. Besides it was she who took care of their books and had discovered what their agent, Chand, was up to. Greystaff shrugged. Molly looked distressed.

"It's no place for a woman," the Major growled, his color deepening, Molly signaling Jamila to change the subject. "Dibrugarh is a dirty river port and even worse with the bloody war going on." Greystaff scowled at Hawk.

"Well, thanks to Alan offering his day off, I won't be helplessly alone." Jamila smiled at Alan. "I'm positive Chand has been up to his old tricks. Possibly even a few new ones."

"And John up to his, too," Molly put in firmly. "Trying to make light of Dr. Gopal's warning. John is going into the hospital at Chabua tomorrow to stay until Dr. Gopal says he can come home."

John Greystaff's lips tightened. He glared fiercely at Hawk. "See you stay with her, Lieutenant. You may think she's all sweetness but underneath she's a tricky minx."

All positions seemingly resolved, they sat a while longer in silence beside the pool before Molly eased the Major, protesting, off to bed. By then it was quite dark. Masoud had turned on some interior lights. The evening was filled with more than the usual air activity, planes still landing from last missions. Jamila reached out and placed a hand on Hawk's arm.

"I think you will find Dibrugarh interesting. Once I thought it was where I would like to live. Not in one of the great ports, Calcutta, Bombay, Marseilles, Rotterdam, not even London. They overwhelm me. I've only seen pictures of your great American ports like New York."

"That also tends to overwhelm, Jamila. Do you have a favorite place?"

"Thera, on the island of Santorini, Greece. One of the Cyclades. We were sailing for France and our ship had engine trouble. We ended up in Piraeus and Molly and I took a two-day excursion to Thera. The Major, who hates sailing, wouldn't come. Maybe you've read of it? The place where a volcanic eruption changed the course of the western world?"

"For me, Jamila, the course of the western world is changing here." He placed a hand over hers. They both looked up at the sky, following the downward slant of a plane to the airstrip. "I guess for me my favorite port is the one where one gets out of a storm, or off some place with you. What time do we leave for Dibrugarh?"

Jamila withdrew her hand from his. "Early. Our office in Chabua is sending a lorry. We'll pick you up at seven. Can you drive a lorry?"

"No chauffeur?"

"Only as far as Chabua. From there we're on our own. It's a long drive."

"We truck drivers are used to that, Jamila." He leaned forward. Their first kiss came naturally, bodies not touching, but her lips open, warm, moving against his. When she drew her head back he rose, lifting her up against him, the scent of bergamot in her hair, her firm body against his. The sounds of many insects fell through the night like rain over them. His fingers followed the inward curve of her spine as a rush of blood consumed his body. She pulled free.

"On our way back from Dibrugarh," he said, holding her away, "we could stop at Most Celestial Dining. Maybe by now Manchu has a place for dancing."

"I was wondering if we might like some iced tea?" Molly's disembodied voice came from the shadows. "I've got John settled down and it isn't too late."

"Later than I thought," Hawk said. "I shouldn't keep Kalim and his tonga waiting half the night. Jamila is getting me up very early tomorrow. We'd like to be off by nine."

Back at the base, Kalim let him off at the edge of the tent compound. Fitz and Robby were playing gin on his cot. "Butler sent word you were to report to him as soon as you came in," Fitz said as Hawk pushed in through the mosquito netting.

"Was he pissed off or smiling?"

"Schultz was smiling. He brought the message on his way to the bar."

Hawk went back out, and walked down to Butler's tent, again pulsing with the hot glow of the lantern. Butler was seated at his table, wrapped in a paisley bathrobe, probing at a camera. He gave Hawk a grim stare.

"You wanted to see me, Jedd?"

"Not particularly, lieutenant." Butler lifted a lens from the table and held it up to the light. "But you've got an early morning flight. Trip down to Taro where you flew some Brits when we first arrived. Your mission, wasn't it?"

Hawk shrugged. "Whatever. Only tomorrow is my day off, remember? You'll have to get someone else."

Butler's teeth clenched. He gave his lens another look, laid it on the table and leaned back. "Look, I've already set the schedule for tomorrow.

We've run out of pilots. We've got this order from Group HQ to get a gooney down to Taro and bring some Brits up to Jorhat. Your take-off is scheduled for six. I've told Chavez to work all night if necessary but to get our last damned gooney operational. Got it, Lieutenant?"

"I had made plans for tomorrow, Major."

Butler relaxed. "Thanks for your use of the past tense. At least you're not refusing to obey orders. I've got my schedule for tomorrow. You should be back here from Jorhat by ten. That should give us time for a run up around Sadiya."

"Look, Jedd," Hawk said, keeping his voice even. "If I get back here by ten I'll probably have time to do what I planned."

"You mean like chasing that Indian broad around the countryside?" Butler's expression became sly.

"Major, I'll make the Taro flight tomorrow morning, but I'm not spending the rest of the day chasing over the Mishmih hills. I should have told you before. I'm not interested in your albino elephant."

"The Mishmis, Lieutenant?" Butler's jaw stiffened, his lips curving into an arrogant slant, reminding Hawk of an unshaven Mussolini. "Colonel Tyrone and I have discussed the possibilities of utilizing the Sadiya airstrip for emergency purposes. To that effect I have been given instructions to do a preliminary fly-over of the Sadiya area. Our flight tomorrow will be official business. Understood?"

Butler gave him a long stare which suddenly softened into a friendly smile. "Come on, Alan, loosen up. Missing one date is not the end of the world. We've got to get on with our plans. Right?"

Hawk straightened. "I'll be ready to take off at six tomorrow morning, Major.

Back in his own tent, Fitz and Robby were still at their game. Schultz had not returned. Hawk went to the tent pole and fumbled in his flight bag for his briefcase, pulled it out, sat down on his cot, found a sheet of note-paper and envelope and wrote Jamila. If possible she should wait with her Chabua driver until he got back from Taro around ten. If not possible, he would assume she had found another driver to take her on to Dibrugarh. In that case he'd get in to Chabua and wait for her at Most Celestial Dining. Please have a note sent to him at Operations.

"Schultz figured you were getting screwed out of your day off," Robby said. Hawk slammed his briefcase back in his flight bag, and left the tent without replying. He knew where Barpa lived, but at night, getting there was like stumbling through a maze. Narrow lanes of bashas, barking dogs, and an occasional word in Hindi flung in passing. Finally he found Barpa. Yes, Barpa would be most pleased to deliver Hawk's note to the Greystaffs' before sunrise.

"I've decided to have Lieutenant Bierman fly with you," Butler told Hawk in the morning. When Hawk made no reply, he went on. "They released him from the hospital yesterday, which means he's cured, if that's what's bothering you."

"I've got several other options, Major. Is Bierman strong enough to get the wheels up and down?"

There had been a few mild cases of jaundice in the squadron, but only Tony Bierman was hit hard enough to be sent to the hospital.

"He hasn't been officially restored to flying status, if that's what you mean," Butler said cautiously. "But he came in to see me yesterday pleading to fly. His clearance is only a matter of a couple of days. Besides, he has to fly because he's the only pilot we've got left."

Bierman was only a couple of months with the squadron. Hawk knew him only through casual conversations and had never flown with him. And hadn't Butler himself, when they were still based at Tunis, commented that Bierman should be kept a co-pilot?

"I'd prefer Chavez, Major, even if he's been working all night. I'll let him sleep most of the flight."

"Bierman's flying with you, Lieutenant! I've already sent him out to the plane, which is where I want you to haul ass to and take off. Remember, I want you out of Taro by 7:30 sharp--back here by ten. I've got a new wide-angle lens I want to try out."

Bierman was waiting at the gooney, its engines running, seated in the cargo opening, a hunched-over, cadaver-like figure in the semi-gloom. He pulled himself erect as Hawk appeared.

"Hi, Tony. You really feel up to it?"

"Rarin' to go, Hawk. The Sergeant said he'd be glad to take my place. Told him no way. I may look like death warmed over but I feel like living. Let's go!"

Hawk sent Bierman forward to have Chavez leave the engines running. He gave the undercarriage, flaps, and tail section a quick inspection.

"Don't worry, Lieutenant," Chavez said, close behind him as he reached up and removed the rudder lock. "She's running smooth, *muy bueno.*"

"Sorry I can't take you," Hawk said.

Chavez shrugged. *"Otro mas tiempo,* Lieutenant. I'll kick your chocks loose and go get some sleep."

The tower was silent on his first two calls. On his third McCabe broke in with a snarl. *"O.K., O.K., Lieutenant, you 're cleared for take-off. Heavy rain reported over the Patkais but clearing up down below. Shin reports everything quiet. Let us know when you reach Taro."*

Bierman got the wheels up with no problem. For a little while they lost what fragment of the dawn had reached Sook. A cascade of rain as they climbed but little turbulence, breaking out into a desolation of torn clouds, gaps of sky, then sunlight as they cleared the hills. Hawk checked his map and set them on a southerly course a few miles west of Shin. He let Bierman take over.

"Go ahead, Lieutenant. Take the wheel, and welcome back to the war.

Bierman gave him a ghostly smile, took the wheel, promptly lost two hundred feet and brought it back up. Hawk leaned back and closed his eyes. A hundred or so miles from Sook to Taro. A hundred miles from peace to war. Probably Jamila was already banging along the road to Dibrugarh. Bierman tapped his arm and pointed ahead and up. Instantly he clamped his earphones straight, hit the alert. A gut-wrenching sense of emptiness as he stared up at the three fighters crossing at twelve o'clock five thousand feet up. Then the immense release of relief.

"American," he said. "P51's. Probably on their way down to the Mandalay section, hoping to pick off a Zero on their way."

"Aren't we supposed to have alert on in combat zones, Hawk? I'm not finding fault. Just a bit nervous."

"Me too, Bierman." Hawk reached forward and gave the radio knob a twist. BBC playing *When You Wish Upon A Star,* followed by the news which as usual spoke of bombing runs over the continent, gross tonnage being brought into

Murmansk by allied shipping. Something was happening on the Russian front.

"Sometimes Radio Moscow comes in clearer," Hawk said, then glanced down, the land opening up and the first long curve of the Chindwin River below Shinbwiyan. "Damn it, I forgot to call Shin. Get them and give them our position. I'll take over."

Hawk put the gooney in a steep descent, circling to the east and then back, catching sight of Taro, bright under a slant of sunlight, the old airstrip glinting with pools of water. Butler should have had information on it. He himself should have known what to expect, then logic telling him they wouldn't have ordered a gooney in if it couldn't land. He dropped down to 300', leveling, coming in over the jungle and shattered remains of the buildings, easing down to 100' as the airstrip came up. A lot of water. The near end looked an impossible bog. Maybe a straight edge of land the last half. He jammed the throttles forward, came up to 300' in a steep bank, circling back, down-wind leg had not a breeze stirring the jungle as he angled a long approach. Bierman took his wheels-down signal. Whoever was waiting down there sure must have heard them. A nice firm look of earth beyond the last pools. He eased the flaps down. Don't drop it in! Might just keep on going -- straight down! The feel of wheels brushing, touching, grabbing the earth. They were down. He braked carefully, letting them slosh through a shallow pool. Tail down, they came to a stop a hundred feet from the end. He stared ahead at the ridge of thorn trees. Maybe Buddha had got them down in one piece.

"Damn, that was a pretty landing!" Bierman said.

"A landing is a landing is a landing," Hawk said. "Now, if they haven't given us too heavy a load we just might get the hell off. Where are they?" He cut the engines.

They both slid back their windows and leaned out. For a long while, it seemed, there was only silence. A troupe of monkeys hooted in the distance. Birds in the thorn trees.

"For God's sake, they must have heard us," Bierman said.

"Maybe they called off the war." Hawk unbuckled his safety belt and started back down the plane.

"Of course," Bierman said, close behind him, "it could be an ambush. You got your .45?"

"I always forget it. Yours?"

"I gave it to Captain Walker when I went to the hospital. He said he'd get me a swap, a Luger. I've always wanted a Luger."

They jumped to the ground. It was, Hawk thought, like a hot summer's day in thousands of places all over the world. Only, on the farther side of silence.

"This gives me the creeps," Bierman said. "How long are we supposed to wait?"

"Not long. I've got a date. Come on, something you'd be interested in seeing."

The temple. Hawk doubted anyone had been there since he'd stumbled upon it. Maybe that was his own footprint, only partly dissolved in mud at the foot of the broken steps, beyond the brush.

"I suppose at one time this was a pleasant place to live," Bierman said. "I guess you could call this their church. Houses. Certainly stores. They played games."

"Probably fell in love," Hawk added. "Made love. Had children. Argued and fought at times. Just like in real towns." He got up and circled back around the toppled walls. Five more minutes. As they turned back to the plane, Hawk saw a glint at his foot, as he pushed through the brush. Another fragment? At that moment, Bierman gave a shout of alarm. An ambush? The heavy sound of engines. Hawk took off past Bierman.

This time there were three vehicles, two British jeeps and a battered van with a large white cross painted on its top. A line of men in camouflage were winding across the airstrip between pools of mud and water, two men on litters. Three soldiers in front, three in the rear, their rifles at ready.

Hawk gave a yell and ran forward, waving, yelling back to Bierman to get the steps down. Why the hell wasn't he told there'd be wounded?

There were three wounded, the two on litters and a third on foot, arm in a sling, tall, using a stick as a cane. One of the litters revealed a protruding nose and eyes dull with pain. The other, less bandaged but bloodier.

"Sorry we're late," the tall one called, flinging aside his stick. "Bloody rotten mess. At the last moment, too."

"Hey," Hawk said, recognition dawning. "You're one of those I brought in here."

"All of us, Lieutenant. Right you are."

"Let's cut the gab and get the fuck out of here," one of the soldiers yelled, glancing back at the distant van.

Bierman had the steps down. They slid the litters up into the plane and secured them. The soldiers took off at a trot back down the airstrip. "O.K.," the tall Brit said, pulling himself erect. "You got us down here, now how about getting the pieces back, what?"

They got the pieces airborne, Hawk yanking the gooney clear as it seemed about to slam off into the brush. Passing Shin, Hawk called in. Bierman spent most of his time back with the three men, all of whom were under sedation, which was beginning to wear off when Hawk brought the gooney shuddering through the last small storm over the Patkais to Jorhat. Cleared for immediate landing, he brought the plane to a stop half-way down its macadam runway. The pursuing ambulance swerved in beside them.

"The guy who could talk," Bierman said, slipping into his seat as Hawk taxied down the runway, turned, asking the tower for clearance to take off, "from what he said I gather they've been behind enemy lines for days. Lost all their equipment. Somebody ratted on them. Then right at the last when they're heading back out they get ambushed -- and one of their own limey platoons rescues them."

"They could make a good war movie out of something like that," Hawk said.

"That fellow with all the blood," Bierman said. "I helped rebandage him. Then I flashed the hash. Didn't make the door. Made quite a mess. Sorry."

"There goes your air medal. How about calling Sook and telling them we've taken off. ETA ten-fifteen."

The note was there for him at Operations. Jamila would not be back in time to meet him at Most Celestial Dining that evening. In fact, she might have to spend the night in Dibrugarh.

Major Butler got up from his desk. "Gather there were no problems with the gooney," he yelled. "I've called to have it refueled. Give you a half hour before we take off."

Hawk stared at Butler. Suddenly he knew what he wasn't going to do. "I'd cancel the refueling," he said. "We've got a bad engine. Had to come in on one at Jorhat. Better get Chavez back on it in a hurry. It sounds to me like we're looking at a new engine."

"Shit!" Butler's face went red. "You know how long I've been planning this!"

"Yes, I do," Hawk said. "I suppose it happens to all of us from time to time."

"Well, then take the rest of your goddamn day off," Butler said.

"Thanks," Hawk said. "I'd planned to." But before I do, he thought, I damn well better find Chavez and Bierman, just in case. It took only moments to wake Chavez and explain his gambit about the bad engine. Chavez promised he'd have the engine dismounted by evening. Bierman wasn't in his tent so he left a note on his pillow, telling him about their one-engine landing at Jorhat. Back at Operations he checked the flight board. Schultz was due in from a drop east of Walawbum and scheduled next for a delivery at Shadazup. What the hell, Hawk thought. Not a chance now to see Jamila. He'd never had a close look at the war. He'd take a ride down with Schultz and see how things were at Walawbum. Maybe even find Fred.

10

"EXPLORE the jungle! You've got to be out of your fucking mind!" Schultz said. Hawk came forward into the cockpit to stand between Schultz and Murphy, the co-pilot. Schultz leveled out just above the dense cloud mass covering the Patkais and motioned Murphy to take over.

"What ceiling they giving you at Shadazup?," Hawk asked. Not that he really cared as long as they could set down, but seeing he'd decided to wreck the rest of his day off he didn't want to spend it slamming around the sky while Schultz found a strip where they could dump the ammo. If he was lucky the rain would hold off. He was ready for some walking, so had worn his boots, slacks, a bush jacket to hold off the bugs, and a pith helmet in case the sun came out.

"Broken clouds," Schultz said, glancing up at Hawk. "You going to another goddamn tea party? Don't you realize it's a fucking jungle down there? Why didn't you bring . . ." He broke off, snapping at

Murphy. "I leveled off at sixty-five hundred, Red Baron, not sixty-eight and climbing! Want a Zero picking off our ass up here? Think we'd make it to the clouds?" He winked at Hawk.

Murphy dove, tried to level at 6,500', dropped past into clouds at 6,200', surfaced, submarined again, and finally wobbled up and held, on the edge of daylight.

"Shit," Schultz said, "maybe we should all take the rest of the day off."

"What I want to remind you," Hawk said, "is to keep my name off your manifest. I'm not on board. You know how Butler is. I figure I can be back at Shad by late afternoon, find someone to give me a ride back to Sook. O.K.?"

"Like I said, Hawk, you're out of your fucking mind." Schultz's glance swept the instrument panel. "Murphy, I was doing one-sixty. You think you're flying a fucking dive bomber!"

Murphy's thin face tightened, jaw twisting. He eased back on the throttles. He looked as if he might cry. Hawk leaned over him.

"Don't give up, Murphy. You should have ridden with the sonofabitch when he was flying co-pilot for me."

"Let's start our descent, hot-shot," Schultz said. Schultz let Murphy bring them down through a swirl of cloud, rain and sunlight, then took over and brought them in with a solid three point onto the muddy Shadazup strip. The tower directed them to the end of the airstrip and up to an earthen revetment. As Hawk came down the cargo-bay steps a battered six-wheeler roared up, did a tight half-circle and backed to the gooney. The driver leaned out, gave Hawk a look and said something to the other two enlisted men with him. They laughed and jumped from the truck.

"The road, Sergeant," Hawk asked the driver. "The one down to Warazup. Which direction?"

The sergeant, big and battered as his truck, climbed down and stared at him. The other two came around the truck and paused. "The soldier here," the sergeant announced, "is making a visit to Warazup." He turned to Hawk. "You got friends there, soldier?"

"I just wanted to know where the road is, Sergeant."

The sergeant placed both hands on his hips. His two unshaven helpers grinned. "Who the hell are you, mister?"

Schultz and Murphy came down the plane steps and paused beside Hawk. "If you'd remembered to wear some insignia, Hawk," Schultz said, "you might get more respect." He gave the men a wink. "I gave the lieutenant a ride down from Sook. He's looking for a friend. He may get lost. He's a pilot."

"It figures." The sergeant shook his head in disgust and frowned at Hawk. "O.K., Lieutenant, if you just follow the tracks out around the revetment and through what's left of Shadazup you'll hit Stilwell's road. Turn right, start walking. Which side is your friend fighting on?"

Hawk smiled. "988th Signal Operations, a unit of theirs with the Third Infantry Company. Fellow named Fred Jilbert."

The sergeant glanced at the other two. They shrugged. "The Third got the shit shot out of them a few days ago," one said. "Maybe they got relieved." He shrugged again, then winked at the sergeant. "You could stop by and inquire at Headquarters. Vinegar Joe might be in. The General might be willing to help you out."

"O.K., enough bullshit," the sergeant burst out, motioning to his men. "Let's get this gooney unloaded." He glanced at Schultz. "You don't happen to have any whisky on board, do you? The going price right now is thirty-five a fifth."

"Sorry," Schultz said. "All we brought you is ammo, and flame throwers for your barbecues." He turned to Hawk. "Take it easy, Hawk."

Hawk followed the ruts out around the revetment and through a wasted stretch of jungle, charred poles and black smears where dwellings had been. He could hear the sound of traffic up ahead. Newly-constructed pole buildings appeared. Rows of tents along narrow trails leading into denser jungle. He was forced to step to one side as several platoons of Chinese soldiers, young, grim-faced and sweating, trotted past.

The sun came hot and full just as he reached the Stilwell Road, the road rumored to reach eventually on beyond the villages not yet captured, to Mitch, Bhamo, and into China. Hawk turned onto it and began a faster pace. It was the same road they had been flying above in its windings down from the Patkais into a war they never saw. A long convoy caught up with him and ground past. Next came two armored cars, followed by several flat-beds with what looked like artillery pieces shrouded in heavy canvas. Finally, a single jeep with two enlisted men in greasy fatigues stopped at his tentative thumb gesture.

He climbed in the rear among rifles, boxed ammo, and food rations. "How far you going?"

They both turned and stared at him for a moment. "Couple of miles," the redheaded driver said. "That is," the other said, "if the boys are still where we left them."

"And alive," his thin companion added. "Where you headed?"

"Towards Warazup. Looking for a Unit of the 988th Signal Operations, supposed to be with the Third Infantry Company. Back at the airstrip they said it got hit pretty badly."

"There were hardly enough men left to give us a few replacements. They should have pulled the company back. They sent us back for supplies." The driver nodded at the stuff heaped about Hawk. "We thought we'd have a party tonight." The driver yanked the jeep onto the shoulder as a six-wheeler came roaring toward and past them.

"Then the signal unit must still be with them," Hawk said. "I'll keep on a ways. How far down is the front line?" He adjusted his pith helmet.

The two stared at him again, mouths agape.

"Jesus H. Christ," the thin one said softly.

"He's wearing nice clean clothes," the redhead said, rubbing his unshaven jaw. "And I love his hat. He wants to know where the front line is! Sweet suffering Jesus!"

"Sorry," Hawk said. "I flew down from Sook. The fellow I'm looking for is supposed to be down here somewhere."

"Just what do you do back there in India, General?" the redhead inquired.

"I fly a plane," Hawk said. They were pissing him off. "Don't you remember me waving to you during my last drop?"

"Why the hell didn't you say so! With a fucking bonnet like yours, how are we supposed to know?"

"So what's wrong with my asking about the front line? Think I'm a goddamn spy?"

"No, not a spy. Just a jerk who doesn't even know there's no such thing as a front line. What the fuck you think this is, World War I?" The driver brought the jeep to a stop. "Look, Lieutenant, or whatever the hell you are, my advice to you is haul ass back to Sook. We'd like to keep you alive so you can keep us alive."

"Thanks, Sergeant, but I'll keep on as far as you're going and ask around."

"Or you could just keep on," the thin one added. "Ask around in Warazup. The Japs might know your friend. Then again they might string you up by your balls."

"Look," the driver offered, "what we're saying is that without a front line the Japs can be about anywhere. We try to encircle one another. Mostly we're gaining." He eased the jeep forward. "But I wouldn't count on it." A couple of light trucks came around a bend up ahead. "Want me to stop them? They're headed back for supplies at the airstrip."

"I'll go on a ways," Hawk said.

The redhead shrugged and pulled off the road. The trucks crashed past. The jeep rolled on, from time to time passing rutted trails snaking off into the jungle. A couple of miles later, they pulled off where trails branched out on each side. The redhead stopped, turning back to Hawk.

"Twelve miles ahead to Warazup, or you can turn around here and start back. If you're smart. A mile down the road they're doing some surveying. You might try them. But remember, Lieutenant, this is a war of encirclement. Be careful."

"Hey," the thin one cried, "the bastards may already have us surrounded. Let's get the fuck out of here!"

Hawk jumped out and watched the jeep vanish along a trail into the jungle. Suddenly it was very quiet. He stared ahead, for the first time becoming aware of the heat. Sunlight flooded through the canopy of branches. He'd go on as far as the survey crew.

He moved on cautiously, his feet making no sound on the muddy earth. Far to his rear came the vague sound of trucks. Overhead the occasional hum of a gooney. The insect noises seemed to rise and fall with his passing. High above him a monkey made a brief silhouette as it swung past. The sunlight held. Hawk felt his body ease. It was almost like walking a woods' road back home. Birdsong and fragrances. Only a distant, heavy clump like thunder gave him momentary pause. The line of the poem Jamila had quoted came unbidden, "Tiger, tiger, burning bright, in the forests of the night." The undergrowth became thicker. What eyes were watching?

He went on more quickly, breath easing, when a long curve brought him parallel to a shallow stream and familiar-sounding voices up ahead. He caught sight of a single soldier leaning against the bole of a giant, vine-veined peepul tree like the one at the Greystaffs'. Jamila had said it was a kind of fig and sacred to Hindus. Just beyond the tree a single charred timber poked from the brush.

The soldier watched unmoving as he approached, an older man in rough khaki who examined him from beneath the rim of his battered pith helmet. Then Hawk glimpsed the single star of a brigadier general, almost hidden by a sweat-cloth crumpled about his neck.

"Sir." Hawk paused and saluted.

The General returned his salute and smiled. "You look like you're a long way from wherever it is you ought to be, soldier."

"First Lieutenant Hawk, sir. Eighteenth Squadron at Sookerating. My day off from flying.

Looking for a friend from the States. He's with a unit of the 988th Signal Corps."

The General studied Hawk. His expression indicated the same disbelief as had those of the others.

"I suppose it's a dumb thing to do," Hawk said.

The General shrugged. "Probably no dumber than what I'm trying to do. My men are a few hundred yards downstream trying to figure how we can bring Joe Stilwell's road closer to the river without risking a washout when the monsoon finally hits."

Hawk smiled. "I didn't expect, sir, to find a general all by himself in the Burmese jungle. Guess I'll move on."

"My advice, Lieutenant: try my survey crew. Two of them are from a local infantry unit. They might be able to help you. If not, I suggest you get back to your squadron."

"Thanks, sir."

"And if you spot any buffalo along the river, stay clear of them. They don't like our smell."

Around a bend the road held straight for some distance along the top of the slope to the river's edge. Hawk had walked about a hundred yards when a dozen or so buffalo appeared, moving out from shade along the river. They stopped and turned his way. Hawk froze, felt his chest go tight. He had the sudden impulse to raise a hand to check the wind direction. Had they smelled him? He took a step forward. Another. One of the buffalo shook his ugly spread of horns. Hawk waited, tried another step. Then he found himself walking quite rapidly, not breathing or glancing back. When he did, the buffalo were plodding on through the mud.

He found the survey crew, rifles stacked handy, running a line into a gash in the jungle. The two officers and five enlisted men stopped work and watched him approach.

It was apparent to Hawk, when he began to explain himself, that they gathered about him as they might about an apparition. They exchanged slow even looks.

"Jesus," an enlisted man finally said softly, "now I've seen everything!" Their captain, tall and thin to the edge of emaciation, removed his helmet, dirty beads of sweat from his forehead and replaced it. "Lieutenant, do you know where you are?" His question had a meditative, almost confessional quality. Hawk toyed with the idea of an philosophical reply but said, "I guess I'm kind of near the front line."

As if in reply, a heavy muffled explosion came from up ahead.

"If there was one, Lieutenant, you'd be beyond it. You're in what used to be called, years ago, 'no man's land.' "

"Well," Hawk said. "Sorry. It's just that the general I talked with back there said somebody here might be from a local infantry unit who might know if a 988th Signal unit is still around."

"What's left of us," one of the enlisted men said. "We're supposed to pull back as soon as Chinese relief shows up. About a quarter of a mile ahead. But I wouldn't go poking about in the underbrush looking for them."

"Well, I've come this far," Hawk said. He glanced up as another muffled, thunder-like thud sounded.

"That was a mortar," the Captain said. "One of ours. The next one might not be."

Hawk glanced at his watch. Later than he thought. Afternoon half shot. Still, he'd come this far. "Thanks," he said and walked on, setting a pace that would make short work of a quarter of a mile. If nothing turned up he'd head back and catch a ride at Shadazup. At least find out if Fred Jilbert is still alive.

The sunlight began to fade. Suddenly clouds were overhead, heavy and pressing down. The jungle darkened. Rain probed the jungle canopy. Another glance at his watch. No sign of the infantry unit. In five minutes he'd turn back. Ahead another, closer, solid clump of a mortar burst. He increased his pace. The jungle closed in. *Tiger, tiger, burning bright.*

He did not know why, but in the middle of a stride, he came to a stop, stood immobile, caught in the center of a strange, waiting silence as if the world had become dumb. It was as if he had reached the border of an invisible country beyond which he should not pass. Then the words came, clear, even and deadly, with a Southern accent.

"Don't even think about sloping, jerk head! Raise your fucking claws, grab the sky, turn to your port and tack until you hit green stuff and whoa!"

Hawk felt the air leave his lungs. Slowly, arms raised, he turned left, knees shaking as he stepped mechanically forward, eyes wide, unseeing. Bushes came against his body. Something small and hard jabbed out of the green into his guts. He looked down at the end of a rifle barrel, then up into the unshaven face of a lieutenant in camouflage. Hawk tried a deep breath; heard his voice come as if from another person.

"I'm sure glad I've done some sailing, Lieutenant."

A heavier figure pushed in behind the lieutenant. "Ask the asshole where he thought he was going."

"You heard the sergeant," the lieutenant said.

"Looking for an old friend supposed to be with a unit of the 988th Signal Company."

"Who the fuck are you?"

"A pilot. My squadron's based at Sook. My day off."

The lieutenant removed the rifle barrel from his stomach. "You'd have had the rest of your life off if you'd gone on another hundred yards."

Hawk stared at him. From somewhere behind them came another jarring thump of a mortar.

"A Jap patrol is just a little ways down the road," the lieutenant said. "They'd have blown your stupid goddamned head off. Let's get going, Sergeant. Things are about to kick up a bit. And keep an eye on this idiot."

"I might, if you think he's worth it."

He turned, motioning Hawk ahead of him. The lieutenant led the way along a narrow trail and up a ridge, past a series of empty foxholes, a couple of manned machine gun emplacements, into a ragged encampment. A beaten-up group of GIs sat around a litter of C-ration containers, rifles across their knees.

"Patrols reporting anything?" the lieutenant called out.

"Nothing," someone said. "No signs of anything except for that fucking mortar they're playing hell with."

As if in reply three mortar shells burst somewhere off beyond the road, the sound sighing through the trees.

"What's Communications report about getting us out?"

"Nothing yet."

"Excuse me, Lieutenant," Hawk said. "Don't want to bother you, but if you got anyone here from the 988th Signal Company, I'm looking for a Fred Jilbert."

The seated riflemen stopped eating and glanced up at him.

"You'd have been less bother if we'd only had to bury you," the sergeant said.

"Fred Jilbert?" one of the seated men said. "I remember him. He was pulled out a week ago. They sent the poor bastard up into the Kumons with Merrill's Marauders."

This time they heard the low whistling sound of the mortar shells before they burst, shivering the air slightly.

"Told you, Lieutenant," the sergeant said. "Like I been saying, the Nips are going to fake an attack up the road, try to get the Chink troops to pull back from Warazup. You owe me five bucks. Listen!"

They listened. Hawk stared down at his boots, wet, stained, clotted with mud. Again the mortars opened up beyond them, but closer, firing steadily, as if searching, up and across the road.

"O.K., men," the lieutenant called. "Let's pull back to our positions beyond the ridge."

"And I guess I'd better be getting back to Shadazup," Hawk said.

All eyes turned on him. They regarded him with the kind of expression that comes when something apparently normal changes to the unknown.

"No, Lieutenant, you're not going anywhere. If you're still alive in the morning we'll wrap you in a strait jacket and send you back to Sook!"

The men were already on their feet, collecting gear and beginning to file over the ridge. Beyond it Hawk saw a well-fortified position of foxholes, timber shelters, and gun emplacements. The sergeant led Hawk to a roofed shelter and vanished, to return in moments with a box of C-rations, a zipperless sleeping bag, a can of insect repellent. By now the mortars had begun a steady bombardment that reached almost to the other side of the ridge.

"You see, Lieutenant," the sergeant said, crouching beside the log where Hawk had sat down, "by now the road above us has been blocked. At least one Chink company has been brought up to prevent infiltration on either side. The Nips are going to mortar the fuck out of the road and then probe forward. Strictly a fake, as I told the lieutenant. An old trick of theirs. But if you'd started back up the road by now you'd be kaput. Enemy fire or friendly fire -- it don't make a hell of a lot of difference if you're dead. Guess I'll go collect my five bucks from the lieutenant."

Hawk remained on the log and tried his C-rations. He'd gotten used to the mortar fire and figured his heart beat was probably running at no more than twice its normal speed. An occasional burst of machine gun fire from the ridge only gave it a temporary jolt. Darkness came slowly with a lowering of clouds, an increase in rain, and fireflies exploding in the jungle canopy. After a long while he spread out the sleeping bag under the sheltering timber. The bag was slightly overripe. He took off his boots and tried to clean off the mud. The sounds of war dwindled slowly, the rhythmic impact of the monsoon rain taking over. He fell into an intermittent sleep. The sergeant awakened him at dawn and led him along a twisting path that brought them out on the road where the survey crew had been working. The way looked clear. And no buffalo prowled the river's edge.

Colonel Tyrone, flanked by Major Butler and Captain McCabe, sat at the cleared table in Operations. Hawk sat facing them. Schultz, Fitz, Bierman, and Chavez were ranged on each side of him. The squadron clerk, a corporal, sat at an improvised desk to the right of the table, his typewriter at ready.

"Lieutenant Hawk," Al Tyrone began, "I'd like to begin our proceedings with your account of why you were not available for flight duty this morning."

Butler gave an exasperated toss of his head. "Because he was AWOL," he burst out. "That's why I confined the lieutenant to his quarters when he appeared on the airstrip shortly before noon. That's why I've called for this hearing."

"Jedd!" Al Tyrone said patiently. "This is merely a preliminary and unofficial inquiry to determine the reasons for the lieutenant's regrettable absence from duty today. He is not being formally charged for absence without official leave. This is an informal investigation. There will be no further interruptions. Lieutenant, proceed with your account."

"Excuse me, sir." The corporal rolled a piece of paper into his typewriter. "So far our meeting has been called a proceeding, a hearing, an inquiry ,and an investigation. It would be a help if I could use just one word for it."

"Since no formal charges have yet been brought, call it an inquiry, Corporal. You may proceed, Lieutenant."

Hawk rose. For the occasion he had put on relatively clean shorts, bush jacket, and a decent pair of sneakers. He'd kicked the disaster that was his boots underneath his cot. "I'll be brief, sir."

"And stick to the facts!" Butler added.

"The facts," Hawk said. "Yesterday I had an early mission to Taro. Lieutenant Bierman flew with me. We had to return via Jorhat where we had a bit of engine trouble." He glanced at Bierman who stared expressionless at the tin ceiling. "Actually it was supposed to be my day off, so once back here, Major Butler gave me the rest of the day off." Hawk paused. He'd decided not to mention Butler's idea to fly up over the Mishmis. That was Butler's business. Butler merely stared off across the room.

"Now, a friend in the States had written, asking me to try and get a message down to her husband, stationed somewhere near Shadazup. That's where Lieutenant Schultz was scheduled to fly. He gave me a ride to Shadazup. From there I went on down the Stilwell Road looking for the communication outfit this fellow was supposed to be stationed with. I started out, did some walking, caught a ride or two, finally learned that this fellow, a Fred Jilbert, had been sent up with Merrill's Marauders into the Kumons. About this time a Jap mortar attack began. It was late in the afternoon. I wanted to start back but by then it seemed there was fighting all around us. So I spent the night there, hitched up to Shadazup this morning and caught a ride back with Schultz."

"I'm thinking of setting up a frigging taxi service," Schultz said, grinning.

"You mean Hawk had arranged with you to pick him up?" Butler demanded.

"What the hell!" Schultz snapped. "How did I know where the fuck Hawk was? I didn't take him to raise. And coming back I didn't let Hawk touch the wheel. I also didn't charge him a goddamn cent!"

Colonel Tyrone held up a hand, waited for the laughter to subside. "So far I've heard nothing to warrant a charge of AWOL against Lieutenant Hawk. Major Butler?"

"So far we've heard nothing, Colonel," Butler said. "But there is the fact that the lieutenant was not given permission yesterday to leave the base, at government expense, and enter a combat zone. He tells us he had a message from some dame in the States to give to her husband. Would the lieutenant be willing to tell us what the message was?"

Tyrone and McCabe exchanged looks. "I doubt," Tyrone said, "it was a message threatening the security of our troops." He frowned, glancing from Butler to Hawk. "Would you mind, Lieutenant?"

"My friend in the States has had a baby. Her husband wasn't getting any mail. She wanted him to know."

"A likely story!" Butler snapped.

"I brought her letter with me, just in case," Hawk said, pulling the letter from his bush jacket. "Would you like to have it entered as evidence?"

Al Tyrone took a deep breath, sighed and looked at Butler, who said quickly, "Lieutenant Hawk had no business using government transportation for personal business!"

"Major Butler!" Colonel Tyrone turned squarely to Butler. "In my opinion you are on extremely weak ground in bringing a charge of AWOL. Sounds like you are making up government regulations as you go. Now, while Lieutenant Hawk has given ample evidence of his capacity for being a damn fool, he has given none for which he can be charged with violation of military regulations."

"How about lying to a superior officer?"

"Major!" The Colonel's fist slammed the table. "What in damnation are you getting at?"

"I'm suggesting the lieutenant hasn't told us everything, Colonel. I'm saying he gave me a false report yesterday of engine trouble upon returning from Jorhat. I'm saying he told me that in order to get the plane grounded and get the rest of the day off."

"Can you prove it, Major?"

"Ask Lieutenant Bierman. He was Hawk's co-pilot."

"Lieutenant Bierman?"

"Sir." Bierman rose. "Any gooney can have engine trouble once in a while."

Al Tyrone leaned back and studied the rust-streaked ceiling. With his eyes still fixed upward he said slowly, "Gentlemen, from where I sit it appears we have a leaky roof. I suggest our inquiry be suspended and an informal discussion be continued at the squadron bar. All in favor?"

He looked over the upraised hands, lacking only Butler's from being unanimous.

"I declare our inquiry suspended," Tyrone said. "However, before leaving, I do have a question for Major Butler." He turned to Butler who sat with his head bent forward, hands clasped in a prayer-like gesture. "Jedd, there is a rumor that you had scheduled another flight yesterday with Hawk, after his return from Taro. What was your destination?"

Butler straightened, his look of reproof plain as he stared at the Colonel. "Another flight, sir? I heard the same rumor, checked the Operations log. No such flight was scheduled."

It was very late when Hawk and Schultz stumbled into the tent. Fitz and Robb had left the bar early, neither of them having done much drinking. Hawk, exhausted, had found his energy increase as the evening progressed and only faded when they ended up reduced to Manchu's flamingo piss, imported from Dibrugarh. Schultz fell on his cot, instantly asleep. Hawk sat down on the edge of his cot. He felt like talking a bit more about his experience on the front line. But there was no response from the other two until Fitz sat up abruptly, flashlight glaring.

"I made a mistake," Fitz hissed. "I should have voted for your conviction. Now shut up!" His light flickered across the tent and fixed on Hawk's boots, immaculate and shining on Hawk's pillow.

"Barpa was still here working on your bloody boots when Robby and I returned. He is very angry with you. I think he wants to kill you. Good night!"

Hawk closed his eyes, felt his body become rigid as the sound of mortars enclosed him, pressed down. I was afraid, he thought. I am still afraid.

———◆———

11

"FOR a time," Hawk said, "I had the feeling somebody down there was punishing me for screwing up our day."

Jamila placed both her hands over his. "Somebody 'down there' punishing you? Not 'up'? But no, I refuse to let your strange metaphysical distinctions draw me into an argument."

They were sitting by the pool's edge, feet dangling in the water, cicadas providing a scherzo of grace notes to the muffled night sounds from the airstrip. Hawk had flown that day, for the first time since coming back from Shadazup.

"Would it be a better choice if I used your word karma?" He took one of her hands in his, bent down and kissed each knuckle.

"Not really." Her fingers tightened on his. "In England I once took a course in Comparative Religion. I compared and gave up. Yesterday evening, when I finally got back from Dibrugarh and

189

learned you had not returned, all I felt was an emptiness, a grief, a desire for -- " Jamila paused. "I was standing on the verandah and then I found myself walking along the road toward the airstrip, with Masoud and Molly calling for me to come back. Planes were still coming in and I kept thinking you must be on one of them. I'd stop and watch each one of them drop below the trees as it landed. I felt everyone believed you were dead and I realized there was nothing up there -- or down there -- to help me. I was angry you had come into my life."

"And I wasn't even flying." Hawk fumbled in his shirt pocket, then took Jamila's hand and pressed into it the fragment of red and gold tile from Taro. "I meant to give it to you for May Day. At home when I was very young we made paper May-baskets for those we loved. So, a little late, I bring a May basket to you, a piece of ruined temple, a shattered god."

Jamila held the fragment up in the dim light from the house. A slight glitter of gold. She turned to him. "So much for the gods, Alan." He pulled her close. The scent of jasmine or bergamot. Her lips moved against his. He traced with his hand the soft curve of her shoulder up into her hair. She drew her head back.

"Was it a bad time, Alan, a bad night?"

"For a little while. Not the being scared. After a while I got used to the mortars and that part became sort of normal. It was later, after the attack stopped, that I began to understand a little. I became appalled at my ignorance. The night filled with the essence of what was at the heart of life. I wanted to live. I wanted to see you again. Lost in part of the war but also removed from it. Whatever happened would happen. Karma?"

Jamila smiled. "It will do."

"I've said it badly."

"No, Alan, but you should have finished by kissing me again."

This time he was sure it was bergamot. The soft yet firm skin under her chin. He explored the long valley of her spine. No need for his hands to tremble.

"Was it bad today, Alan?"

"More or less normal."

Actually it was the squadron's worst day. Certainly, contrary to the popular song, God was not his co-pilot, only Chavez, though Chavez always spoke as if he'd received some special assurance that he would live to return to his beloved Mexican hills. After their last drop, Chavez had returned to his seat from a long look from the bubble, exclaiming with a kind of delight that he had observed a rifle shot, only moments before, as it drilled through their right aileron. Back at Sook they discovered two more, one in their mid-section, the third through the left wing-tip. In all, four of their planes got punctured, Schultz even taking a hit in the gas line and then having to put down at Shin for repairs.

There had also been more sightings of Zeros. And, of course, the rains, all day, quick storms as if the coming monsoons were feeling them out -- obscuring hills without warning, lowering on airstrips, forcing planes to circle too closely while waiting for a break in the clouds.

"When you're kissing someone, Alan," Jamila whispered, "it is bad form to have other things on your mind."

He rose, lifting her up and against him. "Sorry. I guess I was flying back to you. Now we are wholly together." She was only a little shorter so when she looked up and reached, his lips could trace her small, firm chin, her high cheekbones and sloe eyes.

A patio light came on, brightened, and faded. Molly's slippers made a soft swish on the tile and paused just beyond them under a palm, a hesitant wraith in a flowing white robe.

"John has gone to bed early, Jamila. It's the strain of the hospital, and now all that trouble you had to go through at Dibrugarh. May I make you some tea before I go on up?"

"No thanks, Molly." Jamila went up to her and slid one arm around her shoulders.

"It's nice having you back with us, Alan Hawk," Molly said. "I do hope you won't frighten us again that way.

"Never again that way, Lady Greystaff."

"Well, goodnight then." She reached up and kissed Jamila, turned back to the house, fading across the patio.

"Poor thing," Jamila said, returning to lean against Alan, her head on his chest. "She worries so much now about the Major. The hospital thinks there's a danger of stroke. I wish there had been some way of not telling him about Dibrugarh, but then he'd always suspected Chand of stealing. Unfortunately Moslems do not rate high with him. When I told him of the situation at Dibrugarh, he was about to launch into a jihad of his own against all agents. To calm him down, Molly had to agree to double his evening ration of whiskey."

"Your agent Chand's misdeeds have increased?"

"Perhaps it's the war." Jamila smiled. "He's a handy scapegoat. I've handled our books now for three years. My examination of Chand's accounts revealed that he had increased his percentage of swindling beyond acceptable limits. I pointed out the errors. Chand's apologies were profuse. He agreed to rectify things. I insisted he do so immediately."

They stood silently for a few moments, watching a bat stitch the soft light over the pool. "I have a feeling, Jamila, that Molly also worries a great deal over you."

"Not just me, Alan. Us."

"Should she?"

"More importantly, Alan, should we?"

When Molly had appeared he had become aware that Jamila did not turn away from him. Now he held her close. Her eyes seemed part of the darkness. She moved against him, thighs, hips, breasts, arms tight, her mouth finding his, then her fingers tracing his face and lips.

"It is not a night to worry, Alan. Come."

She led the way beside the pool toward the pathway through the flowering shrubs. The iron gate opened smoothly and they went on along the path among the pruned, bulb-like tea shrubs. The gazebo seemed a small white temple in the fain't, almost sourceless light. The screen door squeaked lightly when he opened it. Jamila brushed past him, laughing softly. She took his hand and led him around a chair to a low couch against a bamboo wall. He watched her, in silhouette, unwind her sari, letting it fall to the floor. Naked, she leaned against him, holding him to her. For a little while they stood without moving. The sound of insects, the distant cry of a jackal, the low throb of an engine from the airstrip, all receded, faded, until there was nothing left but a soft silence.

Three days later Colonel Tyrone called a late-evening meeting, because of the increased activity of Japanese Zeros as far north as Shinbwiyan.

"The Japs know we're up to something," Tyrone had remarked that afternoon in Operations. "So every gooney they can knock down will really slow the troops up, wherever they're headed." He had glanced across the room at Butler, glowering at his desk, and at Ericson and Hawk, who were waiting to file flight reports.

"I think it's a dumb-ass move," McCabe banged in and said, "to send Murphy, still a co-pilot, off on a mission with Roden, a navigator acting as co-pilot. I don't give a rat's ass if it's an easy flight to Maingkwan. Murphy is still too nervous and Roden spends most of his time studying maps of California!"

Butler had yelled at Tyrone. "See what I mean, Al. Where the hell is our *esprit de corps?*"

"Take it easy, Jedd," Tyrone said. "We'll try to cover everything at tonight's meeting."

The tower called. Hank Romano was coming in, emergency landing, most of his tail shot away. They all headed for the door and watched as Hank set the gooney down roughly, shreds of his vertical stabilizer still dangling.

The late-evening meeting was held in Operations. "Too much ventilation in the mess hall, if you follow me," Tyrone told McCabe. "Sounds go both ways. Things are tightening up. Security is vital."

McCabe gave him a look. "You don't suspect Manchu?"

"Yes, of someday taking over the world." Al smiled. "But right now he's too busy taking over unofficial sources for squadron supplies. And where in Boston or Dallas can we find delights to equal those of Most Celestial Dining?"

There were two guards at Operations and an extra guard on the airstrip perimeter. Only flying personnel were allowed at the meeting. Tyrone, McCabe, and Butler faced them across a cleared table, in front of a new wall map. Butler had wanted the enlisted flying personnel to sit separately. Tyrone had firmly said "no."

The Colonel rose, and waited for silence. No pith helmet this time, only his dress jungle fatigues. "I'd like to begin," Tyrone began quietly, "with a matter not directly related to our main concern. There's this new rumor that part of the squadron is being moved to an auxiliary airstrip at Sadiya. It's only a rumor, with no basis in fact. I would not consider breaking up our squadron. You're doing a great job the way things are."

"Colonel, if I may say a few words." Major Butler stood up, paused, then sat down abruptly when Tyrone gave him a level stare. "No more on the matter, Major."

Hawk, sitting between Fitz and Chavez, suddenly found himself the focus of Butler's intent stare. Tyrone had obviously not authorized any preliminary fly-over of the Sadiya area, as Butler had claimed. He returned the stare until the Major looked away. Did thoughts of albino elephants dance in his head?

"I'll let the survival of Hank Romano and his crew set the tone of this meeting," Tyrone began firmly. "Hank admits he delayed getting someone up in the bubble after his last drop. That he finally did is the reason they're here. Consider it an order -- from now on keep an eye on what's above and behind you or it may not matter where you're headed. O.K.?"

They waited for him to go on.

"Now," Tyrone said, "I'll begin with a brief summary of what's going on in our war and how things are shaping up. Of course, I only know a small part of what is going on and even less of how things are shaping up. That said, I suggest that my comments not be used for predictions on when we return to Sicily, the date of the Second Coming, or what's promising in Wall Street investments. I would be most pleased if we all remained alive. But that is a matter in which luck does play a part. Right, Hank?"

"Not at all, Al." They stared at Romano. He stood up, straight-faced. "I'd like you all to know that the reason I'm here tonight is because of my superb, if not unequaled flying skill, my high-school years as a star quarterback, which developed my character, and to my parents' guidance, which resulted in their tanning my ass every time I acted like, to quote them, 'a stinking little wop'. Therefore, I believe I deserve, as further reward, a doubling of my ration of rye whiskey." He gave an awkward bow and sat amid their cheers.

Tyrone quelled them with upraised arms. "Thank you, Lieutenant. Exactly what I was about to say. And now -- " he turned and for a moment studied the wall map, then raised a hand and pointed to the dark winding line of the Stilwell Road running up over the Patkais and south through the Hukawng Valley toward Kamaing and Mogaung -- "now, it's a possibility that long before we arrived, Vinegar Joe had already decided to go for Mitch and pay the Japs back for kicking his ass out of Burma two years ago.

Or maybe it's Mogaung he wants. Both are on the rail line. If we take either, we'll be halfway across Burma. Any questions so far?"

"Caramba," Chavez whispered to Hawk, "now we are going to China!"

"Now," Tyrone continued, "on the so-called local scene. Southwest, east of Impal, the Japanese are falling back before the British and Indian troops. Up here we have the Chinese troops. Lots of them, already well down the valleys by the time we arrived. The Japanese have fallen back into the Mogaung Valley, but still show no sign of giving up Kamaing and Mogaung. East of Mogaung is Mitch. So the question is, which is our objective, Mogaung or Mitch?"

"Frankly," Gimbel said loudly, "mine is New York City."

"Maybe the Japs', too, Lieutenant," Tyrone said. "Any more smart-ass remarks?" He waited, then went on. "My guess is the Japs aren't sure either, but have bet on Mogaung, figuring that even if we want Mitch there's no other way than through that valley. Which isn't going to happen overnight. So why worry about Mitch? Reconnaissance indicates that Mitch is lightly garrisoned, as few as a thousand men. And where are we?"

"Some of us are up in the Kumons, dropping supplies to Merrill's Marauders," Ericson offered. "Not even a thousand of them, plus a few Chinese troops. Don't tell me they're going to go over the mountains and take Mitch while the Japs sit waiting for us at Mogaung?"

"Then why so many Zeros all of a sudden?" McCabe put in.

"Exactly," Tyrone said. "It looks like the Japs have figured out we aren't just practicing up in the Kumons. And maybe they're starting to reinforce Mitch. If they do, and the Marauders get stalled in the Kumons because the Zeros start picking us off, what then?" He paused and stared at them, his expression grim. "A fact," he went on, "Group HQ reports that in the last week Zero attacks have tripled. Our squadron has lucked out, but you may be aware the Group has lost four gooneys. Now, starting tomorrow, we're to double our missions, both above Kamaing and to the Marauders. All in all, it's not going to be fun. Any questions?"

There were none.

"So," Tyrone said, "that's my guess of what's going on. Don't take it as an official report from Washington. Whatever happens, for godsake keep an eye out in those bubbles! Meeting adjourned, squadron bar open."

Hawk and Fitz were among the last to file out. Glancing back, Hawk noticed that Butler had not moved, just sat alone at the table, staring blankly ahead.

Joe Cordner brought the news to their tent the next morning on his way to mess. Colonel Tyrone had relieved Major Butler of Operations duty. Butler had been taken to Jorhat for a medical check-up. McCabe was taking over Operations, Ericson and Hawk would handle Information and Intelligence.

"So naturally," Cordner observed, "we'll all be doing even a bit more flying." His glance traveled over their sprawl of clothing and equipment. Only Hawk opened his eyes. The others remained motionless in tangles of sheets. Rain fell softly, steadily, whispering against the canvas. "Ceiling supposed to lift by ten," Cordner went on. "McCabe wants everyone on line by nine. You give them the message, Hawk?"

Schultz reared up suddenly from his cot. "Cordner, just go stuff your fucking fat face and let us rest!" He collapsed abruptly back on his cot.

Robb and Fitz hadn't moved. Hawk sat up as Cordner pushed out through the tent flaps. He leaned from his cot, checked the earth for footing and stepped to the tent pole. Grappling through his flight bag, he located his briefcase, wiped the slight skim of mold from its surface, and sat on the edge of his cot. The only way to handle communications, he thought, is on impulse.

After staring for a moment at the paper he carefully printed the date in the upper right hand corner -- *MAY 4TH, 1944*. From the airstrip came the sound of the first engine roaring to life, idling to a mutter, roaring again and falling silent. Overhead the birds of morning began to answer. The only one he'd learned to distinguish was a bronze-winged dove. Or was it a parrot? From somewhere far off on the jungle's edge came a chattering of monkeys.. Robby moaned and twisted restlessly. A distant clash of metal from the mess. Hawk stared at the paper and in a careless, looping scrawl wrote *JAMILA,* paused, added a question mark, crossed it out and tried some exclamation points, added a flourish to the "*J,*" then abruptly crumpled the paper and pulled another sheet from his briefcase.

He found it impossible to write to her. What could he say to someone who now was a part of him? The whole business defied dissection, which in itself was a stupid word to have even come to mind. Was he in love with her? To say as much was to say nothing. His feeling was more as if he had slept, a chrysalis, to awake finding he had changed. "Nothing of him that doth fade, but doth suffer a sea-change into something rich and strange." If he quoted that, would it please her? He took out another piece of paper.

Now he saw his father, at first seated at his church organ, playing as if summoning the hosts, this dissolving to a rocky Atlantic ledge, his father's quick white fingers baiting their hooks, their bamboo rods bending as they cast the speared periwinkles into the white surf for rock cod.

"Cod!" his mother exclaimed, unwrapping the soggy newspaper and wiping her hands on her apron. "I told you not to bring any home. They're filled with a million bones!"

He went on, used the paper now for commonplace phrases and words, not thoughts. *I AM WELL. LOVE, ALAN. P.S. TELL ALMA JILBERT I WAS UNABLE TO LOCATE FRED.* On the outside of the envelope he scribbled *CENSORED*

12

BARPA didn't appear the next morning until after Hawk had returned from mess. Schultz hadn't bothered to get up. Fitz and Robby were already off to the airstrip. McCabe, having checked Fitz out, was sending him off on a mission as first pilot.

"We've still got ten minutes," Schultz said, dressed but stretched out on his cot. "No point getting there early, McCabe on his new job and swearing at everybody."

"I find his language simply dreadful," Hawk said.

"Fuck you." Schultz gave him a look and closed his eyes.

The tent flaps were thrown aside and Barpa appeared in the entrance cradling a polished wooden box in his arms instead of the usual large leaf from an elephant-ear plant. Since the episode of the muddy boots below Shadazup, Hawk had become aware that a certain formality had developed in their relationship. His boots, restored to their pristine condition, had been placed each day on a fresh leaf. But a warmth had vanished from Barpa's voice. Jamila had identified the problem.

"Barpa is obviously displeased," she said, "at the cavalier treatment you gave your boots that day in the jungle."

"I have brought you a gift, sir." Barpa stepped to Hawk's cot, knelt, examined the boots, brushed the toe of one with his sleeve, then slid the boots into the box. They fit exactly. "This way they remain dry, sir." He closed the small, brass-hinged perforated door. "And safe, sir."

"It is a beautiful box, Barpa," Hawk said.

"I made it myself, sir."

Barpa's seriousness was almost too much. "But Barpa," Hawk said, "I was just thinking that today I might wear them flying. My first mission is to Shadazup and back. There's hardly any mud there."

Barpa, still kneeling, opened the box, withdrew a boot, buffed it lightly on a sleeve, replaced it, closed the little door and rose, his expression inscrutable.

"I don't think he's going to let you wear them," Schultz said.

"Sir." Hawk noticed that Barpa's glance did not focus directly on him. "I make this box from very hard wood. What you call ma-ho-gany. Two day ago I find bad ants in boots. Also it is where snakes like to go."

"Now you tell me, Barpa," Hawk said, then saw immediately Barpa did not understand his remark. "Thank you, Barpa. I think it is too hot and I will wear my sneakers."

Schultz gave a snort of disgust and lurched from his cot toward the entrance. "Keep this up and he'll have you flying fucking barefooted."

Three days had passed since Butler's departure, and Ericson and Hawk had worked out a reasonably smooth takeover of Butler's duties. During his spare time, McCabe had carefully packed up Butler's photographic equipment. Word was Butler's period of examination at the hospital for mental stress would be of some length. Hawk and Ericson had worked out a split schedule for each, half in Operations, the other half in the air.

That morning McCabe was clearing out the rest of Butler's gear from the desk Hawk and Ericson would share. Colonel Tyrone was at the wall map. Already, a sifting of sunlight indicated clearing. Hawk went over the flight assignments. Fitz had requested Robb for co-pilot. Hawk hesitated, then wrote Robby's name beside Fitzgerald's. Routine supply missions into the Hukawng Valley. No drops. Robby, though a navigator, had flown twenty missions as a co-pilot. Hawk turned from the flight board as Ericson entered. Ericson strode to the flight board and studied it.

"You're giving Fitzgerald a navigator as co-pilot on his first mission, Hawk?" Ericson glanced at Tyrone.

"As you know, Lee," Hawk said, "I checked him out yesterday. He did a first class job. I've no problem giving him Robb."

"What do you think, Colonel?" Ericson, cautious as always, glanced at Tyrone.

"I think I'll stay out of this one," Tyrone said. "You two are handling the scheduling."

Ericson turned to McCabe, busy sorting Butler's papers into a carton. "What do you think, Captain?"

"I don't give a rat's ass who flies with Fitz. Send Manchu along if you like."

"Gimbel is free this morning," Ericson said, turning to Hawk. "I don't think he'd mind. Might make Fitz feel a little more steady."

"Fitz doesn't need someone to help him feel steady," Hawk said. "Besides, Gimbel is from Brooklyn."

"So?"

"So is Fitzgerald. But from a different neighborhood. They don't like each other much."

For a few moments the sound of engines being revved up shuddered through Operations. Hawk glanced at Tyrone, in whose eyes the shadow of a smile lingered.

"My only observation, gentlemen," Al said, "is that it would be too bad to send the two together and risk the chance of having our entire New York contingent wiped out."

Ericson shrugged and turned to McCabe. "How about finishing up with Butler's desk? Hawk and I need some space of our own." He turned to Hawk. "Who's flying this morning, you or I?'

Hawk nodded at the board. He had scheduled himself for a drop at Talpha Ga first, the second up into the Kumons, Murphy as co-pilot. "Murphy's the one who still needs some steadying. The only official co-pilot we have left. Maybe you could check him out this afternoon."

"More goddamn animal pictures!" McCabe exploded behind them, waving a handful of Butler's photos. "And that albino one again. An enlargement of that one at the Greystaffs'." He held it up to them. "Butler warned me if I didn't take care of his equipment he'd kill me." He slapped the photos down on top of a carton. "You guys want your goddamn desk, it's clear."

Hawk went to a window and stared up. Slats of blue were creasing the dirty drape of clouds. The first gooney came taxiing up for take-off. He'd scheduled Fitz for his last. No way Fitz could get in trouble in any of his three flights. Shinbwiyan, Maingkwan, Shadazup. Pieces of cake.

"You want the left hand or right hand side of the desk?" Ericson had opened a briefcase and was sliding out neat bundles of papers.

"Makes no difference, Lee," Hawk said.

"Come on," McCabe said to Tyrone. "My best tower man is down sick with jaundice. Want to help me get the clowns in the air?"

"And back," Tyrone said, turning to Ericson and Hawk. "Both of you are a bit ragged so far, but I imagine you'll get done whatever has to be done."

Hawk caught himself taking a deep breath, a sigh of relief, when he stepped from Operations into the damp, heavy air, the clouds again closing against the sunlight, the gooneys edging up the line for take-off. He wondered whether his feeling of ease was due to having escaped briefly from Operations and its new demands. Murphy was waiting at the plane, the kickers and ground personnel still loading from a six-wheeler that had backed too close. A little tense, Murphy showed him the dent on the cargo entrance.

"Yeah," Hawk said, "but we can still probably get her into the air. Check the ailerons and tail section."

"I already have, Hawk."

"Check them again."

"Yes sir, Lieutenant!"

"And Murphy. Take the left seat. You're flying first pilot today." Murphy's pimple of a chin seemed to harden. He turned away, red-faced. So, Hawk thought, it'll be Murphy's first drop in the Kumons.

Hawk pulled himself up through the cargo entrance. The two kickers were lining up the heavily-wrapped bags of rice. They were dropping to the Chinese troops moving up through the mountains behind the Marauders.

In the cockpit he called the tower. McCabe was there. Yes, Fitz had gotten off O.K. What in hell was he worrying about? McCabe cleared them for take-off. Murphy taxied up and into position, glancing at Hawk.

"O.K., Murphy, it's all yours. You get us off. I'll get the wheels up."

Murphy gave him a wide-eyed look.

"Come on, Murphy. You heard me!"

Murphy grabbed the throttles abruptly, shoving them forward. The plane lurched ahead, gained speed quickly. Half-way down the air-strip the tail lifted. Murphy held the plane on the ground for a moment, then brought it into the air, held it level, aiming at the rise of trees ahead, then pulled into an easy climb. The Greystaffs' pool made a shiny blue spot beside the white house as they passed over. Murphy took the gooney into a steep climb, then gave Hawk a puzzled glance.

"She's not climbing right, Hawk."

Hawk glanced up into the thickening clouds. "Maybe she's trying to tell us something, Murphy."

Murphy gave him a look, stared ahead, worked their nose down a bit, then up. He flushed red again.

"Wheels up." He jerked a thumb up.

"It helps," Hawk said easily, reaching for the lever. "Now let's see how you are on instruments."

Murphy was rough on instruments. They staggered and rocked up through layers of cloud, emerged suddenly into the purity of open sky, the clouds below them blanketing the Patkais but fraying out ahead over the Hukawng Valley.

"I'll have a look from the bubble," Hawk said, unbuckling his seat-belt and stepping back into the passageway, bracing himself on a metal cleat. The translucent Plexiglas bubble was clean. From it, he could make out several gooneys ahead, two already in their descent to Shinbwiyan. Above them the clear sky reached almost to the horizon.

"You know where we're dropping, Murphy. How do you figure on getting there?" Hawk returned to his seat and handed him the map. "I'll take the wheel while you look it over."

"I've already studied the map," Murphy said. "Seems the best route is to the road, down to Shadazup, then over to Talpha Ga. The drop zone is only a couple of miles east of the village."

"A lot of air traffic up and down the Road-- Shinbwiyan, Yupbang, Taipha Ga, Maingkwan, Shadazup. Might have a little more elbow room if we cut through the hills east of Walawbum. Especially if the weather closes in."

Hawk leaned back. Murphy continued on course, straight and level, engines purring. Hawk got up again, took a look through the bubble, returned to his seat.

"How you feeling now, Murphy?"

Murphy gave him a smile. "Much better. You know, I really like flying a gooney.

"Then why cut your chances of continuing?" Hawk said. Murphy gave him a puzzled look.

"What's our altitude, Murphy?"

Murphy leaned forward and peered at the altimeter. "Five thousand feet."

"Why?"

"Well, you haven't said anything about changing it."

"Who's the pilot, Murphy? Or are you hunting for Zeros?"

Murphy flushed, put the gooney into a steep descent. One of the kickers came forward wanting to know what the fuck was wrong.

"One of the wings felt loose," Hawk said. "We wanted to see if it was going to fall off."

"Fucked up again, " Murphy said. "Sorry."

The Jaino hills below Walawbum climbed up as they approached, a jagged, green dam. Hawk pointed out the opening. "Wide enough for a turn at one place," Hawk said, "but stick to the middle. About eight miles -- that is, unless I've picked the wrong opening."

This time Murphy smiled, a tight smile, his lips turning a bit white as they went through, over the ammo drop zone of a few weeks before, now unused, emerging into the Mogaung Valley, the beaten-up village of Talpha Ga dead ahead.

"O.K., Murph," Hawk said. "I'll take over for the first two passes. Then you give it a try. . . . Now, when I signal a drop don't hesitate."

The mission went smoothly. A well-marked, long drop-zone and, unlike the other drops, no troops milling about in the zone like a bunch of ants. The story was probably apocryphal, Hawk thought, of one early drop when someone had told the native helpers they were supposed to run out and catch the ninety-pound bags of rice. Unfortunately, one had.

They had a heavy load. It took eight more passes to get rid of their cargo. Murphy took over, handled the gooney roughly, after coming in too low on his first pass and forgetting to tell Hawk to signal the kickers. But with his second pass, Murphy, sweating profusely, had things under control. The last drop completed, he pulled up and sat back, motioning Hawk to take over.

"Sorry," Hawk said. "I'm a bit tense. Think I'll take a little nap."

He watched through slitted eyes as Murphy took them back through the Walawbum Hills, holding close to the jungle all the way back up the Hukawng, doing a gentle climb up over the Patkais where the clouds had vanished, and down to receive the Sook tower's directive that they were clear and number one to land.

Murphy landed and taxied back to their loading zone. Hawk handed him their log book to fill out. "Next one we do is the Kumons," he said to Murphy. "See we're loaded properly. It's chutes again. I'll go up and see Ericson about changing your status. You are now, having passed the basic tests, qualified as a limited first pilot."

The temperature in Operations hung just below a hundred. Ericson was sweating over a stack of forms, the tower radio turned up and McCabe there, screaming at someone for having tuned in the BBC while in flight. A new enlisted man named Ben, installed as a second clerk, was pounding at a typewriter while Jim, first clerk, made changes on the flight board.

"You think that's wise about Murphy?" Ericson said to Hawk. "I mean, it wasn't really a proper check-out. And what about the written part?"

"Give it to Murphy when we get back from the Kumons."

Hawk turned to leave.

"Sir." It was the new clerk in the corner. "Sorry, I almost forgot. A communication for you from Group HQ." He held out a yellow, sealed envelope.

"Ah!" Hawk exclaimed, taking the envelope and ripping it open, "my orders for R and R at Agra. The Taj Mahal dancing girls! Scented nights and the exotic sounds of tambourines or whatever it is they play."

He read the few lines over several times, then folded the paper and shoved it in the hip pocket of his shorts.

"Anything wrong, Alan?" Ericson said, his voice seeming to come from a great distance. The room came back in focus for Hawk.

"No," he said. "Not any more. My father died a week ago." He moved toward the door.

"I'll take your flight, Alan," Ericson said.

"Thanks," Hawk said. "But I'll be better off flying."

The telegram had said "peacefully in his sleep." Hawk came up to the plane and slid into the left seat. Did his mother really know if it was peaceful? "To die, to sleep, perchance to dream." He watched a gooney slide in on a long approach, slapped on his earphones. Tower reporting Rogers with a blown tire, McCabe expostulating. What in Christ, Rogers snapped, did McCabe expect him to do, change it before landing? McCabe's voice loud, warning the airstrip, the fire truck suddenly tearing alongside the line. Rogers, a sailor from Connecticut, was going to buy a schooner after the war and sail around the world. Hawk watched the gooney touch, lift, touch, skim the airstrip, and ease down as if releasing a long-held breath.

"C'mon, Hawk!" McCabe's voice blasted. *"Let's move it on out! Ericson wants to get in a couple of missions this afternoon. Murphy's already at the plane."*

This time Hawk wanted his own hands on the wheel, the solid feel of the rudder pedals against his feet. Before boarding the plane he'd made sure his sneaker lacings were tight, yanked in the belt of his shorts another notch, tucked in his shirttails. Suddenly it was important to be in control of things. He glanced back down the plane. The two chute men were standing by the cargo opening, checking the chute cords, the tightly wrapped supplies lined behind them in neat rows.

He started the engines, checked the mags with quick thrusts of the throttles, signaled out for chocks away. The chute men sat down, backs against metal, and gave him a "thumbs up." He picked up the mike, the gooney shivering lightly as he eased it forward. *"Tower from Hawk. Taxiing out."*

"Cleared," McCabe said. *"Come on fast and I can get you off before Walker gets on his final approach."* A pause. *"And Hawk, sorry to hear about your father. Just take it easy."*

"Roger and out." Hawk was scarcely conscious of Murphy beside him as he moved quickly onto the airstrip. McCabe cleared him. The gooney lifted nicely, the white gleam of the plantation and pool flashing past. Hawk signaled

wheels up. He suddenly wondered, had his father ever flown in a plane?

The clouds had thinned over the Patkais so he could avoid climbing, permitting them to skim the jungle over the abandoned strip at Likhani where Weed had been killed, its long basha already a crumbled ruin of vines, poles, and thatch. He dropped with the fall of the land, leveling at 500 feet over the long beginning reach of the Hukawng Valley, the Stilwell Road a brown snake weaving through the jungle off to their right. Much traffic moving south. Murphy switched to alert channel. It crackled but remained silent.

"I could try Maingkwan," Murphy said. "They might have a weather update."

Hawk pointed ahead to the dark lifting of hills on the jungle horizon. "There's your weather, Murph. Clear to the hills below Walawbum, just like before. It's what's beyond them that counts."

Their course was exactly the same as earlier, as far as Talpha Ga, then on into the Kumons and their drop zone. They were already past Maingkwan. A couple of gooneys were lifting from behind a low range of hills.

"Hey!" Murphy said, leaning forward suddenly, pointing to their fuel gauges. "Both tanks are half empty. They forgot to refuel us!"

"No," Hawk said, "I told them to skip us. We've more than enough to get down and back and the gooney always dances better on an empty stomach. What if we had to do a loop?"

Murphy looked at him, grinned and shrugged. "What if the weather closes in and we have to fly to . . . to . . . ."

"I'd rather be ready for the dance, Murph."

The low, green darkness of the Walawbum Hills shouldered up before them into a thin gray haze threading the tops. Hawk found himself toying with the gooney, a slight dip, a touch of left rudder, a skid to the left, back and up a hundred feet. Precision flying, he thought. An updraft sent him up two hundred feet. He corrected. Now a long, ragged stretch of burned land, skeletons of trees, charred ruins. Not even an elephant herd to buzz. He eased down to 500 feet just as the alert signal rasped through the cockpit.

"Two Zeros at 10,000 over Kamaing, heading two-hundred-seventy degrees -- repeat, two Zeros at . . . " The alert broke off in a rush of static.

"Not in our ballroom," Hawk said.

The long-ago image came abruptly, clearly: a dance floor on the second story of the Masonic Temple, a high school freshman dance, and the girl clinging to him had round dark eyes and smiled bravely every time he stepped on her feet. He couldn't recall her name. She was squat and dumpy and played the piano, his father had said, with some talent. His mother had arranged for him to take her to the dance.

Murphy got up and stepped back to the bubble. Balancing on one foot, his head poked up against the Plexiglas. Then he returned to his seat.

"They don't know we're here yet," Hawk said. "Or, they're waiting until we get jammed up in the Kumons. They've probably got Jap observers hanging from the trees to call in the Zeros."

This time Murphy's chin barely tightened. His look became impenetrable. The Walawbum Hills closed about them, the valley winding in, the morning's drop zone busy with Chinese troops, certainly not expecting them, scattering as they roared over and on into the upper Mogaung and to Talpha Ga, ahead.

Hawk began his climb, a thickening of the air, visibility deceptive, the Kumons rising and vanishing in thickening rolls of clouds. He spotted the entrance, climbed into its green gap and the jumble of hills which marked the first upward thrust of the mountains. How many days before had the Marauders slogged along the muddy, barely visible trail below to vanish in the jungle?

The mountain gaps closed. A sudden spill of cloud as Hawk rounded an upward tilt of land, a blinding smear of rain across their windshield. Ahead a dark, seeming dead-end of jungle and cliff. Murphy, both hands gripping his knees, snapped forward, a figure carved of stone.

"Jesus H. Christ!" he muttered and crossed himself.

"I hope they've got the tunnel built," Hawk said.

Murphy gaped.

The gooney shuddered as Hawk banked, flicking just over the jungle, leveling under a long layer of clouds.

Murphy leaned forward, hands pressed together.

"It's O.K.," Hawk yelled. He gestured ahead toward a short, narrow cleared strip bisected by a thin white line. "This is it! Get the chute boys off their asses!"

The long, ragged valley appeared entirely encircled by hills. A movement of men along the edges of the drop zone. A blast of static from the radio, a heavy voice - *"O.K., O.K., nice you dropped in. Just keep the goddamn chutes out of the trees. Over and out."*

Hawk lined up on the guiding marker, then pulled up as it vanished under him. At least they'd picked the widest part of the valley. He banked right, then into a tight arc left for the first drop. Murphy sat turned in his seat, eyes on Hawk as they approached the white line at 300 feet.

"Now!" Hawk yelled. Murphy's arm jerked down. Then they were over and beyond, Hawk banking for his next one eighty sharply enough that they were able to catch sight of the string of orange chutes, supplies swinging like pendulums, falling perfectly onto the drop zone. Hawk lined up and came in again.

"Now," he yelled. Murphy signaled back quickly. They were over, reaching into another one-eighty, seeing again the dull orange moons of the chutes falling toward the white line.

It took four more passes before they were done. Hawk lifted, swung into a gentle turn, came back over the drop zone. Men were already out, obscuring the white line into the earth. One chute had hung up in a tree at the edge of the zone. Then they were weaving out of the valley, lifting into an easy climb until the last hills were behind them and Talpha Ga visible just ahead. Murphy leaned back in his seat, stretched and smiled. The alert came on.

"Two Zeros in vicinity of Warazup and Shadazup. Looks like a hunting expedition. One gooney hit and doing a wheels-up at Shad. All aircraft take evasive action."

"Which means?" Murphy yelled, tense again, glancing at Hawk, then ahead and up.

"It means get your ass up in the bubble while we go down and hide in the jungle." Hawk glanced back down the plane where the two chute men were working by the cargo bay, stowing away the gear from the drop. "And get the men forward."

Less than twenty miles now across the flat stretch of jungle, past Talpha Ga and then up the Mogaung Valley. Once through the pass they should be O.K. Get back in over the old ammo drop zone and do three-sixties until an "all clear" was given.

Talpha Ga flashed past a hundred feet below them, the hills looming up ahead. Only minutes and they'd be safe in their cover. Murphy's yell knifed through the gooney.

"Hawk! Hawk! One's after us! Looks like a Zero! High up and diving!"

"Stay up there," Hawk yelled. He put the gooney into a skid -- left rudder, right turn, then a slide in the opposite direction. He straightened, dove at the jungle, then jerked upward. He just might spoil the bastard's aim. A yell from Murphy, a metallic shuddering, the dark shape of the Zero flashed over them so close it seemed he could reach up and touch it. The pilot would be back on their tail in less than a minute. Hawk rammed the throttles forward. The green mass of the hills loomed, closed about them. "Get down, get down," he whispered to himself, hands hard on the wheel, treetops seeming to slap at them. If he could reach the drop zone there might be a chance to . . . .

"It's on our tail again!" Murphy's voice wrenched into high panic.

The zone loomed ahead between the hills. Hawk dropped full flaps, throttles back, banked hard right. The gooney shuddered, seemed to stumble. Were they already hit? The final moments -- the Jap pilot already chalking up his kill?

Again the Zero flashed overhead, close, in a steep bank. They were still airborne. For moments Hawk held the gooney in its shuddering turn. Ahead, the Zero reached for the opening that would bring it out of the hills, pulled up abruptly but too late. The plane seemed to merge with the jungle. The hill which the pilot had misjudged seemed merely to take it in quietly. A bright orange flower of fire lifted above the green. Hawk eased the gooney from its labored flight, angled into and through the gap in the hills, his mind blank until the lovely valley of the Hukawng reached out before them and he became aware that Murphy had returned to his seat, sat staring ahead.

"I think we've got a hole in our bubble," Murphy said softly, after a while.

The alert came on -- *"No enemy aircraft now reported. Cautionary 'all-clear' has been issued."*

Hawk glanced at Murphy, whose hands were grasped together and shaking a little. "I'm going back and check on the chute crew," Hawk said, unsnapping his safety belt and rising. "Mind taking it for a few moments?" Murphy's hands came apart and slammed onto his wheel. "Just a slow, climb, Murphy."

The chute men were sitting with their backs against a metal partition halfway up the plane. "Pretty rough flying, Lieutenant," the older one said. "The kid was yelling he saw a Zero. Did he?"

"Yes, he saw one."

"Shit, if we'd stayed in the rear," the other said, "we might have seen. I ain't never seen one."

Back in the cockpit Hawk let Murphy keep the wheel until they began the climb over the Patkais. The clouds had thickened and rain fell heavily as they came over and down on instruments toward Sook. McCabe gave them a 300 foot ceiling and an east-west landing. Planes stacked up at 1,000' foot levels to 6,000'. Hawk took over. They were a half-hour getting in, no chance for even a glimpse of the swimming pool. Down and taxied off the strip, engines cut, Hawk sat motionless behind the wheel.

"You all right?" Murphy said, sliding from his seat.

"Write up the log," Hawk said, "and go on along. I'll sit here for a while." He waited there until his hands were no longer shaking and the hard knot in his stomach dissolved, the taste of fear dry in his mouth.

When he entered Operations things were in sort of a melee. Flights being canceled. Ericson pissed off. Weather forecast for the next morning not good. He'd be stuck again in Operations. Would Hawk like to trade for the afternoon?

"How about for the next month?" Hawk said.

Colonel Tyrone,, who had been on the phone, looked up at them. "Guess what? Major Butler has disappeared from the hospital at Jorhat. He's now listed AWOL."

The clerk's phone rang. The Jorhat line again. Group HQ calling: if Butler showed up at Sook he should immediately be confined to quarters.

"Ask them if they have any idea where he went? Did he grab a vehicle? How was he dressed?" Colonel Tyrone turned to the wall map, and with a finger traced the rail line that ran southeast beside the Brahmaputra River. "Maybe he's taken off for Calcutta," Tyrone said. "He sometimes talked about going there to visit the zoo."

The clerk hung up his phone. "No one has a clue," he reported. "They say he seems to have taken off last night. Took only the clothes he was wearing, khakis they think. And a couple of cameras."

"I think I know where they should look," Hawk said. "Sadiya. Tell them to check in Sadiya."

"Good idea," Tyrone said, smiling at Hawk. "Hey, McCabe was telling us you got an alert this morning. See a Zero?"

"Not really, Colonel. It went past too quickly."

13

HAWK, awakening to the cry of jackals, not bothering to check the time, sat up and tossed his sweat-soaked sheets aside, letting his feet down cautiously onto the damp earth.

Fitz had warned him: "You ought to check on those night-sweats." Fitz had decided to study medicine after the war. From the English library in Chabua he'd borrowed an old and massive textbook into which he delved every evening. After Hawk's third attack -- four days after the business with the Zero -- he'd read aloud to Hawk," . . . often indicative of psychological imbalance due to stress or malfunction of the eccrine glands."

"A stress," Hawk had replied, "resulting from Manchu's failure to get me the decent bottle of Scotch he promised."

Schultz, who had been sleeping, stirred on his cot but did not open his eyes. "Romano has the same problem. Claims it's from lack of fucking."

"No," Fitz had said, running a finger over the page, "that has to do with the apocrine glands."

"That's why you don't see me sweating none," Schultz had replied. His voice lifted in a cracked bass. "'Born in a whore house, raised like a slave, fuckin' an' fightin' is all I crave'."

That was last night. Tonight no one else was awake. Hawk grabbed up his soaked sheet, crumpled it in a ball and flung it under his cot. It hit the box Barpa had made for his boots, thumped against a metal cot leg. Fitz and Schultz slept on. Robby grunted, thrashed about, came up on one elbow.

"Hawk," he whispered, "your meeting in the Colonel's basha. What was it all about?"

"Secrets," Hawk said. He shivered, felt goose bumps come along his arms, reached out and found a clean shirt among the tent pole hangings, slipped it on and lay down, hands under his head, staring upward, the black murmur of soft rain against the canvas. Robby fell back to sleep.

Only the Colonel, McCabe, Ericson, and Hawk had comprised the meeting earlier that evening. Tyrone's tent was well lit, a guard posted out front.

"Evening, Lieutenant." It was one of his chute men the day of the Zero. He gave Hawk a brief sweep of light. "How you been feeling? Quite a ride you give us."

"Thanks, Slim. If it stops raining I'm scheduled for another ride tomorrow. Want to come along?"

"Thanks, Lieutenant, but I'm scheduled up until Christmas."

Hawk gave a rap on the canvas and pushed in. Ericson had arrived, sat at Al's big table cleared of its usual centerpiece, Al's ancient wind-up phonograph. In its place were four glasses and a decanter, set between bottles of gin and their standard-issue rye. Newly roofed, with a solid wooden floor, screened windows and thatch siding, the only suggestion of the tent's former use was the slight odor of cow.

"Scotch?" Al said, turning from placing a record on his phonograph, now resting on top of a newly acquired British officer's field desk. He gestured to the decanter. "Manchu swears it's the real stuff."

"I'll risk a test run," Hawk said.

"Lee? A touch of gin laced with quinine? Good for malaria, Lee."

"Nothing, thanks." On principle Lee Ericson did not drink alcohol and after his bout with yellow jaundice was even leery of water.

"Let's listen to Bessie until McCabe arrives," Al said, cranking up his machine and letting the needle arm down gently on *Empty Bed Blues*.

Hawk poured some Scotch from the decanter. Bessie Smith slid into her blues over a sad horn. Hawk sipped.

"Well?" Al said.

Hawk took another sip. "A real malt taste, Al. The genuine article. My compliments to your bootlegger."

"Unfortunately, he still doesn't do as well with the gin," Al said. "But there's a rumor from Group HQ that our usual rye might be augmented by a shipment of bourbon."

"A sure sign we're winning the war," Ericson said sharply. He looked up at Al. "Isn't that why we're here tonight?"

"Signs and omens are rife," Al said. He turned to his desk, ran a hand carefully over its sleek surface. Its brass pulls and protective brass corners had been newly polished. Even the heavy iron handles on the ends glowed darkly. Al had come across it a couple of weeks before in the Chabua bazaar, bought it and brought it to Sook, after a stop at the Greystaffs' plantation for an appraisal. The Major had pronounced it authentic, even discovered a military numeral that suggested the desk had first been used in the Crimean War.

"At least a hundred years old!" Major Greystaff had claimed. "In those days every officer had an orderly. Things were done properly. Some sense of military tradition, *esprit de corps.*"

"My problem," Al said, coming now to the table and pouring himself a gin tonic, "is how to get the desk back to the States. No problem getting it to Sicily, but no way they'll give me a gooney to fly it home."

"Oh, so we're thinking of going home?" Hawk said, glancing at Ericson. "Is this a preliminary planning session?"

Al Tyrone stared at them, finished his drink. "Where the hell is McCabe? I told him this was important. He's already five minutes late. He could have one of his enlisted men take the tower."

"Sorry!" McCabe pushed hurriedly in. "I might even have been a day late if those assholes had their way! A couple of Pentagon bird-colonels were just flown over from Group HQ and demanding immediate transportation to Chabua. Some sort of joint British, Chinese, American meeting. Vinegar Joe is there from Shadazup. No notice they were coming, just a call from their gooney. How about a drink, Al?"

"You deserve it, Terry. Nothing like a couple of colonels to screw up the war. Scotch?"

"I said a drink, Al." McCabe grinned and took the glass of rye Al handed him. He tasted, nodded at Ericson and Hawk. "You told them yet, Al?"

"I was waiting for Bessie to finish, Terry." Al turned to his phonograph and carefully lifted its needle arm, slid the record into its worn jacket. "Might as well," he said. "It's *Merchant of Venice.*" Al smiled. An enigmatic smile, at which he wasn't very good.

"The USO," Hawk offered, "is sending in a troupe to put on a little Shakespeare for us. The two colonels are to play Rosencrantz and Guildenstern."

"I think the rank of colonel has been maligned enough for one evening," Tyrone said. His expression sobered. "*Merchant of Venice* is the code which will indicate the Marauders have captured the Mitch airstrip and it's clear for landings. That means no matter what we're doing we stop and start hauling fresh Chinese troops and supplies to Mitch. All scheduled drops to the Marauders are canceled. They've moved too far up into the Kumons. With the monsoon pushing closer any more drops are out. The Marauders are moving too fast."

"How soon?" Hawk asked.

"Today is the eighth. Stilwell is counting on the Marauders taking Mitch by the twelfth of May. I doubt they'll make it. But until then we're cutting our flights back to purely local supply missions."

"How will the flight crews be notified that the strip has been taken?" Ericson asked.

"Those in the air by radio. All pilots will be told that *Merchant of Venice* means return to base. We've got four days to set up our crews and cargo. Questions?"

"If there's a bit more Scotch," Hawk said.

For a moment Hawk saw the Colonel's irritation sharpen his eyes, then vanish. "And perhaps you'd like another song from Bessie, Lieutenant?"

"Yes, sir," Hawk said. "It would help."

Al Tyrone took a deep breath, lifted the decanter and sloshed Scotch into Hawk's glass, then turned to Ericson. "Nothing for you, Lee?"

"Thanks. Just a little water. No ice."

"Some of us will be going in at night," the Colonel said. "There's bound to be some fighting around the airstrip. Two of the squadrons will be bringing in gliders the first morning once the strip is secure. We'll be hauling Chinese troops, artillery pieces, supplies and ammunition, even a few mules."

"My guess," McCabe said, taking a refill of rye, "is that the Japs have now figured out Mitch is our main target, in spite of the Chinese push toward Kamaing and Mogaung. So naturally the buggers must be starting to reinforce Mitch. Now, after two weeks climbing over the Kumons, the Marauders and Chinese are going to be pretty beat up. I'd say Mitch ain't going to be a picnic for either them or us."

Tyrone stared at McCabe, then rose and stepped to his desk, yanked open a drawer and pulled out a handful of records, slipped one from its faded jacket and placed it on his phonograph, cranked up the machine and let the needle arm down carefully.

"*Rainy Day Blues* sounds like it should be our theme song." He returned to the table. "Let's get to work making up our crews. I want the squadron ready to go the morning of the twelfth."

Four days to the twelfth, Hawk thought, as Bessie Smith's sad warm voice sighed through the basha. Too late tonight to see Jamila.

Hawk awoke in the middle of the night. The sweats again. He'd had to fight like hell with Tyrone about having Chavez fly as co-pilot for the coming Mitch landings. A partial victory. He groped for and found his notebook in his flight bag, hunched up on his cot, flashlight close to the lined paper. He glanced over his previous entry. What am I to Jamila? Would Jamila be all tears? His hand gripping the flashlight tightened, the light slipped free, a minuscule lightning flash through the tent. He picked it up, sank back on his damp sheet. It was important to get it clear just what he was afraid of, important he get it down.

"What is this, the fucking Fourth of July?" Schultz snarled from the darkness. He groaned and thrashed into silence. Hawk flicked off his flashlight.

Next morning Hawk, Chavez co-piloting, had two supply missions down to Shadazup. There the rumor was that the Marauders were stalled by the terrain and heavy rain, and had been losing mule transport over precipices in the Kumons. Taking off from Shadazup, on the return from the second flight, the ceiling dropped abruptly in a cloudburst, a sudden electric storm that tossed them about. Hawk climbed high and broke out at 12,000 feet into an explosion of sunlight and a clear sky north to the Patkais. It should have eased things but his too-hard three-point landing at Sook caused Chavez to give him an inquiring glance.

"You don't like the way I fly," Hawk snapped at Chavez, "maybe I'll let *you* take over from now on!"

He was no more than through the doorway at Operations when Ericson, a flak jacket slung over his shoulder, was up. "You were right, Hawk. They found Butler somewhere in the jungle north of Sadiya. Flew him back to the hospital at Jorhat this morning, in bad shape. How's the weather down there?"

"Shadazup was socked in when I took off. Should be rolling over Maingkwan about the time you arrive."

Ericson shrugged and left. Hawk filed his flight report and sat down at their desk. Operations was tranquil. Only the new clerk, Ben, was on hand, who gave him a nod and went on typing. Hawk stared down at a list of the crew assignments for the Mitch operation. Ericson had pencilled in a note at the top:

HAWK, TYRONE WARNS WE'VE GOT TO HAVE INFO ON CONDITION OF MITCH, ESPECIALLY. OUR FIRST LANDING COMES AT NIGHT. THE JAPS MAY HAVE THE WHOLE

AIRSTRIP STREWN WITH LOGS! WE'LL HAVE TO KEEP CHECKING WITH GROUP HQ. ERICSON

The odd thing, Hawk thought, was that though I realized from the beginning that I might be killed, I merely thought of it as the unspoken bargain I'd made for a chance to have a look at some of those faraway lands I'd only read about. Death, if it happened, would probably be short if not too sweet. But certainly nothing like what was happening to those poor bastards up in the Kumons, where getting killed was a twenty-four hour business.

When he joined the squadron in Africa there had been death. First a gooney lost over the desert east of Tobruk, another vanishing in the desolate mountains south toward Constantine. Friendly navy fire during the invasion of Sicily had picked off four of the group's planes. All that was part of the unspoken bargain. But now, in this backwater eddy of the war, could it happen? Was he going to be killed?

Colonel Tyrone, followed by Robb, pushed in, Robb holding a parachute. Robb stopped, held up the chute, pointed. "It's in there!" he exclaimed proudly. "Groundfire. A bullet. Wasn't sitting on my flak jacket but the chute stopped it near Walawbum."

Tyrone grinned. "However you want to phrase it, Robb." He looked at Hawk. "You heard about Butler? Did you know he was up there looking for that elephant?"

"I guessed," Hawk said, staring down again at the flight crew list for Mitch. Suddenly it came in focus. Chavez was not down to fly with him. He'd been given Robby. He looked up, about to speak to Tyrone when the tower broke in.

"Tower to McCabe. Sorry sir, you'll have to hang up there a while longer. Got a special flight cleared for a straight-in approach from Jorhat."

"Bierman went on sick leave this morning," the Colonel said. "McCabe had to take his flight. That emergency strip below Shin -- Nathkaw."

Hawk nodded down at the crew listings. "Sir, I asked for Chavez. You haven't got him listed."

"Chavez is our top mechanic, as you know," Tyrone said. "We've got to keep every plane flying when Mitch opens up. I want him here, on the ground. Besides, what's wrong with Robby? You can let him sit on his chute and he'll suck up all the lead flying your way.

The tower came on again: *"Tower to McCabe -- sorry, hold at 500. We've got two bird dogs coming in after the gooney from Jorhat."*

"I don't give a rat's ass. Squeeze me in!"

"Sorry, McCabe. VIP's. Over and out."

"Inspection team in the gooney," Colonel Tyrone said. "They're hot on Butler's case. Wanted an immediate meeting. Know where they found Butler? Somewhere up along the Dibang River north of Sadiya. He was with an old guide and a crew of natives. HQ is suspicious. Want to check on Manchu too. A possible Chinese connection?" Tyrone shook his head and shrugged. "God knows who's in the two little bird dogs."

Hawk glanced over Ericson's neatly ordered desk. Ericson always left things in order. Did it really matter who he had as co-pilot when they went into Mitch? *If* they did. Maybe the whole war will stall out in the coming monsoon. He watched Tyrone step to the wall map and stare at it. The phone rang. Ben answered.

"Colonel," the clerk called. "It's about those two planes coming in. Jorhat calling."

Tyrone took the phone. "Colonel Tyrone speaking." That was all he said, then he only listened, which meant brass on the other end. Finally, with a "Yes, sir, I'll see they're taken care of," he hung up, handed the phone back to the clerk and returned to the wall map.

The tower speaker came on. *"Tower to McCabe, we have the gooney on the ground, the bird dogs on approach. You are cleared for your downwind."*

"Roger. Who we dragged in this time, Lord Mountbatten?"

The tower clicked off. "Actually," Tyrone said, still staring up at the map, "in one bird dog we've got a couple of *Life* reporters who must be taken in on the first Mitch landings. In the other, two unnamed Pentagon brass who want ditto."

"Maybe I could get one of them to fly in for me," Hawk said. He stared down over the pilot listing. Fitzgerald to co-pilot for Schultz. Hawk pointed it out.

"It will bother Fitzgerald," Hawk said. "They don't get along well at all."

"I'll look into it," Tyrone said.

"And a request, Colonel," Hawk said. "I realize we're supposed to stick close to the base with Mitch on tap. But I'd like permission to leave for a while this evening."

Tyrone turned and studied him, his expression serious 'You know what you're getting yourself in to, Hawk? Make sure you have a clear line available."

"Did you, Al?" Hawk returned.

Al Tyrone turned back to the map. "All flight personnel must be available at all times, Lieutenant. Just remember, that means keeping in touch with the base. See if the car pool has a spare jeep."

They were sitting beside the pool, the last light fading over them. Major Greystaff tugged a small brown envelope from his bathrobe pocket. "And you know, just the other day I was wondering if the old chap was still alive. Think you might find this interesting, Lieutenant." He fumbled a single folded sheet of paper from the envelope and handed it across the table to Hawk. "From

Ramesh Raju, Jamila's uncle." Hawk took it, glancing at Jamila.

"Yes, Alan, my uncle," Jamila said tonelessly. She looked at Molly, then out into the darkness beyond the pool. A recent decree had forbidden outside lighting in a wide area around the airstrip.

"Read it, read it," Major Greystaff said fretfully. The letter was in pencil, the printing precise.

SAHIB GREYSTAFF

GREETINGS. THIS LETTER I TRUST FINDS YOUR HEALTH GOOD. I WISH TO INFORM YOU OF MOST INTERESTING HAPPENING. AN AMERICAN MAJOR SEARCHED ME OUT, WISHING ME TO GUIDE HIM TO THE LAND OF THE ALBINO ELEPHANT. THAT IS THE WAY HE EXPRESSED HIS WISH. HE SAYS HE HAS SEEN A PHOTOGRAPH AT YOUR TEA PLANTATION. HE ASKS IF THE ELEPHANT STILL LIVES. I TELL HIM YES. I TELL HIM I MUST HAVE PERMISSION OF THOSE IN AUTHORITY AT NIZAMGHAT. IT IS THEN I LEARN THIS AMERICAN WISHES NOT ONLY TO SEE THE ALBINO ELEPHANT BUT TO BUY THE ELEPHANT. I TELL HIM IT IS NOT POSSIBLE. ALSO I SAY THOSE AT NIZAMGHAT WILL CERTAINLY REFUSE PERMISSION IF THEY LEARN OF THIS WISH. WOULD YOU PLEASE BE SO KIND TO GIVE MY RESPECTS TO MEMSAHIB AND LOVE TO MY MOST WELL-REMEMBERED NIECE, JAMILA. NAMASTE.

RAMESH RAJU.

"Major Butler has been found and brought back to the Jorhat hospital," Hawk said. "He has a few problems."

"Yes, an odd chap with all his fussing with cameras." Greystaff settled down in his chair and closed his eyes.

Hawk caught the warning glance from Molly to Jamila. "We thought," Jamila said, "we would go to Most Celestial Dining for dinner."

"I understand," Molly said, giving Jamila a cool look, "that the establishment is now a place where one would hope not to be seen."

Jamila leaned back, smiling, shaking her head. "Molly, dear, dear Molly, we do not live any more in the days of the Raj. It is a perfectly proper place for an Indian girl, even accompanied by an American." She smiled.

"Thank you for your support," Hawk said.

Major Greystaff's eyes popped open. "Used to be a proper place. Held the gymkhana there, and all that. Too many changes these days, what!" His eyes closed.

"Time we were off," Hawk said

Molly accompanied them out to the verandah. Masoud was waiting below and led them to the jeep with a flashlight, letting its beam sweep the jeep so Hawk could see it had been washed clean of mud.

"Thank you, Masoud," Hawk said.

"Put out your torch, Masoud," Molly called down.

Most Celestial Dining was still in the process of renovation, the parking lot partially resurfaced with loose stone, shrub plantings still wrapped in palm and burlap, separate spaces lined for vehicles, an area for the men and horse-drawn tongas. From somewhere out behind the long, low building came the heavy throb of a generator. A thin weaving of stringed music. Only the absence of bright lights, the dim glow from windows shaded with slitted bamboo, suggested the presence of war.

The entrance was open and had grown in importance, the ceiling raised, walls paneled and decorated with mounted heads. Waiters milled around the arched, columned entry to the main dining room, from where Kumar suddenly appeared, smiling, beckoning, leading them not in but down a side passage of many doors, some open, revealing glimpses of white tablecloths, cut flowers, water carafes and tapestry screens. Passing a side entrance to the main dining room, Hawk glimpsed a mosaic of green and black tiled floor, paneled walls, an arching ceiling of white held almost delicately by three golden Byzantine columns twisting up from palm-shrouded bases.

"Why, it's beautiful!" Jamila exclaimed.

"In Xanadu did Kublai Khan," Hawk said. "Only the uniforms have changed."

"Here," Kumar said, pausing and opening a polished door, then stepping back to bow them into a gleam of silver, candlelight and shadows. "Most Celestial Dining welcomes you."

A single table set for two; Paisley drapes over the two bamboo-shuttered windows; the punkah suspended from the ceiling turned slowly, its palm fronds whispering through the air.

"Sahib send greeting," Kumar said with a gesture about the room. "You like?"

"It's very special," Jamila said, as Kumar held her chair.

Hawk sat opposite her. "I only mentioned to Manchu we might be coming one of these nights," he said. "I didn't say anything about a private room. Sure you wouldn't prefer the main dining room, Jamila?"

"Oh, this is lovely, Alan. The dining room looked a bit, well, crowded." She and Kumar exchanged quick glances.

"Sahib is much pleased you make mention of his place and wishes to appreciate you, Lieutenant," Kumar said. He passed them large folding menus done in a swirling calligraphy. "You would like pleasant drink? I am to mention a fine red wine from Samarkand."

"I expected no less, Kumar. Thank you." He waited until Kumar left.

"Samarkand?" Jamila framed her question in a smile. He saw again how beautiful she was, her skin warm against her light, patterned sari wound and curving up over one shoulder.

"Where you must have come from, Jamila. Samarkand on the old silk route where treasure was brought out of China. Manchu's connections are incredible."

"Molly asked me about him. She wondered about his name. I told her what you had told me. She said, 'How typically American. They do so admire power!'."

"A human trait, Jamila. But also of some concern to the English over several centuries, if I've read history correctly." Hawk paused. "Why did Manchu see we have a private room?"

A look came in her dark eyes he had not seen before. Somewhere in them a stranger was observing him.

"Because I am black, Alan. I'm sorry. There's no reason why you should have known."

"You are Indian, Jamila."

She held out both hands toward the candles, sliding the folds of her sari from her arms. "See? In English eyes we are black, not white. That is the way they have spoken of us ever since they claimed India. That is why your very thoughtful Manchu gave us this private room. He did not want to embarrass me. After all, he knows what it is like. He is, what you Americans call, a 'chink'."

He reached and took both her hands in his. "I know so little about India. For instance, there was a massacre of your people back at the end of the first World War, by the British."

"At Amritsar." Jamila's hands remained motionless.

"Mahatma Gandhi. Too bad more of our leaders don't have his courage. Do you think the British will give up India?"

"Not 'think,' Alan. They will give up India. But not until this other war is done."

"You see how little I know, Jamila."

Her hands tightened on his. She smiled. Kumar entered bearing a tray, a bottle, poured for Hawk and waited. Hawk sipped. "Also ignorant about wines. Tastes to me just as if it has been imported from Samarkand. Salud, my love."

They touched glasses. Kumar left. Hawk said, "One time when I was hitchhiking about the States I lived in California. The wine I drank there we called dago red."

"Dago, Alan?"

"We Americans have names for all the different peoples. Dago meant Italians. The French we called frogs. The Mexicans were greasers. The Jews, kikes. The colored people, niggers."

"What did they call you, Alan?"

He smiled. "That was to be the center of my thesis on ethnic appellations which my ancient college advisor reluctantly approved, remarking only that he wondered why they would call us anything."

"Damn Yankee? I learned that in England but I'm not sure what it means."

"Whatever way it fits, I suppose." Hawk raised his glass, Jamila hers. Their touch made a bell-like sound. Then Kumar was back. Were they ready to order?

"Even Manchu cannot produce beef," Hawk said, glancing down the menu.

"Most sorry, Sahib Hawk."

Jamila traced a finger down the menu. "There is some lamb that looks nice."

"You order. I want to hear the sound of your voice."

Jamila ordered, her voice low and soft. Overhead the punkah whispered. Faintly from the main dining room, the lilt of string music. From outside, the occasional rasp of a jeep horn, and the distant thunder of high planes heading over the Hump to China.

"Now," Jamila said when Kumar had left, "I will tell you the true story of why there is no beef in India. In ancient times the Indian princes were faced with a problem. The peasants were eating so much beef, so many cows, that there were not enough bullocks to pull the carts that carried the goods the peasants produced which made the princes rich. So they consulted with a wise man -- of course in those days there were no wise women -- and the wise man told them all that was necessary was for the princes to declare beef holy, the Indian cow a reincarnation of one of their gods. So the princes declared the cow holy and the peasants stopped eating beef. That is why there are so many cows in India and no beef."

Alan stared solemnly across the table, reached and took up one of Jamila's hands, leaned forward and drew it to his lips. "I kiss the hand of my wise black love."

"So," Jamila said, smiling, "what is holy in your country?"

"I'm not sure. Certainly money, but also right now a kind of patriotism."

Kumar appeared with their meal.

"I hope you will be pleased," Jamila said, "though I was not very imaginative. Curried lamb. Kumar strongly urged the fish but we are too far from the ocean and the river fish are always questionable. Now, what do you find holy, Alan?"

He shrugged, watching Kumar leave the room, hearing again the high thunder of the planes, seeing a vision of the Kumons, and the Marauders struggling toward a remote jungle airstrip. He shrugged off the thoughts.

"I don't know. I've yet to discover what is holy."

She smiled, reached and touched his arm. "Like you, I'm not sure. But my voyage of discovery began on that boat I told you about when Major Greystaff brought me down the Brahmaputra from Sadiya. We were not close. For a while I was afraid of him, the power he seemed to have. But now I am sure of one thing, my loyalty to the Greystaffs."

For a while he did not speak. For Alan it was enough to sit across the table from Jamila, aware of the moving shadows in her eyes, her English accent softening, as if leaving something unsaid, not quite resolved lingering in her tone. She spoke of her months and years in England and how she had come to understand India through English eyes. But there remained a loyalty to her own country, her belief that its slow yet implacable progress toward freedom could not be denied.

Kumar appeared with coffee. From the main dining room a swell of voices, singing in German of *Lili Marlene.* He listened. Above the sad sweet song, the sound of planes again. He reached and took her hands, saw the quick tears in her eyes. Suddenly he realized what he had been hiding from himself since that first night awakening to his drenched sheets. He was afraid, because he had found Jamila and now might lose her. Before this, the possibility of death had not been part of the equation.

"I would like to leave, Jamila."

She hesitated only a moment, then rose. "Yes, Alan, it is time to leave."

They returned through the rare clear night, the plantation dark except for an inner hall light. He cut the engine and they got out, followed the path that led out around the pool, through the door in the brick wall. The bergamot was still in bloom.

The gazebo appeared a miniature pagoda under the sourceless light of the night sky, a place Kublai Khan might have dreamed of. Jamila took his hands, brought them against her face and they moved together.

14

FITZ sat on the edge of his cot, dressed, medical book open. He looked over at Robb and Hawk, both still in their cots, staring up at the water-beaded canvas, on which the mid-morning rain drummed heavily down.

"Hey, listen to this, you guys." Fitz placed a finger on the page and read slowly. "The autonomic system contains only motor nerves. Although its impulses originate in the central nervous system." He smiled up at them. "Like, you know, discovering a Zero on your ass -- you perform more or less automatically, without conscious intervention of higher brain centers."

Hawk and Robb continued to gaze at the canvas.

"Some muscle responses," Fitz read on, "may be triggered simultaneously, as when a person shudders and jerks away from the touch of an insect." He paused. "I suppose you guys know about Pavlov's famous experiments with dogs?"

Hawk closed his eyes and began a low howl that rose through the octaves. Robby punctuated it with a series of sharp yappings. Barpa appeared in the tent opening, eyes wide.

"Hey, Hawk," Robby said, remaining motionless, "here's your shoe-shine boy."

Hawk sat up, found a smile. Barpa glanced first beneath Hawk's cot, then at Robby, and at Fitz with his book, finally at Schultz's empty cot.

"You're late, Barpa," Hawk said. "Besides, none of us are in the mood to have things picked up."

Barpa blinked sadly at them. "So sorry, Lieutenants. Much water comes all along the road. I must help to take the little children away. Also, there are many trucks with the Chinese soldiers making camp and others to unload large guns. Much mud and I am asked to help."

"Guns, Barpa?"

"37-millimeter guns, also mortars -- 60-and 81-millimeter."

Robby sat straight up. "Where'd you hear that, Barpa?"

"I listen to the soldiers, Chinese and English, and your people. They put guns near the airstrip where you will fly them to Mitch."

Fitz closed his medical book with a slap. "Did you hear when we would be taking off, Barpa?"

"No." Barpa gave them a knowing smile. "I am thinking that is a thing not said." He glanced down at the wooden box under Hawk's cot and bent over.

"No, Barpa," Hawk said. "The boots are fine. I looked at them earlier. Now a little mouse lives in the box and guards them."

"A mouse!" Barpa's eyes went wide with alarm. "It is eating the boots!"

"No, Barpa!" Hawk said sharply as Barpa started to kneel. "No mouse! I make an American joke. Now, please, go away. When you find out when we're taking off for Mitch come and tell us."

Barpa straightened, regarded them all with a frown. "I go, Lieutenants. I do not understand. Today all I meet look cross at me and do not speak!" He turned and strode from the tent.

"Today is the twelfth," Hawk said. "I hope Barpa will let us know when the Marauders have taken Mitch."

Schultz pushed in through the flaps, wiping rain from his unshaven face. "What the fuck's wrong with Barpa? Bastard wouldn't even look at me."

"He's worried about a mouse eating my boots," Hawk said. "What's the word?"

Schultz shrugged. "Tyrone's been talking with Jorhat. Nothing. McCabe's been listening in from the tower. Not a fucking word. By now Vinegar Joe probably has that wild hair up his ass pushing out his tonsils. Only decent thing that's happened, Manchu's been serving pancakes this morning. Aunt Jemima pancakes. I saw the goddamn boxes. Where the fuck you think he got them?"

"Samarkand," Hawk said, leaning back on his cot.

From the airstrip, which had been quiet all morning, came the muffled roar of a gooney being throttled up. It was joined by others. Fitz, about to open his medical book again, paused. Robb sat up.

"I could go down and check with Chavez," Hawk said. "He'll probably know before we do."

Schultz collapsed on his cot, let loose a prolonged fart, "You really ought to try Manchu's pancakes."

Fitz slammed his book down and jumped for the tent aside, stuck his head out into the rain and took several deep breaths. "If Aunt Jemima walked in this instant," he said, "I'd shoot her."

"It always puzzles me," Hawk said, "why condemned criminals make such a fuss about last meals. They don't even have time to digest the food."

"Something bothering you guys?" Schultz said softly. "It's only a war. Not like you were going somewhere to get killed. How about quieting down so I can get a little sack time."

The rain ceased at noon, giving way to a dark, slatting but lifting, cloud layer. Hawk walked to the mess with Robby. Pancakes were still available, but Hawk chose boiled eggs and strong tea. Manchu, reconnoitering the food line, remonstrated, assuring Hawk of the fine flavor of the pancakes.

"Thank you, but today I'm not very hungry."

Manchu smiled. "But afterwards, at Most Celestial Dining, you will bring your most lovely friend and I will surprise."

"Afterwards? After what?"

Behind the broad smiling face and kind eyes the Manchu he did not know regarded him, bowed slightly down. "But there is always an afterwards, Sahib Lieutenant."

Robb ate little. The mess was very quiet. A little bitching about the overdue mail. The new rumor: it was being held for them in Sicily. Chavez came by, complaining of McCabe accusing him of being more valuable on the base than co-piloting around Burma.

"*Caramba*, Hawk," he muttered, "I want to get into Mitch while the action is going on."

"You need medals, Chavez? Overdrawn on your rye account?"

"I'm going to get down there somehow!"

"Think the Marauders will take Mitch today?" Robb asked.

"This kind of weather?" Chavez shook his head. "Rain half the day. McCabe says Shadazup is still socked in. What do you expect the Marauders to do, come charging down the Kumons yelling 'Geronimo,' dragging their artillery behind them?"

"From what we hear," Hawk said, "their artillery is parked down by the strip waiting for us to haul it in."

"Maybe first you haul in the China boys," Chavez said. "You should see them. Just kids. Trained for maybe two weeks. They don't even know where the hell they are. Like they never seen a tent before. I helped them put up a couple."

"How about the guns?" Robb asked. "Many?"

Chavez nodded. "Shouldn't take us more than a couple of weeks to get them all to Mitch. Artillery and mortars. Plenty of ammo, too."

"Oh good," Robby mocked. "That's what I want for a load, ammo! Let's take a walk down and have a look, Hawk."

"And remember, Hawk," Chavez said as they left, "you don't get me to Mitch, I cancel your invitation to Mexico!"

The 37-mm. artillery pieces were under tarpaulins, lined up back of the flight line. Behind them, loosely stacked crates containing the 60 and and 8l-mm. mortars, boldly labeled in black print.

"You know," Robby said, "I've never heard a mortar go off, except in the movies when an enemy emplacement gets knocked out. Artillery only during those ceremonies when they're hauling a flag up or down. What's it going to be like when we hear real mortars go off ?"

"My one night in the jungle," Hawk said, "did little to enhance the entertainment factor." He stared across the airstrip where the Indian workers moved in their endless pattern, tipping gracefully from their heads the baskets of rock. Both men and women moved without breaking pace. Along the flight line mechanics were inspecting tail sections and landing gear. In the tower a corporal, chin propped on his hands, stared down at the planes, then abruptly straightened, adjusting his headphones. Down at the end of the line a gooney came abruptly to life.

"Maybe it's happened!" Robby exclaimed.

They watched the gooney taxi out from the line to the end of the strip and into position for takeoff.

"Colonel Tyrone, it looks like. Tyrone wouldn't be taking off if anything was doing."

They watched the tower operator speak into his mike as Tyrone revved up and checked his engines. The plane rolled forward, lifting off in a long easy climb to the west.

"Probably another HQ meeting at Jorhat," Hawk said. "Which means no one's expecting anything to happen today." He glanced at his watch. "I'm due in Operations. Ericson has been a bit short-tempered lately if I'm not on time."

At Operations Ericson was sitting tense on the edge of their desk, briefcase under one arm. Ben, the clerk, looked up from his typewriter and grinned.

"You damn sure took your time! A little sight-seeing along the strip?" Ericson inquired caustically

"Just checking to make sure the guns are loaded, Lee. Where's the Colonel off to?"

"HQ conference." Ericson gave him a disgusted look and strode to the door. "Vital to our war effort. The Group has finally managed to bring in some beef. Enough for all four squadrons. But naturally HQ wants its share. There seems to be a little argument over who gets how much."

"Well, we can't let the capture of Mitch interfere with a major beef effort."

"Mitch is out for today." Ericson turned from the door. "Tyrone got some kind of word. Probably not tomorrow, either. The Marauders are having a rough time. Incidentally, the final list of flight crews is on the desk. Better look it over." He went out, kicking the door closed.

Hawk sat down at the desk, glanced down at the flight assignments. It looked O.K. to him. He leaned back, then noticed Ben's grin.

"Look who's flying with Schultz," Ben said. "Roden."

"So, what's so funny, Ben?"

"They're both Germans."

"I was under the impression they're both Americans."

"You know what I mean. It happened yesterday afternoon when Schultz came in to check on assignments. When Schultz saw who he'd got he told Ericson he wasn't flying with a Nazi navigator. He slams out. Then Roden comes in, steaming. Says he absolutely will take a court martial before he'll fly with a damn atheist Kraut. Well, Ericson got really pissed. Tells Roden both he and Schultz are Germans and he's just arranging to get them both killed off." Ben grinned. "Or maybe he's gonna to do the job himself."

"Right now," Hawk said, "we're all a bit on edge." He glanced down over the list. Assignments on all Mitch flights were supposed to be permanent. Tyrone had surprised him by deciding to use Murphy for his co-pilot. Neither he nor Ericson were about to suggest Tyrone take someone with more experience.

"Then possibly -- " he paused as McCabe with Ericson slammed into Operations -- "maybe the Marauder assault on Mitch has been canceled."

"Well," McCabe snapped, pausing and glaring at them, "it damn sure ain't going to happen today! Know what? The weather is lifting and Jorhat has cleared routine supply flights to Shin and Maingkwan. Where's the Colonel?"

"Checking into that beef distribution we still haven't got," Hawk said.

"And I give you ten to one whose going to end up with most of it." The phone rang. He stared at Ben who paused in his typing, grabbed it, looked up at Ericson. "It's for you, Lieutenant. Jorhat."

Ericson reached and picked up the phone, listened, placed a hand over the mouthpiece and looked at Hawk. "They need another first pilot."

"I'd tell them we're fresh out of not only firsts but seconds and thirds."

"Sorry we can't help you out." Ericson paused, listened, looked heavenward. "Sorry, sir. No, sir. Sorry, sir but Colonel Tyrone is not here. No, I don't know when he'll be back. Sorry, sir, that you feel that way." He hung up abruptly. "Bastard accused me of being evasive."

"Hey, Ben," Hawk said, "come to think of it I'm going to need a lookout in my gooney when we head into Mitch. You could pick up a bit of flying pay."

Ben stopped typing and stared hard at the paper before him. "You know I'd be glad to, Lieutenant, but when I fly my ears pop, my brain goes all funny and I start puking. Besides that I'm already overpaid."

McCabe moved up close to study the wall map. "What's going to happen," he said, "is this fucking rain is going to keep up, the big invasion into France begins and we're left here in Burma, sucking on the Salvation Army's soggy doughnuts!"

With evening the rain had increased, sighed in sheets. At the mess bar, conversation tending to the confrontational.

"Where in hell are the Marauders?" Romano exclaimed, downing his drink in a gulp.

"No sense using up your booze ration in one night, Romano," Fitz said. "Medical authorities say excessive drinking is often an unconscious attempt to avoid hysteria."

"Up yours with a meat-hook, Fitz."

"Someone call up General Stilwell and ask him what the hell is going on."

"Perhaps," Colonel Tyrone said, "I ought to send a few men out on a search for our beef."

"I volunteer," Schultz snapped.

"The last we'd see of you or the beef," Roden said.

"And you mean what in hell by that, Kraut!" Schultz slammed down his drink and advanced on Roden.

McCabe got between the two before they could close. Tyrone had brought his phonograph to the bar. He slapped on a record, *Maple Leaf Rag*. Outside in the night came the thin ping of Manchu's rifle. Several shots. He appeared in the entrance, announcing he had driven off the cowardly jackals. He wore a broad grin. "Also, gentlemen, I am saying that again I serve pancakes for breakfast mess."

"I say," yelled Robby, "anybody want to help me kill Manchu!" Manchu disappeared back into the night. At midnight Hawk found himself sitting at the bar, refusing McCabe's order that he sign the chits for drinks he hadn't ordered. What he wanted to do was walk to the Greystaffs'. He and Jamila would go swimming. Manchu returned to say he must have time, please, to get the mess ready for breakfast, when again, pancakes would be served.

It rained steadily for the next two days. Ericson was on duty at Operations the third morning. The skies had broken enough to let off a few badly-needed supplies to Shadazup where, Hawk reported, returning at noon, everybody was really depressed. At Sook, the Chinese troops had hunkered down in their tent shelters, the airstrip was a mud lane, rumors a dime a dozen. Ericson had sent over three planes to a temporary airstrip near Jorhat where a Glider Group had just been stationed. Aside from Tyrone and McCabe, no one had ever towed a glider. By the time they got over to Jorhat and set up to tow the ceiling had dropped. They couldn't even return to Sook. An order from HQ informed them that after the Mitch airstrip was captured any of their idle gooneys and crews would be placed on temporary duty with the Glider Group.

"Idle gooneys!" McCabe exploded to Tyrone. "Tell them to go piss up a pond! We haven't had an idle gooney since we left North Africa!"

"I told them," Tyrone said, "that we would be delighted to lend them any available gooneys and pilots as soon as Mitch was secured, which I figure is about the time we're ordered back to Sicily or next year. No sense hurting their feelings."

"Who gives a rat's ass about their feelings!"

"I do, Terry. They're about to distribute the beef shipment. I suspect your eloquent rejection would lead to instant reprisal, like a substitution of C rations for steak." He winked at Hawk. "So, what rumors from the front today?"

"The main one is that the Japs have started to reinforce Mitch. " Hawk walked over and stared at the wall map. "The guessing is that the Japs have pulled in enough troops to stall the Marauders up in the Kumons. However, another rumor says observation planes report no activity near the airstrip. Which means maybe the Japs only intend to defend the town and railhead."

"And maybe blow our ass out of the sky if we try to move in on Mitch!" McCabe said.

"That would be your rumor, Terry." Tyrone joined Hawk before the map. "The way it looks," Tyrone went on, "if the Marauders can't take Mitch then the Japs are free to reinforce Mogaung on the rail line. Then the monsoon settles in. The Japs then become a threat to the British and American forces to the south, driving toward Mandalay. Then everything bogs down for another year. That's how the logic goes."

"Might as well start another rumor," McCabe said, turning and heading for the door. "Steak on the way!"

"Maybe Manchu's already serving," Hawk yelled, as the Colonel joined McCabe.

"I'll see he sends you down a couple of burgers," Ericson added as he left.

"But the beef hasn't even been delivered yet," Ben said.

"But we've got Manchu." Hawk sat down at his desk. "That's how the logic goes."

Next morning the weather cleared. Six missions to Shadazup. Rumors the Chinese Division was now driving hard on Mogaung. Zeros spotted throughout the day coming from the east below Mitch. Reconnaissance? American P-51s from the southern forces chased them away. No word of the Marauders. In the afternoon Hawk got in two missions, one to Maingkwan, the other to Shadazup. Back at the strip, Chavez reminded Hawk he was to be worked into the Mitch business.

Meanwhile, word had come in from Jorhat. The Squadron's supply of beef was ready for pick-up. A plane should be sent over immediately.

"So, not off to war but off for beef," Hawk said. "Come on along." He headed back to his seat, while Chavez pulled the chocks from the wheels. The tower cleared them. Hawk took off low over the Greystaffs', gunning the engines twice. Jamila would understand.

A half hour and a hundred miles, and the Jorhat airfield lay below them. Heavy air traffic arriving from the west. They held for another half hour at 3,000 feet before being shunted to an auxiliary airstrip ten miles to the west. Landing, they were directed by the tower to a deserted area and told to wait.

They waited. Trucks circled the airstrip's perimeter, only to vanish in the night. Hawk called the tower. A British voice responded. Was Hawk calling from Jorhat? Hawk explained. The tower was sorry: he had just changed crews for the night. He'd check with supply. Hawk had come for beef, was that correct?

"Make it two double cheeseburgers," Hawk said.

A long pause. *"I say, old chap, you've got us a bit confused."*

"Sorry," Hawk said, irritated. *"Actually I'm calling from Mitch, that place where there's supposed to be a war going on. I've got a couple of Jap friends who've never had a cheeseburger. Would you make that four?"*

"Bloody Yanks," a background voice from the tower said. The first voice: *"We have your message and understand. A lorry has just arrived and is being dispatched to your location with cargo."*

"We'll go back and give them some light and a hand," Hawk said.

Minutes later, the lorry, a six-wheeler running only parking lights, rumbled out from the darkness, turned about and backed slowly up. Two Indians leaped from the cab, came to the rear of the truck and pulled aside its canvas flap. One climbed up and in a moment slid the first wooden crate over the tailgate. The other took it on his shoulder and carried it to the cargo opening, heaving it up to Chavez, then returning for another. There were three in all. Hawk and Chavez stared at one another. Hawk jumped from the gooney. Two Indians were tying down the lorry's canvas flap. A uniformed Brit sat behind the wheel dragging on a cigarette.

"Three crates?" Hawk said. "For a whole squadron? Some mistake, friend. We're collecting for our whole outfit!"

The Brit shrugged. "Sorry, chum, that's all we got." He handed a paper out the cab window. "Almost forgot. Do need your signature, and we'll be off."

"I'd like to look in your lorry," Hawk said.

The driver gave him a hard look. "Don't you trust us?" He shrugged. "Go ahead, Yank."

Hawk returned to the rear of the lorry. The canvas had been loosely retied. Chavez came up, flashlight in hand, squeezed the canvas aside. Hawk peered in. The lorry was empty. As he stepped back the lorry's engine throbbed to life. The lorry jolted forward, as if trying to shake them off.

"I guess, *amigo*," Chavez said, "we've been just *un poco* screwed."

Back at Sook, near midnight, Manchu, in the presence of Tyrone, McCabe, Hawk, and Chavez, weighed the squadron's beef allotment. Still partially frozen it weighed in at just under a hundred and fifty pounds. Manchu sniffed. Satisfactory, but he recommended its immediate consumption. "Tomorrow we have a party," he said, glancing at the Colonel.

"Tomorrow," Tyrone said grimly, "Tomorrow we shall ..." His voice faded, he vanished into a darkness, touched with the sad ragtime of Scott Joplin.

———◆———

15

THE first message from Shadazup Control came just before sunrise The Marauders were in position three miles north of Mitch. Airstrip under surveillance. Colonel Tyrone ordered the squadron on alert, all flight personnel to report to Operations. Under a thin sift of rain the crews began revving up the gooneys. Behind them the young Chinese troops and their nervous young officers milled about forming lines. Trucks loaded with mortars and ammo moved up from below the airstrip. Day seeped in. The gooneys fell silent. The Chinese troops broke lines and squatted. It was nearly nine before Group HQ at Jorhat sent the word -- the Marauders had moved and Mitch was in the ring!

Twenty minutes later the Marauders swept over Mitch. It was *Merchant of Venice!* Colonel Tyrone strode to the wall where a new, detailed map of the Mitch airstrip had been thumbtacked.

"O.K. men, this is it! You've studied this, now we're going to see it." He tapped with a pointer at the strip. "West to east, muddy and not very wide. He drew a line east to the outline of the town by the Irrawaddy River. "Three miles. Only three goddamned miles and the Nips with plenty of mortars. We land west to east, pull off, unload, get the hell out east to west The Marauders are responsible for clearing our western approach. Avoid all terrain between the airstrip and town. Questions?"

Schultz turned impatiently from Operation's window. "Why don't we start loading up? The Chinks are milling around like cattle."

"Green troops," Tyrone said. "Nervous troops. They've been in training less than three weeks. They don't know where they are. They don't know where they're going. Packing them in the gooneys now will not improve their morale. What if the airstrip isn't clear for landing until tomorrow?"

"What if it never gets cleared?" someone said.

"A possibility," Tyrone said, "but I'm betting on the Marauders." He looked them over. "And you. Now, another thing. All of you are wearing side arms, as ordered, while on your planes. Any outbreak or disorder among the Chinese, any sign of panic, use your sidearm. We've gone over this before. Any questions?"

"What if we have trouble with our co-pilots?" Lieutenant Cordner asked.

"Or vice versa?" added Lieutenant Roden.

Their laughter ceased as Chavez appeared at the door. "Colonel, sir, our gooney is carrying mortars and two 37-mm. The men want to load and break for noon mess."

"Loading begins when I give the order, Sergeant!" Tyrone snapped.

"Yes, sir, Colonel. But word just came about the hamburgers being served."

Tyrone frowned, glanced at McCabe who shrugged. "O.K.," Tyrone conceded, "no point in keeping it a secret."

"Manchu claims," McCabe put in, "there wasn't a decent steak in the load. He's chopped it all up."

"Ground personnel will clean us out before we have a chance at it!" Lieutenant Bierman yelled.

Tyrone turned to Ben. "Corporal, contact mess and tell Manchu no hamburgers served today."

Operations fell silent. A clerk relayed the message, paused, covered the phone with a hand. "Sir, Manchu says he's already started cooking and besides, he doesn't have enough refrigerator space to save the meat."

Colonel Tyrone paused, looked from Ben over the men and up at the wall maps. "I hope you men understand," he said in a level voice, "how difficult we in command find it when pressed to make vital decisions." He glanced down at Ben. "With that in mind, Corporal, contact Manchu and tell him all hamburgers will be cooked up and enough sent down here to supply all flight crews. What's left is for ground personnel."

"Does that include us?" someone asked from the back of the room. The two Life correspondents, heavily loaded with their camera gear, were standing against the back wall. The older, bearded one had spoken. The other, thin and grinning, had produced a small notebook and was scribbling in it.

"No. I'll tell you just one thing," Tyrone said evenly. "You jokers send out one hamburger story and I promise you'll never get to Mitch!"

Ben's phone rang. He turned to Tyrone. "Colonel!"

Tyrone listened only seconds, smiled as he slammed down the receiver and faced them. "Gentlemen," he said softly, "the production of *merchant of venice* is on. Let's move on out!"

Five after three by his wristwatch. Hawk, lifting off from Sook, glimpsed three gooneys cross above him in their climb through a slash of sunlight toward the Patkais. He gunned both engines twice as the Greystaffs' pool glittered below. Behind the pilots, standing in the companionway, the two correspondents leaned forward, the thin one with camera at ready. Suddenly it seemed the air was filled with gooneys.

"Looks like we'll have quite a gathering at Mitch," Hawk yelled back to them.

"Don't mind us," the bearded one said. "We let you make the news. If we don't like it we'll change it." Evidently an in-joke. His buddy raised cautionary eyebrows. "For instance," the bearded one went on, "that business of using your side arms on the Chinese troops. You really would?"

"That question," Hawk said to Robby, "is what they might use as a 'human interest' story." He throttled forward a bit, climbing to slide over a gooney angling across their course. "We use our side arms on anyone," he called back. "But no bullets, just beat them over the head -- co-pilots, passengers, makes no difference."

"Hey!" Robby said. "You mean your .45 isn't loaded?" He stared at Hawk. "Neither is mine!"

The correspondents grinned. The bearded one glanced back into the cabin. "We'll make it a human interest story: THE AIR FORCE GOES TO WAR."

Hawk leveled, the Patkais close below, then over and down. Distantly he could make out the dark wall of the Kumons beyond the Hukawng Valley. An air current gave them a brief shake.

"Better go back and check the lashings on the mortars. Might get a bit rough."

Robby unbuckled and squeezed back past the correspondents, remarking, "And one of those 37-mm. breaking loose would take us all out."

"Hell," the beard said, "we don't even have any way to stay buckled in."

"Another human interest story," Robby said. "We always like to give passengers first chance out in case things get rough."

Robby returned with a report of a few lashings loose. He peered at their compass. "You've changed heading."

"Keeping to the east looks better. Less air traffic. Looks like we'll even have some gliders coming along. If I were the Japanese and aware of all this sudden traffic I might be tempted."

"What's our ETA?" the beard inquired.

"Roughly a hundred miles. About an hour."

The fading sunlight dimmed and went out. A thick layer of dark cloud enveloped them, the plane lurching roughly. Hawk eased into a long climb. Too much traffic down the valleys. He'd go over the Kumons at 10,000 feet, come out over the Irrawaddy River. Approach Mitch from the north.

"I hope it clears beyond the Kumons," Robby said, checking their map.

"With any luck," Hawk said.

"And if we don't have any luck?" the bearded one said. The plane was shaken briefly by another hard upthrust of air-current. Both correspondents leaned forward, peering into the dark wrapping of clouds.

"In that case," Hawk said, "what we usually do is fly in circles, scream and shout. Is Burma your first assignment?"

"I'm beginning to perceive it more as my last," the beard said.

Thirty minutes later the clouds thinned. Air currents buffeted them again. A glimpse of the storm-shrouded Kumons below, and ahead the long green valley of the Irrawaddy. Hawk eased throttles, banked south into a steep descent, motioned to Robby. "Doubt they'd have any Zeros up this way, but go back to the bubble and keep an eye on things as we close in. We're down here a little sooner than I expected."

There were a few sampans on the river. Nothing he could do about them. At 1,000 feet, and by the map about twenty miles north of the town of Mitch, he leveled. The waning afternoon dissolved in a gray soup, accented ahead by a leaning smudge of dark smoke. He nodded to the correspondents and pointed ahead. The buildings of a town were visible along the water.

"Mitch," he said. "Some kind of fighting going on." He swung slowly toward the beginning rise of the Kumons on their right, beckoned Robby back to the cockpit, flicked on their radio. The airstrip came in sight. Beyond it, coming in high from the west, a single gooney. The radio burst into a panic of static.

"Try and make contact," Hawk told Robby. "I'll keep heading straight in, let the other joker land first." He turned to the correspondents. "You guys go back and sit down, hold on." They disappeared.

Hawk slid his hands over the wheel, dried each palm on his shorts, took a deep breath. About two miles to the airstrip. Under them the land was flat, pocked by scrub growth and green checkerboard rice paddies. The plume of smoke from the town had thinned. For a moment he relaxed. It was like a scene from a medieval painting, a small quiet town by a broad river, surrounded by green fields, tall clouds building to the west. Abruptly the radio crackled clear.

"...got one gooney over the field, also some crazy coming in from the northeast near the town, hey, come straight in, avoid east end, machine gun fire reported, hey you up there to the west, get your ass down here or do a one-eighty and try again if you can't make it!"

"Mitch tower," Robby called, *"we're not crazy, can get in from the east before the other makes its one-eighty."*

"O.K., jerk-head.. Come on, both of you. When you're on the ground, dump your loads at the east end and get the hell out! Over and out!"

Hawk came in along the deserted edge of the airstrip. Near the west end another gooney, already down, tilted to one side on crumpled landing gear. Banking, Hawk signaled Robby to drop their wheels. They came down, hitting hard, bounced into a short skid. He wheeled about and taxied across the airstrip. The airstrip control broke in.

"Gooney on the strip, get off, get off, you got someone ready to chop your ass off!"

A mumbled message came from the gooney landing behind Hawk.

"I don't care if you-all got a fuckin' admiral on board," control snapped. *"Get down now!"*

"I wonder who'll be directing traffic when we come back tonight," Hawk said. He slowed nearly to a stop opposite a sand-bag building under construction.

"Go on, go on!" the control yelled. *"Off the east end. We'll have men out to unload. Then get out, go back and get some more of whatever you've got. Any spare whiskey on board?"*

Robby turned to the two correspondents who were back again behind them. "Either of you guys got any whiskey?"

They shook their heads. Robby shrugged. "They may send you back with us."

The other gooney stopped at mid-field, discharged a few passengers, then came taxiing to the east end. A raggedly-dressed group of men came down through the brush from a rise of land beyond. Hawk and Robby, out of the plane now, worked the metal ramps into position and slid the first 37-mm. into place for unloading. As a group of Marauders came forward a machine gun crackled viciously a little way off in the brush. The men flattened. Robby, Hawk, and the correspondents stared at one another. After a few seconds the machine gun fell silent.

"We'll get you unloaded and out of here," one of the men called as they came to their feet.

The Marauders eased the artillery piece down the metal ramp. The two correspondents jumped from the plane, reached back for their flight bags and camera gear. Robby loosened the lashings of a mortar and worked it to the cargo opening.

"Hey, flyboy," a gaunt, raw-boned Marauder yelled up at Hawk, "Where are the men?" A corporal's stripe hung by threads from his sweat-stained shirt.

"What men, Corporal?"

The corporal gave his friends a look. "The men that are going to shoot these fucking guns you brought."

Hawk nodded down at the two correspondents. "All we brought are these two. They came to take your pictures."

The two correspondents paused. The thin one hauled out his pencil and notebook.

Distant machine gun fire erupted, followed by the closer crump of a mortar. The two correspondents crouched under the gooney's wing, the bearded one already drawing his camera out.

"Jesus," the corporal said pleasantly, "you guys better be careful. There may be a bayonet charge. Either of you want to borrow my jack-knife just in case?" He motioned his men forward. They took down the first mortar.

"Excuse me, Corporal," the bearded correspondent said, "but could you point in the direction of your headquarters? We've got to report in."

"We ain't got a headquarters, Mister." The corporal pointed down the strip toward the partially-built wall of sandbags. He paused to watch another gooney coming in low from the west. Behind it two more. "Maybe one of them's got whiskey, Jack," he yelled to one of his men. He turned again to the correspondents. "Or you can try Signal Company back up there beyond the rise." From the direction in which he pointed a line of pack mules appeared, followed by a column of six men, each two carrying a litter. "Come on, you guys, let's get the plane unloaded. The fly-boys have some passengers for their return trip." He looked up at Robby, working another mortar to the cargo opening. "You got any blankets, Bud? These jokers are going to be in bad shape. We ain't even got a fucking first aid station set up."

"How many are there going to be?" Robby asked.

"We give everyone a choice, friend. Maybe you'll have the whole damn Marauder outfit on board!" He looked around him. "We've taken the strip. We're going to hold the strip. But we're fucking well ground down."

"When you come back, bring us some whiskey and boots," another man yelled above the noise of the arriving gooneys. One of these came taxiing down past them. The approaching mules erupted for a moment into a melee of kicking before their handlers calmed them down. The men with three stretcher cases came up.

"Twelve more coming, " the lead man called. "Captain says you get them aboard and take off." In the direction from which the men had come, another group of bearers appeared.

Hawk and Robby got the plane unloaded. The mules had mortars slung on each side of them. Somewhere beyond the airstrip's east end heavier fire now erupted, this time answered by fire from the direction of the signal unit. Other gooneys taxied past with a blast of prop wash. Hawk beckoned the stretcher bearers forward.

"All we got is three blankets," Robby said, kneeling in the cargo opening.

They lifted up the first stretcher and slid it carefully into the gooney. The GI on the stretcher stared vacantly up at Hawk, his tongue moving slowly along split lips as if searching for something.

They got fifteen stretchers on the plane and secured. In place of blankets they improvised coverings from the two 37-mm. gun coverings. There was little way to tell whether the men were sick or wounded or both. All were bearded. What was left of their clothing was wet and mud-stained. Two were either unconscious or dead, and had rolled limply as the stretchers had been passed up into the plane.

"No," one of the bearers replied at Hawk's question. "They're all breathing. All they need is another life." He grinned, fished out a cigarette and lit it. "Come to think about it, so do I." He jumped down from the cargo opening.

East beyond the airstrip the machine gun fire eased up. From farther back a new thunder of mortars began, sending up small, dark pillars of smoke.

"I'd like a goddamn drink of water," one of the stretcher cases said.

Robby came up with a canteen and knelt beside the man.

Hawk went forward and tried to raise airstrip control. Robby returned to his seat. "Poor bastards," he muttered. The right prop slapped over, caught. The left engine, nearest to the mules with the loaded mortars, kept grinding, refusing to catch, then exploded with a roar. The mules erupted again in turmoil, one mortar loosening in its bind. One mule driver raised a fist violently up at Hawk.

Hawk tried control again. A crackle of static. Hawk glanced toward the east end. Things looked calm. He edged the gooney away from the loaded mules and faced the airstrip. Another gooney was coming in from the west, one from their group -- looked like Romano. Hawk waited until it had touched down and flashed past, then gunned his engines, moving straight ahead onto the airstrip and turning west. A dead Japanese soldier lay just ahead off to his left.

"Gooney on strip, where the fuck you think you're going!"

"I can make it," Hawk replied. *"Plenty of room."*

"Not if one of them gliders crossing in from the north gets in your way."

"There's the first one," Robby said, jabbing out his side window. "About a mile off, I'd say. Why the hell they sending gliders into this mess?"

Hawk hit the throttles. The gooney lurched forward. Directly ahead, near the end of the airstrip, a glider appeared magically, extremely low, scraping the airstrip and skidding left into some brush, where a small tree tore off one wing. As they lifted past it, armed figures spurted from it like ants from a disturbed log.

Hawk felt the plane lift off as the airstrip ran out. Robby brought the wheels up. Hawk climbed straight ahead. Robby slid his window open and looked back.

"Two more, on the ground," he yelled, "one right in the middle of the airstrip."

"So I didn't have plenty of room," Hawk yelled back. "Want me to go back and make another try?"

Robby closed his window, gave Hawk an idiotic stare and peered forward. "Where we headed?"

"At the moment, just up." The plane rose slowly toward the cloud-wrapped Kumons. "Are we going to lose any passengers?"

"Naw." Robby shook his head. "They're all mad -- and much too happy to die. I mean, they stare up at you and don't even see you. Their eyes look sort of burned out, but smiling. We going back the same way?"

Hawk nodded, continuing his turn, with a last glimpse of the Irrawaddy River in the closing darkness as they went on instruments. He let Robby take over. At 8,000 feet he angled westward, caught Maingkwan for a fix. They were told to contact Shin for instructions. Shin directed them to Jorhat. The clouds began dissolving, scattered lights below. A flight of four gooneys off to their right, headed south. They came over the Patkais, thirty miles out from Jorhat, made radio contact. They were cleared for a straight-in approach. Transport for wounded would be waiting.

"Just as if they had things all planned out," Hawk said. "The only way to run a war."

Two ambulances moved up as Hawk taxied to a stop and kept his engines running. Men leaped from the ambulances, Robby was already back unlashing the stretchers. He returned, reporting all alive and swearing.

They were cleared again for takeoff. A few minutes out, Sook responded to their call. "*Return immediately to base. Food available at Operations. Another cargo for Mitch.*"

When they entered Operations, Ben was sitting on a stool gnawing at a hamburger. Jim was pecking at his typewriter. Ericson was pissed off.

"Sure, things are going well," Ericson said, "only I've been on my ass here in Ops all morning while, you guys get to Mitch! Sh--" He broke off. "I'm stuck here until Romano shows up."

"He landed at Mitch O.K.," Robby said. "Don't know whether he got off or not. Sort of a mess down there so far."

"What you got for me this time, Lee?" Hawk asked.

"Some of that Chinese division we're supposed to get to Mitch by evening." Ericson managed a smile. "I hear some of them have been acting up. Just don't take any sh--, well, you know what I mean."

"Speaking of food," Hawk said, "where is it?"

"Mess tent set up out back, sir," Jim said from his typewriter.

"You've got twenty minutes," Ericson said. "Chavez is checking your gooney."

Out back were a couple of Manchu's kitchen boys -- and Barpa, smiling broadly from under a turban-like chef's cap.

"Hamburger with curry is very good, Lieutenants," Barpa said. He picked up a cloth and slapped at the insects clouding the temporary hanging bulbs.

"Dig in," Hawk told Robby. "Be back in a minute."

Inside Ops he found a pen and paper, leaned on the edge of a desk, and wrote.

JAMILA, LOVE--YOU KNOW BY NOW, OF COURSE. THERE WILL BE SOME DAYS BEFORE WE CAN MEET. BUT I SPEAK TO YOU EACH TIME I FLY OVER--LOVE, ALAN

Jim gave him an envelope. He tucked in the paper and wrote her name on its face.

Out back, Robby was seated at a make-shift counter, two hamburgers before him. "One for the next picnic at Mitch," he explained.

Barpa placed a mounded plate before Hawk. "Nice and warm, American style, Lieutenant."

"Thanks, Barpa." Hawk handed him the envelope. "Tonight, Barpa. You will please see this gets to Miss Greystaff."

"Sooner than possible, Lieutenant."

Romano and Bierman appeared at the counter. "Three holes in our rudder," Romano said, his voice flat. "Got too close to the east end. Fuck 'em! Gliders coming in like a bunch of blind crows. Why didn't they wait a day?"

"Be sure and tell Ericson," Hawk said. "What about lights at Mitch tonight?"

"Portable lights of some kind." Romano shook his head. "Maybe they'll just have GI's out there with candles -- they light up when a gooney appears. Blacker than Sip's ass down there."

"Who the hell is Sip?" Robby demanded.

"A sort of guardian angel, Robby," Hawk said.

"Not of Chinamen, that's for sure!" Bierman said.

"So we had a little trouble loading up our troops," Romano said. "They didn't want to get on here or off down there."

"So you shot them," Robby said.

Romano grinned. "Nope, just told them to get the fuck on the plane. At Mitch I told them to get the fuck off. Even helped a few in a sort of airborne way."

"Hey, you guys." It was Ericson over them. "You want to have a party, maybe I can find some music for you. Hawk, your troops are waiting to load. Chavez has O.K.'d your gooney. Get your ass in gear. And Romano, I'm taking your flight. Go get some sack time. You're off early again at six a.m."

Hawk and Robby found Chavez standing protectively beside the cargo opening of their plane. Facing him, sitting cross-legged on the ground, back-packs and carbines beside them, were forty-eight young Chinese soldiers, sitting expressionless. Before them their officer paced nervously back and forth. He stopped abruptly, spoke sharply to his men. They remained motionless.

"Gooney O.K.," Chavez said. "Only an aileron nick. No problem."

"O.K.," Hawk called to the Chinese officer. He pointed to the plane. "Time to load up."

The officer gave a sharp command. His men did not look up. No one moved. The officer's voice rose a pitch. A few men looked up. One reached out and pulled his carbine close.

"I wonder what's going to happen," Robby said softly.

"I suppose their rifles are loaded," Hawk said.

The officer's voice went into treble.

Hawk stepped forward, smiled and saluted. "Maybe I can help." He turned to the young Chinese who stared blankly up at him. He smiled. Slowly a few of the men came to their feet. Their officer stepped forward, grabbed at the nearest, yanking him forward.

"Please!" Hawk said sharply. "Sir!" He saluted again. This time the officer returned his salute. Hawk turned again to the men. "O.K.," he said easily, gesturing toward the gooney. "It is O.K. A very safe plane."

The officer glared. Slowly the men came to their feet, picking up their packs and carbines. They were very young -- hairless faces, eyes of wary animals. The first one moved to the cargo steps, paused to look back at his comrades, and climbed up into the plane.

Robby went after him, motioned them forward into their spaces. They loaded, twenty-four on each side. Robby knelt and showed them how to snap themselves into the safety belts.

"I think we've got a good bunch," Robby said as Hawk came last up the steps. The officer had placed himself at the rear of the plane, stood stiffly, back against the bulkhead. Robby gestured to him and pointed forward. The officer shook his head, folded his arms and remained standing. "I stay here. They no run away." He was, Hawk saw, little older than the rest.

"Hey *amigos!*" Chavez stuck his head in from the cargo steps. *"Estan equivocado de avion!"*

The troops stared at one another, then back at Chavez, and abruptly broke into laughter, reaching to clap one another on the shoulders.

"You see, Hawk," Chavez called, "it always helps to know a little Chinese. Next time I should come with you?"

Robby gave a "thumbs up" as Hawk slid into his seat and started the engines. Chavez appeared below them, jerking the chocks aside.

"Clear for take-off," the tower called. *"You're number one."*

As they lifted over the Greystaffs', Hawk twice eased the throttles forward. They rose into the dusk. Far to the northwest a thin line of light edged the high Himalayas. They banked east, climbing over the Patkais. Shin reported a thin overcast at 3,000 feet. Two returning gooneys gave them a blink of lights and word of light rain at Mitch. Combat going on near the east end of the airstrip.

Maingkwan, Walawbum, and Shadazup in turn remained silent. Five minutes beyond Shadazup, Hawk, on instruments, turned again into a climb over the Kumons that would bring them down over the Irrawaddy. An intermittent breaking of clouds, an occasional spark of light as they descended. Was it still raining at Mitch? Perhaps socked in? He checked his instruments, time and distance. No hint of the river. Was a wind, some monsoon current, carrying him off course? He held, letting down slowly: twenty minutes, long enough. He motioned Robby to keep trying Mitch. Seconds of silence, then Mitch in loud and clear *"... light rain, a strong northerly wind."*

"We'll nose down and have a look around," Hawk said. "I've a feeling we've come too far."

They had -- emerging from the cloud cover at 2,000 feet, over a flat nothingness dotted with a spark of light here and there. He didn't see the river until Robby pointed. The Irrawaddy, an ebony snake lacing a blacker earth. Holding altitude, he made a one-eighty. "We'll follow it back until we see some lights. We're probably thirty miles below Mitch."

At a speed of 160, ten minutes should bring them up to the town of Mitch. It took them nearer fifteen. Suddenly Robby pointed ahead. A spread of scattered lights, a flash of artillery, the vague outline of clustered buildings, a glitter of water. Hawk swung down and away, already spotting the airstrip to the west. Robby made contact.

"O.K., think we have you in sight off to the southeast," Mitch called. *"Doing a little sight-seeing? Lot of fighting around the town. Things quiet down here. But come in from the west. Bastards keep sneaking in and taking pot shots. We got a few lights in place."*

Hawk eased down to 1,000', headed west parallel to the airstrip, turned in and on to his final approach, slid in smoothly.

"Get off the runway quickly," Mitch said as he touched down. *"You've got another gooney on your tail. What's your cargo?"*

"Friendly troops from China."

"Get 'em off wherever you can find a place. Just mind the disabled gooneys. We've got three so far. East end seems safe at the moment . . . . Shit!" A long pause. *"Avoid east end. Something's kicked up. Hold up and taxi back this way!"*

Hawk hit the brakes, staring ahead at sudden arcs of tracer fire. What you have to do, he told himself, is take a deep breath and do what you're told, even when you're not sure what they're telling you.

He half skidded onto the rough earth beside the strip, slid in and braked to a stop by a gooney with a bent wing.

"Get the troops off!" he yelled. "I'm not cutting engines."

From behind them in the plane the voice of the Chinese officer rose. A shrill cry of lament. Robby slid from his seat. Hawk switched on the cabin lights. Robby yelled back at him from the cabin. "The crazy bastard has his pistol out!" Outside, above the low throb of the engines, came the sound of gun-fire and the distant crump of mortars. Hawk joined Robby.

Just beyond the first bulkhead, four of the Chinese had crowded in a corner, clinging to one another. All four were crying.

"Where are their weapons, Robby?"

"How the hell should I know!"

"Here, let me see what I can do. Go cut the engines before any of the troops outside run into the props and lose their heads in the literal way." Hawk knelt before the nearest soldier. Tears streaked his cheeks. When Hawk touched him he began trembling.

"O.K.," Hawk said softly. "O.K. It's O.K., O.K." The soldier opened his eyes, kept on trembling. His eyes were wide, dead white with black points. "O.K., O.K.," Hawk repeated. "It's O.K." He reached beyond the boy and touched the next one. Boys, that's all they were, young faces, boys of his own past. Had he once cried like that? He rose slowly, urging the nearest one up. "It's O.K., O.K., O.K."

The boy stood up, pushed himself free. Then another. The four stared at him, wiped their faces, reached down for their gear and carbines. The gunfire seemed to ease a bit.

"O.K.," Hawk said. "Let's go."

He led the way, the first boy following close, a hand on Hawk's shoulder. At the steps Hawk went first, the four following quickly, jumping to the muddy ground. Their officer came up, his automatic out, his voice again a high treble of rage as he raised his weapon.

"No!" Hawk yelled, knocking the weapon aside. He stood between the four and the officer. "It's O.K., O.K., they are coming!"

The officer stared grimly at the four, abruptly jammed his automatic into its holster, turned on his heel and marched off into the semi-darkness beyond the plane, where the rest of his men were again squatting in a close group, heads down, motionless.

"So O.K.," a GI yelled, emerging from the darkness, a carbine slung over his shoulder. "So we finally got things under control? Good. The buggers can fight once they get over the first dive." A flare of fire erupted across the airstrip. "You guys better get out of here while you're still in one piece."

"Let's go," Hawk said. He followed Robby up the plane, pushed by him into the co-pilot's seat. "So O.K.," he said. "I'll handle the communications. You drive us home. O.K.?"

Once out and up, over the Kumons, Hawk tried to relax. He couldn't get the faces of the Chinese boys out of his mind. Faces mottled with tears. So, all right, maybe the Mitch airstrip had been taken. Good for the Marauders. But right then he didn't give a good goddamn. He didn't feel any better until Robby brought them down over the Patkais into their final approach. As they slanted down over the Greystaffs' he reached out and gently goosed the right engine twice. Finally everything, for a little while, was O.K.

16

ON the morning of the third day, when Hawk and Robby landed at Mitch, the body of the Japanese soldier still lay crumpled, face down at the edge of the airstrip. Hawk angled off, cutting engines beyond two gooneys east of the command post, now roofed by a draggled strip of canvas that gave it the appearance of an unfinished Navaho hogan. A short distance below several battered gliders and a gooney with smashed landing gear had been shoved into a heap.

The Chinese troops were talking, unbuckling, as Hawk came from the cockpit to the cargo opening. Behind him Robby was managing some conversation with the Chinese officer. As Hawk paused in the opening the familiar chatter of machine guns interspersed with the measured clump of mortar fire rose from the direction of the town. A couple of the young Chinese soldiers lowered the steps into place. A line of stretcher bearers appeared from the brush, headed toward them.

"Looks like another bunch for Jorhat," Hawk called back to Robby as he descended the steps. Behind him the Chinese officer leapt to the ground, turned and barked up a command. The troops emerged, each pausing, blinking, at the top step, as if newly hatched from some monstrous creature. On the ground they formed double lines, carbines crossways across their chests, standing at rigid attention.

"I'll stay in here and get things cleaned up," Robby yelled, giving Hawk a weary head-shake. "A couple of them puked up."

Hawk counted the waiting litter cases. Fourteen, plus two ambulatory. Another gooney was coming in from the west. Looked like Cordner and Roden. As he'd guessed, Schultz and Roden had not worked out as a team. Though originally a navigator, Roden had developed his own ideas about flying, and complained that Schultz wouldn't let him touch the wheel. Today Schultz had Murphy.

He watched Cordner as he landed long, kept on, was close to the east end when he turned off. Not a good place to stop. Yesterday a heavy Jap mortar attack had reached the airstrip. A couple of GIs appeared, running toward Cordner's plane, gesticulating, cautioning Cordner, carrying ammo, to stay away from the other planes.

"Hey," the leader of the approaching litter column yelled, "how about getting them Chinks out of the way so we can load up?"

Hawk motioned to the Chinese officer. In moments the Chinese were up and marching away in formation toward the command post. For moments the distant guns fell silent. No sound of planes. The sunlight seemed to draw a scent of grass into the air. To Hawk a suddenly remembered open field in Western Maine, the Kumons becoming the shadowy uplift of the White Mountains. When the first mortar shell burst he turned almost casually, staring out across the airstrip to where a dark plume of smoke was rising. Then another burst beside it. A third. Then silence again.

Robby appeared wide-eyed in the cargo opening.

"Nothing to worry about," the lead stretcher bearer called out, coming up. "Those are ours. A squad up near Signal Company. Just checking range. Some Japs tried to sneak in again last night."

The stretchers were placed in a line beside the gooney. A medic went along, checking bandages, offering the men water. The two ambulatory sat down in the gooney's shade. The one nearest Hawk had a bloody head bandage and huge eyes in a ravaged face.

"It's O.K., buddy," he said, catching Hawk's look. "I'm not going to die on you, not when I'm this close to getting the hell out of the bloody mess."

"Come on!" Robby yelled impatiently from the cargo opening. "Let's get loading!"

Back of them, behind a brush-covered rise, a heavier artillery piece blasted off. There was a lull of a few seconds, followed by another blast.

"Dumb fuckers!" the lead stretcher bearer cried out. "They've set up no more than fifty yards from Signal Company, close to the new medic evac station. Somebody better spike that goddamn popgun or it will bring in the Jap mortars!" He gestured to his men. "C'mon, let's load up and get this gooney in the air."

Hawk counted fifteen rounds from the artillery piece before it fell silent. They got the stretchers in fast and lashed down. Hawk and Robby pulled up the steps as the stretcher bearers jogged off back toward the rise. The artillery piece opened up again. Hawk stared up at the rise.

"What the hell!" Robby snapped. Across the airstrip, machine guns opened up in a wasp-like frenzy. The Command Post control cleared them for take-off with a cautionary note -- Japanese patrols had been spotted two miles to the south and moving up. Gliders were coming in from west of the Kumons. An unidentified aircraft was reported over the river. As Hawk taxied onto the airstrip two heavy pillars of smoke rose over the town, followed by the distant rumbling of a B-25 American bomber away south. Tower control reported Jap troops being ferried across the river to the town.

"There was a rumor," Robby yelled as they headed west down the airstrip, "that it would all be over when we took the airstrip."

They lifted off over the dead enemy soldier. "The least they could do is cover him," Hawk said.

"Shall we take the sunshine route back home?" Robby said.

Jorhat was ready for their litters. In exchange for them they got four young American correspondents, all headed to Mitch. They were about to move out when the tower held them. Two Brits wheeled up in a jeep and ran for the plane. One was tall, somewhat familiar. Hawk recognized him from Taro. He appeared whole again. Once they were airborne, the tall Brit came forward -- clean shaven, with new jungle camouflage, a sidearm, beret, and colonel's insignia.

"And all the time I thought you were a lieutenant," Hawk grinned.

"Just an English country boy working my way up, Yank. I suggested they make me a general. Stingey buggers. Think you can get me and the lieutenant down to Mitch?"

"From what we just left I'd say they need you down there more than -- " Hawk gestured back in the plane. The correspondents, clad in clean jungle gear and GI issue rubber boots, were all busy with their back-packs and camera gear. One of them came forward and stuck his head in past the Brit colonel.

"I hear you've taken Mit-y-yinka," he said. A Bronx accent.

"Took it myself this morning," Hawk said. "No problem." The correspondent withdrew his head. "Matter of fact," Hawk said to the Brit colonel, "it looks like we're just barely holding on there."

The Brit nodded. "We've got some gear to pick up at Sook. Hoping you can squeeze it in with us. We'll need it, but the matter of priorities might rule it out."

"Should be able to manage," Hawk said. "What is it?"

"Two twelve-foot rubber rafts, with outboard motors."

"Ah!" Robby said, "One if by land, two if by sea!"

"Something like that," the Brit grinned.

Back in Operations at Sook they found Ericson at his calm, frustrated best. How about Hawk taking over the rest of the morning? He felt like killing the next man who came at him with a complaint. Hawk was sorry. Normally he took all opportunities to avoid the war but he needed one more look at Mitch. Something he'd forgotten. He skipped the reheated hamburgers and caught a ride back to his tent. No word from Jamila.

Returning, he found the gooney almost loaded, cases of ammo stacked and lashed forward. Behind these were cartons of medical supplies and the two uninflated assault boats. The two outboards were tied down in the rear. After a great deal of shouting, and the intercession of Tyrone, Ericson put the four correspondents on board. The two British officers sat buckled in just forward of the cargo opening.

Chavez appeared. "No holes," he yelled. "The right tire looks a bit roughed up. I'll try and find a replacement tomorrow." He stepped away. "When are you going to let me have a look at Mitch, Hawk? Maybe if I joined the Chink troops?"

The day held clear. Heading south, beyond the Patkais, thin plumes of smoke marked the road, reaching on to Shin, which reported all quiet. Convoys of trucks moving south. The first alert came as they passed to the east of Maingkwan at 3,000: *"Zeros in the vicinity of Mogaung."* And moments later --*"Zeros attacking Mitch! All aircraft hold off! Take evasive action!"* Hawk peeled left and down, leveling close over the jungle, headed toward the hills below Walawbum.

"We could go back and wait until tomorrow," Robby suggested, then slid from his seat and stuck his head up into the bubble.

Their passengers sat forward, hunched down, motionless. Minutes later, as they approached the Walawbum Hills, the alert was lifted. *"All aircraft clear to proceed to destination. Enemy aircraft have left vicinity."* Hawk swung up towards the Kumons.

Again approaching Mitch from the north, things looked the same except for one gooney off the strip, its fuselage wrapped in flames under a tower of black smoke. Three others, parked at angles, were apparently untouched. Beyond the command post the smashed jumble of metal that had once been a plane.

"Come on straight in," control directed. *"Ain't nobody here except us heroes proud to be wracking up the purple hearts."*

The dead Japanese soldier still lay beside the airstrip. Control brought them in near another gooney unloading troops.

As Hawk cut the engines, a loading squad and three mules appeared, led by a young second lieutenant. The two Brits and the correspondents were out of the plane quickly. A mule-skinner brought his mule up close to the cargo opening, peered in and turned back to the lieutenant.

"Shit, the captain was right. Boats! Rubber ones. We goin' cruisin'?" He glared angrily at the four correspondents and the two Brits.

"We heard there was good fishing on the Irrawaddy," the tall Brit said.

The correspondents moved off, kneeling, cameras focused on a gooney lifting off over the body of the Japanese soldier.

"Get those boats and motors off and loaded on the mules!" The young lieutenant's voice was high-pitched, so it sounded like screaming. He glanced up at Hawk and Robb in the cargo opening. "They been throwing mortars at us all morning."

"The burning gooney?" Robby questioned. It wasn't from their squadron.

"Three Zeros," the lieutenant said. "Only one pass. Missed all but that one. Don't know if the crew got out or not. If so, they're probably still in the fox holes. One officer killed in the command post." He pointed back into the brush. "They came in real low from the town, I'd say too low -- "

"Excuse me, Lieutenant," the Brit colonel said softly but very firmly. "Could you save the lecture for tiffin? We'd like our boats and outboards. Fishing, chum, we've got to go fishing."

Hawk and Robby helped drag the boats off the plane. The outboards were loaded on the third mule. The correspondents trailed off toward the command post, cameras at the ready. Machine gun fire opened up beyond the farther end of the airstrip. In the distance the crump of mortars began.

"They'll be bringing some stretcher cases down," the lieutenant said as his men began unloading the ammo. He put his hands on his hips and looked up as three American P-51s streaked high overhead. "Hey!" he said exuberantly, still staring, "hey, how about that!"

"Robby," Hawk said, "I'm going up to command post for a minute or so. Soon as the stretchers arrive, get them on and lashed down."

"O.K.," Robby said. "I'll give you ten minutes."

The command post was a hive: radio gear, improvised file cabinets, a couple of clerks banging away at typewriters, the walls stacked with machine guns and carbines. When Hawk tried to enter a burly sergeant blocked his way.

"You looking for somebody, chief?"

Behind him a haggard major in fatigues was screaming about some fuck-head slow in getting machine gun emplacements set up on the perimeter of Colonel Seagraves's Hospital Station.

"Signal Ops, Sergeant," Hawk said. "I'm looking for someone in the 3rd Infantry Company"

Most of them are dead." The sergeant's glance took in Hawk's sneakers, shorts, and unbuttoned shirt. His eyes narrowed. "Rank and outfit, soldier?"

Hawk told him. The sergeant gave him a disgusted look and pointed. "That rise up there, maybe a hundred yards beyond. Visiting hours is when the Japs don't sneak in close enough for mortar practice."

Hawk followed a beaten path up past a bullet-torn cluster of trees, pausing to watch a gooney come in. The burning gooney still darkened the sky with its smoke. Beyond the airstrip on the other side a group of soldiers, crouching low, was fanning out over a rice paddy. The sound of gunfire seemed to hang in the air.

Signal Ops lay down a slope in a saucer of cleared land, a motley collection of tents, six GIs sitting on a bench outside the largest one. They watched his approach with studied indifference.

"Hi," Hawk said. "I'm looking for Third Infantry Signal Company. Fred Jilbert, a corporal, I think."

One of the GIs turned toward the tent. "In there. Sack time for Fred." He raised his voice. "Yo, Fred, you got a visitor."

"Thanks." Hawk stooped in past the GIs. Beyond him an array of improvised tables covered with radio gear. A figure appeared beyond a small table in the rear. "Yeah?" He stared at Hawk. It was almost no one Hawk had ever seen before. A ragged beard, a narrow pinched face, a body on which baggy khakis hung as if from a wire hanger. Only the squint was familiar.

"Alan Hawk. For Christ's sake!"

They had never been friends in high school, merely acquaintances. Hawk vaguely recalled the slight, shy boy who, Hawk now remembered, spent his time putting radios together in the basement of his small, shingled home a couple of blocks from Hawk's. Another memory -- Fred coming out for track one spring. They gave him a try-out for the mile. He made it halfway, stopped, bent over and threw up, turned and walked away from the track forever. Yet the sonofabitch must have climbed over the Kumons with the Marauders.

Hawk pulled Alma Jilbert's two letters from his pocket. "Alma wanted you to know, Fred. Looks like you have a son."

Fred took them, read each one, folded them together, turned back to his table and placed them under a coil of wire. "Thanks, Alan. I thought when you came in it was about my request for R and R."

"Sorry," Hawk said. "We could all stand a little."

"I remember reading in the paper, that was some time after Alma and I got married, how you got your pilot's wings." Fred managed a half smile. "Guess you couldn't fly me out?"

"Sorry." Hawk smiled. "I'll be flying in here for a while. Anything I can bring you?"

Fred looked down at his feet. One was covered with a dirty bandage. The leather of his left sandal had a green scum of mold. "Some whiskey would help. Also some rubber boots. Medics just keep dumping iodine or something on 'em. Every time I get 'em wet the scabs come off."

A distant but steady mortar fire from the direction of the airstrip swept over them like a gust of rain.

"See what I can do, Fred. Gotta go now!" Hawk was out of the tent. The lounging men had scattered. He started running. When he topped the rise he could see Chinese troops moving out beyond the airstrip. Off to his left a couple of artillery pieces opened up. One of the gooneys that had been there when they arrived was taxiing fast toward the east end. It braked abruptly, whirled about and, engines roaring, angled onto the airstrip, then was down the strip and off.

Hawk saw Robby standing in their cargo opening, jumping up and down like a marionette, his voice a high distant wail of anger.

"You crazy dumb bastard," Robby shrieked as Hawk reached the gooney. "Off visiting in the middle of a goddamn battle! Let's get the hell out --
"

The first mortar shell hit a hundred yards away, directly across the strip from them, a second hit ten yards closer. A machine gun opened up behind them, firing into the brush. The third shell, and its plume of earth and smoke, hit another ten yards closer.

"Come on!" Hawk yelled. "Find a foxhole!"

Robby jumped out, racing after him toward a scattering of foxholes on the other side of their gooney. The next mortar shell exploded close to the edge of the runway. Hawk followed Robby head first into the nearest hole. They pulled themselves around and peered back over the edge. The next shell splattered dirt over them.

"They've got us lined up!" Robby yelled. "One more and they've got us. I'm getting out!"

He moved too quickly. Hawk grabbed for him and missed, and for moments stared after him as he seemed to scoot straight for the Kumons. The next clump shook fragments of earth from the sides of the hole. Hawk dropped, curling up, wrapping his arms about his head, all his guts seeming to melt away. Then came a silence that went on too long to be his own obituary. The shelling had ceased.

There was only the distant chattering of a machine gun, and voices from the direction of the command post. He drew himself erect. Robby was lying face down, motionless, a few yards from the tail of their gooney. Reaching Robby, he knelt and touched him. No sign of blood. Rule was you didn't move a body. The memory of headless Weed flashed before him. Robby turned his head, stared up at him. "My spine," he whispered. "I think my spine is shattered."

Hawk saw the spreading red stain on Robby's khaki shorts, near the hip. "I'll try and stop the bleeding, Robby," he said softly, glancing toward the command post. Where the hell were the fucking medics?

He reached around and loosened Robby's belt. Robby moaned. Gently, he worked Robby's shorts down from the wound. The torn undershorts bore a wider stain of blood. He parted the cloth until the wound was visible -- a two or three-inch groove on the hip, into which a pencil might fit. Hawk dabbed at the wound with his shirt as two medics and a stretcher arrived. Both knelt, yanked at Robby's shorts, peered closely. One produced a colorless bottle of liquid and dumped it over the wound.

Robby howled, eyes open and imploring. "Do you think I'll ever walk again?"

"Not if you keep jumping out of foxholes when under mortar attack," Hawk said. A medic slapped and taped a bandage on Robby's hip. "We'll take him up for a look-over." He glanced up at Hawk. "You might as well wait, Lieutenant, that is if you can still fly." Hawk looked over at the gooney. Shrapnel had made a neat pattern along the fuselage. "I don't think Colonel Seagraves will keep your buddy very long."

Hawk watched as they eased Robby onto the litter and carried him toward the rise of land, then turned toward the gooney. He was still checking the shrapnel damage when Robby hobbled back, on his own steam.

"You know," Robby said, pulling himself cautiously up the steps, "Chavez is really going to be pissed off at what you've done to his plane."

The rain returned on the afternoon of the sixth day. A sense of order was emerging to the war. Mitch had become an elongated oval of machine gun emplacements and mortars. Perimeter attacks were easing off. The command post had acquired additional canvas, joined by a row of tents for correspondents and visiting brass. Fox holes covered strategic areas like a cribbage board. Back over the rise Signal Ops had mushroomed into a small encampment. The Japs had, aside from occasional desperate, brave, and doomed forays, been forced back to the Irrawaddy and the town.

Robby was grounded for three days, in spite of his insistence that all he needed was a good soft pillow. The medics in Chabua had found no metal fragments, though he had returned barely able to walk. Fitz offered to aid in Robby's recovery. After consulting his medical books he vanished, returned with a small jar of amber-colored cream. It was to be applied three times a day.

"I've been assured," Fitz told Robby, "that it will restore your ass to its pristine and ugly shape."

Robby gave Fitz a fishy glance. "Who assured you it would cure me?"

"Manchu. It's an old remedy of his."

Robby snarled. "You're not putting any dragon grease on my ass, buster!"

Schultz and Hawk were watching. Fitz gave them the eye. They grabbed Robby and held him while Fitz worked off the bandage, administered the ointment, and taped on a clean bandage. Robby glared up at them.

"What does Manchu put in that stuff?"

"Stuff from his animal pens," Fitz said. "A combination of chicken piss and jackal shit."

Robby looked around at them. His smile became beatific. "Oh, O.K. then. I just thought it might be something I was allergic to."

Chavez confronted Hawk. He wanted to fly to Mitch. He deserved to. Hawk argued with Ericson, who objected strenuously. "Look at the beautiful job he's done repairing gooneys," Hawk said. Ericson gave in.

Now most of the sounds of war at Mitch came from the river. Chavez was first out of the plane after landing the next morning. He stared at the Jap, a small shape still beside the runway. "Hey," he said, "why don't they bury that guy?" Hawk left the plane, carrying a knapsack.

"I'll be right back," Hawk said. "We're going to have another load of wounded. Make sure you've got enough line ready to secure the litters."

A soft steady rain fell as Hawk crossed behind Command toward the rise. Then, just as Signal Ops came in sight, the perimeter guns to the east and south of the strip exploded into action. Looking back he saw men running toward the command post for cover. Along the side of the airstrip a line of troops appeared. Everyone seemed to be looking west -- a single gooney was coming in, very low, wheels down. Then he saw the Zero, a stubby-winged hornet closing in. For an instant the gooney seemed to stand out in sharp relief. Just over the airstrip Hawk glimpsed its two pilots, bent forward. The explosion stopped it in midair. It nosed straight down in a stab of fire. A second explosion sent a shock through the earth. At first only the towering pillar of flame.

Hawk had no recollection of reaching Signal Ops, only knew that he was there, in the midst of

GIs staring out at the flame and smoke. A few pointed higher.

"I saw it!" one yelled excitedly. "A Zero!"

Hawk went on into Signal Ops. It was empty, but somebody followed him in and tapped him on the shoulder.

"Hey," Fred Jilbert said. "That was really something!"

Hawk swung the knapsack around on his shoulder and pulled out the rubber boots and a bottle of rye.

"Gee, thanks." Fred took them but kept staring at Hawk."You look kinda funny. Was it -- ?" He stopped, blinked.

"Yes, it was one of ours," Hawk said. "A load of gasoline." There was no point in saying their names.

Lieutenants Rogers and Gimbel had bought their farms. Returning to the airstrip, he did not look at what was left, a dark sullen marker already imbedded forever in his memory. It could just as easily have been himself as Ericson who had given the assignment to Rogers and Gimbel.

Chavez had all the wounded on board, stretchers lashed down. "We picked up a couple of wing holes coming in," he said. "Nothing serious."

"Let's go home, Chavez."

North of Walawbum the sky had cleared. Behind them was the high dark roll of clouds, ahead a sharp etching of jungle against sky. Smoke from Walawbum drifted lazily upward. A few planes. The radio silent. A very peaceful day. Unexpectedly the face of his father slid like a ghost from that vague corridor of memories he seldom visited. With his father's death he had discovered how little he knew of him.

"How about the dead?" he said suddenly to Chavez. They were over the Patkais, turning on course for Jorhat. "Do you ever think of them?"

"*Caramba*," Chavez said softly. "We think always of the dead ones."

The ambulances were waiting at Jorhat. A few officers in neckties were catching a ride via Sook to Chabua. It wasn't until they were coming down over the tea plantation, Hawk gunning both engines, that Chavez spoke again.

"You know, *amigo*, you get me thinking. Now I can't see anything in my mind except that dead Jap at Mitch, lying beside the strip. I wonder if anyone's thinking of him."

Next morning the weather had shoved in again with a solidity they had not experienced before. Hawk and Chavez took off with a load of ammo, Schultz following with a load of mules. On instruments most of the way, they found a ceiling of only 1,000 feet at Mitch.

Where Gimbel and Rogers had gone down there remained only a circular patch of scorched earth. The Jap's body had vanished. In the scrub growth on the airstrip's western approach a large group of Chinese troops were drilling. Beside the command post a Salvation Army unit had set up a booth serving coffee and doughnuts. Schultz, landing, began cursing. One of the mules had broken free and kicked loose a side panel on his gooney. Control was in a mellow mood, suggesting Schultz taxi down to the east end, now safe, and get another mule to kick it back in place. Hawk was to take his ammo down to the western end to a newly-erected log bunker. Both he and Schultz should be prepared for stretcher cases.

Gunfire came sporadically from the town and river. While fresh troops were unloading the plane, Hawk suggested to Chavez they try out the chance of salvation through doughnuts. Chavez merely gave him a weird look. *"Loco gringo."*

The newest rumor at Command -- the town of Myitkyina would fall within days -- was turning out to be very wrong. Merrill's Marauders had done more than enough, but the Japs were still dug in by the river. Relief, rest and relaxation weren't even a rumor.

Chavez took two doughnuts and his coffee and headed off down the airstrip to the eastern end, where a 37-mm. artillery piece had been set up and was lobbing shells in the direction of the distant town. Infiltrating Japanese units could be a pain in the ass. Hawk gave him fifteen minutes, keeping an eye upfield on the ammo unloading. He passed a few words with the elderly civilian manning the Salvation Army booth and was beginning to look for Chavez when all hell broke loose.

Command Post stirred like a troubled hornet's nest, then erupted in a frenzy of machine gun action. An enemy mortar hit close in across the strip on its southern flank. Rifle fire swept from all sectors like a harsh wind. Hawk heard Schultz's gooney come to life, watched as Schultz came about in a tight circle at the east end and headed up the strip. His just-unloaded mules, breaking from their mule-skinners, headed for the Kumons. Chinese squads jog-crouched past.

"Better grab yourself some cover, shithead!" someone yelled at him.

Hawk glanced back down the strip. Chavez had disappeared. He started down the edge of the strip, running bent over. A network of paths fanned out into the brush past old, water-filled foxholes. Machine gun fire was dense ahead, then was joined by the heavy slam of a 37-mm. piece. He came up behind a low log bunker. Next to it the gun crew was stripped to the waist, feeding in the ammo. Chavez, in the middle of the line, gave him a grim smile. A GI, slumped beside the field piece, looked very dead.

"Chavez!" Hawk yelled, crouching low as a mortar shell exploded just off to the right. "Get your dumb Aztec ass back to the plane or I'll have you court martialed!" Another mortar burst blew apart a clump of small trees nearby. Chavez turned away, clapped one hand to the side of his face and staggered back, a smear of blood from cheek to chin. He knelt slowly as the GI next to him reached out, hand to Chavez's shoulder. Chavez shoved him aside and stood up, moved toward the gun again. A lieutenant bounded forward from the bunker, grabbed Chavez and whirled him about, ran a hand up over Chavez's face, then pushed him back toward the bunker.

"It's O.K., soldier," the lieutenant said to the protesting Chavez. "It's just a scratch. Thanks for your help. Now you and your lieutenant clear out!"

At Command, a medic patched up Chavez's wound. "A piece of wood, a flying splinter," he told Chavez.

The attack dwindled away as they walked back to the plane. Chavez strode ahead but halfway there turned abruptly and faced Hawk. "Get this straight, *gringo*, I'm no Aztec. I am Maya."

The stretcher cases had been held up because of the attack. Not until noon could they be loaded. Gooneys came in all morning. There were rumors at Command of Jap reinforcements spotted moving both down and upriver toward Mitch. The Salvation Army ran out of doughnuts. A Zero alert was announced, then canceled. The ceiling lifted, returned. The rain came heavier. Finally they were cleared for take-off. Airborne, safely on instruments over the Kumons, Chavez worked off his bandage. The bleeding had stopped.

"I've got a really great idea," Hawk told Chavez, who looked duly unimpressed. "You know how Butler was always steamed up because the squadron had no *esprit de corps?* Well, here's the way we can pull ourselves together. A big ceremony. Manchu supplies the food and drinks. Everybody in uniform with all our fruit salad displayed. Tyrone must have some old Sousa marches for his machine. We play those. Colonel Tyrone gives a speech praising the squadron for their part in turning the tide of battle. And then the crowning event. Seargent Chavez and Lieutenant Robb are awarded purple hearts for wounds suffered while displaying exceptional dumb-ass courage under enemy fire."

In his dream, Manchu was shaking him awake to join in fighting off the jackals. It had been a long night with the jackals. Hawk awoke to Fitz standing over him, just as the jackals had worked out a new strategy and in a series of encirclements had decimated a newly arrived flock of what had looked to Hawk like Plymouth Rocks.

"A meeting," Fitz said, shaking him from sleep. "Big news! You're supposed to see the Colonel at twenty minutes of."

"Of what?"

"Noon. Robby is still sleeping. Schultz has gone off to Chabua. The monsoon season is with us. All missions are canceled. You'd better get your ass in gear."

Hawk sat up. "Where is Barpa?"

"Been and gone. Not much he could do. He took away your boots to polish. He took away some laundry for the women. Listen to it. The damn world's awash!"

The rain was a solid pressure over him as Hawk walked past the rows of tents to Tyrone's basha. A mocking, bright rhythm of sound made him pause before entering, a song he had heard long ago, and the memory flooded over him. A single scene: his father at the piano and his mother in a loose dress whirling about their living room. Not the usual heavy classical music his father loved, but one of Scott Joplin's ragtime tunes, making a brightness that for moments seemed now to gild the crevices of the monsoon.

"My gosh," Ericson said as Hawk pushed into the basha. "You really got yourself soaked."

"Just hiding my tears in the rain," he said, wiping his face and taking the bottle of beer Terry McCabe, swollen eyed, held out to him.

Al Tyrone, casual in shorts and a white shirt with epaulets and insignia, rose and lifted the needle from his phonograph.

"So, gentlemen, if we can get on with the business of our departure. I want to get off to Chabua." He smiled. "I'm not sure what Terry has in mind." He smiled again. "Ready for anything, hey, Terry?"

"With this hangover there's only one way I'll probably go."

"Could I get together a pyre for you?"

McCabe folded his arms on the table and put his head down. "I'll bring the matches," he said.

"So to business," Tyrone said. "First of all, mail business. Group HQ informs us no more mail. We're going home to Sicily. I've been instructed to release the information in a way that will not suggest our imminent departure from the CBI. Questions?"

"None printable," McCabe mumbled from folded arms.

"Second item. An unofficial communication from General Stilwell's command, complimenting our squadron for our work at Mitch. Signed by General Stilwell himself."

Hawk spoke up. "Command at Mitch says it will be another two weeks before the town is taken and the Japs driven south."

"In a rat's ass two weeks!" McCabe exploded, raising his head and glaring about. "The Japs are pulling in all their outpost garrisons. They're rushing up supplies and reinforcements from the south. I hear they've still got a few Zeros left. Anyone want to make a bet we'll be here the whole goddamn summer?"

"One thing I'm certain will be here all summer," Al said quietly, "is the monsoon. Our stop here is but the first on our long journey. There are rumors that not everything is well with Chiang Kai-shek and his Nationalist forces, that Mao and his Communist army are making advances. The world needs us."

"You know," McCabe croaked, his head still down, "you listen to Radio Moscow too much." He cocked an eye up at Tyrone.

"Please," Al said, "keep your eye closed. A Cyclops himself couldn't look worse." He paused, picked up a scrap of paper before him. "Oh yes, based on a telephone call from Jorhat. Jedd Butler has escaped again, along with his cameras. Once found, he is to be flown back to the States."

"It's one way to get there," McCabe said. "Anyone got a camera I can borrow?"

"Next item," Tyrone said. He picked up another paper. "Lieutenant Hawk, what's this business with Sergeant Chavez down at Mitch yesterday morning?"

"Nothing much, sir. I guess both of us got a little too close to the action for a few minutes."

McCabe raised his head again. "Who the hell gave him permission to play soldier?"

"I guess I did, Captain," Hawk said.

"His responsibility is with the plane, goddamn it!" McCabe straightened and slammed a hand down on the table. "As is yours! What the hell were you doing?"

"Wait a minute, Terry." Hawk turned to Tyrone. "Has Mitch Command sent up formal charges or something?"

"Here, let me read this," Tyrone said, taking up a paper. "SERGEANT LUIS CHAVEZ, TREATED AT COMMAND HQ FOR A MINOR FACIAL WOUND, IS TO BE COMMENDED FOR HIS ASSISTANCE TO BATTERY B

YESTERDAY MORNING WHEN A JAPANESE ATTACK ATTEMPTED TO OVERRUN ONE OF OUR ARTILLERY POSITIONS. I FIND I CANNOT INITIATE FORMAL ACTION BUT BELIEVE SERGEANT CHAVEZ'S ACTION SHOULD BE RECOGNIZED . . . etcetera."

Tyrone glanced at Hawk.

"Is that an accurate report, Lieutenant?"

"Yes, sir."

"I questioned Sergeant Chavez earlier this morning. His report does not agree with yours. He told me he was running away from a bombardment and ran into a tree. He showed me the scratch on his face."

"He did scratch his face, sir. A branch from a tree."

Colonel Tyrone leaned back in his chair. "Well, Lieutenant, under the circumstances there is nothing I can do along the lines of a formal investigation. However I do suppose you are aware that your plane is your primary responsibility and to leave it unattended while dashing off to whatever you and Chavez participated in a full two hundred yards from your plane, is most serious."

"Yes, sir."

"If you were in my position what action would you recommend?"

"Sir, if I were you I would see that formal charges of some sort be made."

"Of what nature?"

"Of a nature that would make it necessary that I be detained in India for a thorough investigation of the matter."

Tyrone smiled and gathered up his papers. "I could suggest another beer, and another tune from Scott Joplin. However, days like this occur so seldom and we must all be about our affairs. Terry and I are planning on dinner this evening at Most Celestial Dining. Please join us if you wish."

"I've got a lot of letters to write," Ericson said. "Oh, by the way, Hawk. I haven't had a chance to tell you. Those two Brits with their boats and outboards you took down the other day? I learned at Mitch Command they were captured somewhere down river. One of our teams scouting along the river saw them being led into town under guard by some Japs."

Hawk stepped first out into the rain. From down on the airstrip came the rumble of a few engines. His tent was empty. His polished boots were back in their box. He kicked out of his sneakers and into his rubber boots, borrowed Schultz's muddy slicker and walked down the row of tents and out through the compound perimeter.

He needed more time, more than Jamila and he would ever have. But how? It was quite clear that time was ending here.

17

May 22nd, 1944

TO: All personnel - 18th Squadron - Sookerating.

FROM: Lt. Colonel Alfred Tyrone.

RE: Squadron return to Sicily.

Two days from this date Group Headquarters at Jorhat will issue orders returning us to our base at Comiso, Sicily. On May 31st all flying personnel will meet at Cairo. On June 2nd all planes will arrive in Sicily.

This unofficial caution from your commander is merely to anticipate possible problems that might occur during our move. Captain McCabe, Lieutenants Ericson and Hawk are now completing

PLANE AND CREW ASSIGNMENTS. PREPARATION FOR DEPARTURE WILL BEGIN IMMEDIATELY.

OF FIRST IMPORTANCE. RUDIMENTARY MATHEMATICS HAS OBVIOUSLY MADE EVIDENT TO THE MORE PERCEPTIVE OF YOU THAT OUR DATES INDICATE WE ARE GIVEN EIGHT DAYS TO REACH CAIRO FROM SOOK. WE DID IT IN TWO COMING OVER. IT APPEARS THAT GROUP, IN ITS HIGHER WISDOM, IS GIVING US A FEW UNOFFICIAL DAYS OF REST AND REHABILITATION. THEREFORE, ON THE ASSUMPTION THAT A LEISURELY JOURNEY TO CAIRO IS POSSIBLE, I OFFER THE FOLLOWING CAUTIONS, RESTRICTIONS AND ORDERS:

1. FAILURE TO REACH CAIRO BY MAY 31ST WILL BE GROUNDS FOR POSSIBLE COURT MARTIAL.

2. ALL STOPOVERS ENROUTE TO CAIRO MUST BE WHERE AMERICAN BASES ARE LOCATED, SUCH AS CALCUTTA, AGRA, DELHI AND KARACHI.

3. ALL PERSONNEL MUST WEAR PROPER MILITARY DRESS AT ALL BASES. HERE AT SOOK WE HAVE BECOME A BIT CARELESS.

4. THE FOLLOWING BASES, REGARDLESS OF AN AMERICAN PRESENCE, ARE OFF-LIMITS - BAGHDAD, CEYLON, KATMANDU, MOSCOW. ALSO, ANY ATTEMPT TO RETURN BY AN EASTERLY ROUTE, SAY VIA CHINA AND THE PACIFIC, WILL BE CONSIDERED AN ACT OF DESERTION. DON'T TRY IT!

5. ONLY THE CARGO AND PERSONNEL LISTED ON YOUR TRAVEL ORDERS ALLOWED ON YOUR PLANE. THERE MAY BE OR POSSIBLY HAVE ALREADY BEEN, ATTEMPTS BY NON-MILITARY PERSONNEL TO ACQUIRE TRANSPORTATION TO VARIOUS LOCATIONS. FORGET IT!

A GOOD JOURNEY TO ALL OF YOU!

AL TYRONE

$$\text{———◆———}$$

18

IT took Hawk only seconds of awaking to adjust to the nearly deserted tent, the strange quietness that hung over the pre-dawn compound. A whisper of gray rain. No growl from the air strip of gooneys getting their morning pre-flights. Schultz already gone three days, called by the bordellos of Cairo. Fitz off yesterday. Hawk listened to the wash of rain on the canvas. Robby, humped on his cot, gave a deep sigh and went on sleeping. Their last morning of this war. He balled up a shirt and hurled it.

"Let's go, Robby! Another day, another war!"

Robby abruptly sat up. "I just dreamed they tried to give me a purple heart. I refused it. Think how the Bronx would handle my being decorated for getting shot in the ass. What's Manchu feeding us this morning, breaded jackal?"

The squadron mess had been dismembered, only a single table, many dishes, fruit and a steaming coffee urn. Manchu appeared from his kitchen bearing pancakes, sausages and eggs, pulled up a chair and sat down. His smile was enigmatic.

"Tea," Hawk said. "and some mango juice."

"Nothing," Robby said. "With Hawk it's better flying on an empty stomach."

"So now," Manchu said softly, "we fly to another war."

"Another country," Robby said. "The same war."

"All wars need cooks," Manchu said. "Those who win the wars have the finest cooks."

Hawk pulled a bright paisley from his pocket and handed it to Manchu. "For you. From Alexandria when I was on my way to this war. Thanks for everything."

Manchu unfolded the bright patterned silk, flourished it like a butterfly about his head and fastened it about his neck. "Most many thanks, Lieutenant." Something in his smile changed. "I think now for me also another country." His look deepened. "Who knows, perhaps I voyage also to Sicily. With a friend." The excision of his question mark was perfect.

Hawk smiled, shook his head sadly. "It is not possible, not even if you were to promise us a white elephant. However it would be most pleasant, should you appear, to see you again."

Robby stood up. "Or should we dress you up and sign you on as navigator?" He shook hands with Manchu. "Good luck." And to Hawk, "I'll go get my gear down to the plane."

"Most certainly," Manchu said,"I be a very fine navigator."

"We are certain also," Hawk said. "*Buen suerte.*"

Barpa had not appeared that morning but when Hawk arrived at the airstrip he stood by the cargo door steps clutching a paper bag. Chavez was checking the landing gear.

"I bring your boots, Lieutenant." Barpa pulled them from the bag.

"I left them for you, Barpa. With me they will always be muddy or the mice will eat them."

"But you have no shoes, Lieutenant."

Hawk glanced down at his sneakers. "Not to worry, Barpa. I hear they make very fine ones in Agra."

Barpa shook his head, fished in his bag and pulled out a pair of polished sandals, held them out to him. "These for you, sir Lieutenant. Exact to size. I measure from your boots. The shoemaker choose finest leather of crocodile. And for your boots I am full with thanks. *Namaste.*"

"Hey!" Robby's head poked from the cockpit window. "Let's get the show on the road. The dancing girls are waiting!"

Hawk climbed the steps, followed by Chavez who slammed shut the re-hung cargo doors. Hawk made his way forward between stacked crates and filing cabinets. Below them Barpa waved from a swirl of dust. McCabe, in charge of final departures, answered Hawk's call for permission to take off.

"*O.K. hot shots. Clear for take-off. Just make sure you make our Cairo party.*"

Chavez leaned between Hawk and Robby and took the mike. "*Lo siento,* major. Sorry but we fly straight on to Mexico."

Hawk held the gooney's nose down, passing low over the Greystaffs'. A final glimpse of the pool. A vulture dove clear of them. Jamila had been gone two days. She should be in Agra by noon. "O.K. Robby, give me our heading."

Robby pulled down and unfolded a chart. "As if you didn't know! And look, no mountains. Piece of cake. One thousand miles to Agra. Rest and rehabilitation begins this afternoon!"

Chavez leaned over them. "Sack time for me, *amigos*. Up all night putting things together. Wake me over the Taj Mahal."

"*Buenos noches,*" Hawk said. "Robby, change of orders. Make our heading bring us to where the Brahmaputra and Ganges join."

"Sightseeing, Hawk?" Robby bent over the chart. "That gives us over a hundred extra miles. Why don't we fly up for a close-up of the Himalayas? What about my soft bed and dancing girls?"

"Shut up and give me a heading."

"Try 275 degrees and see where we come out."

Two hours later Hawk made out the joining of the two great rivers below a thin sea of cirrus clouds over the western reach of sky. Below the mosaic of old land shelved off under a distant storm to the south. To the north the white teeth of the Himalayan range. Ahead a drift of smoke from the Ganges plain, a train winding the Ganges course. Sometime later the distant voice of the Agra tower. Above them a dark wheel of vultures.

Hawk said abruptly, as much to himself as to Robby, "What the hell do we know of this country? All the history below us. All the plains and mountains and jungles, the cities, oceans and peoples? What in hell do we know about them? We don't even know what the hell we are fighting about!"

"Spoken like a loyal fighting man." Robby leaned forward and peered down at the disk of light smog over Agra. "Look, I know New York. Manhattan, the Bronx, Coney Island, the Cloisters. I used to go there to see the unicorns."

"Perhaps that is how we all end up," Hawk said, "riding the unicorns of our own futures."

Robby gave him a funny look. "You going weird on us, Hawk? Why don't you let me take over?"

Hawk stared ahead. It was as if he could see beyond India and Arabia, the wine-dark pirate seas, Gibralter, the Ocean Sea, his own country, Maine, and Chavez's land of the Maya. Maybe Robby was correct -- weird. The gooney's props slid out of sync, a counterpoint of throbbing. He worked them back to a smooth, solid sound, then startled by Robby tapping him on the arm, pointing ahead as he adjusted his earphones. Ahead through the city's haze he made out the four minarets of the Taj Mahal.

Hawk pointed. "Where I am going, Robby?"

Robby pointed straight ahead where a coil of vultures swept across their way. He banked away sharply and down. Robby began his call for landing instructions.

Part of the airport had become a small American base, a miscellaneous of cargo and fighters. A couple of gooneys from their squadron already in. "I hear," Robby said, "base housing here comes with sheets and pillows, ice cream and soft toilet paper."

"If you ever write your war memoirs, Robby, don't bother to send me a copy. Fill out our log. Make sure Chavez refuels before he leaves the plane." Hawk scribbled out the address and handed it to Robby. "Where I can be reached. I'll keep in touch with the base. You and Chavez have fun with the ice cream and dancing girls."

Robby gave him a half smile, shrugged. "Like it's a hell of a time to fall in love, Lieutenant. But it's your -- well whatever it turns out to be. Give her my best wishes."

Hawk got his flight bag. Chavez was already up on a wing, motioning a fuel truck in for fuel. He waved, yelled down at him. The only word Hawk caught was tequila. A passing jeep gave him a lift into Operations. A well-groomed sergeant signed him in, turned and pointed to the sign over the counter. AMERICAN PERSONNEL GOING IN TO AGRA MUST WEAR REGULATION UNIFORM.

"Sorry, sir." The sergeant's finger tips tested the razor creases of his khakis. "But I'm afraid your shorts, bush jacket pith helmet might present a problem downtown." He smiled.

"I'm just out of Burma, Sergeant. We haven't been dressing for downtown for months."

"They won't let you out the gate in that rig." He leaned forward over the counter and looked down. "Sneakers? Come on, Lieutenant."

"Corns," Hawk said, then remembered, leaned to his flight bag and zipped open a pocket, jerked out Barpa's sandals.

The sergeant shrugged. "It's a start. And your shorts?"

"Regulation tropic wear, Sergeant. I'll get them washed."

"And get that missing button on your fly replaced. As for your pith helmet and bush jacket?"

"For elephant hunting."

"We got hunting here, Lieutenant, but not that kind."

"I've got a couple of shirts with me." He removed his pith helmet and handed it to the sergeant.

"And a tie, sir?"

"No."

"I've got a spare one. You can change down the hall, door on your right. I'll hold the British cap until you return. When you leaving, Lieutenant?"

"When the call comes, Sergeant. Thanks and how do I get to town?"

"Transportation every half hour. The shack down by the gate. Welcome to civilization."

The transport driver shrugged at the address Hawk showed him and left him off in what he called the English Bazaar. "Big place for the troops, sir. Try your address on the wallahs. They should know."

Evening was still distant beyond thin clouds, the air dusty, with the sounds of the city -- cars, trucks, bicycles, tongas, the cries of the rickshaw wallah men. The minor notes of Indian music. A high, sad voice singing *Lili Marlene*. Hawk paused with his back against a broad-leafed tree. Surely that was the cry of a muezzin from a minaret. He thought -- I have never been in India until now. He picked up his flight bag and started along the crowded street. The window of a small shop caught his eye. Ivory carvings and the soft sheen of silver. Inside, behind a counter a gray-haired woman in a blue sari rose a smiled at him.

"Please, if you could help me." He pulled the address from his wallet and handed it to her.

She slipped on pair of glasses and peered at it, her voice warm. "It is quite far from here, sir." She leaned forward and glanced down at his flight bag. "Yes, a long way. Perhaps I may help?" She turned and called back in Hindi. A small boy appeared from the shadows, darted out around the counter and picked up Hawk's bag.

"Here, let me take it," Hawk said, but the boy was already past him toward the door.

"Go with him," the woman said. "He will get you a wallah. And please, if you are passing my shop again while in Agra it would be of pleasure to show you what my husband and I have. Our ivory pieces are very fine and not expensive. Also our silver work is of the highest quality."

He thanked her. Outside by the curb the boy had already hailed a rickshaw. The wallah was a wiry, youngish man. He tossed the flight bag on the seat and motioned to Hawk.

"My uncle will take you, Sahib," the boy said.

Hawk handed the boy some change and the address to the driver who squinted and then nodded, gave a soft cry as they joined in the traffic.

Their progress was erratic at first, caught in the massing of traffic at each intersection -- a mingling of horns, bells and shouts of the wallahs. Then gradually their route took them from the bazaar into a modest suburb of low white houses, a few stores and an occasional garage, a flowering of old jacaranda trees. Then a wide boulevard jammed with military vehicles. The wallah worked his way across, using a small lorry as a blocking back, entering a neighborhood of more opulent buildings shielded by vine-covered walls, their entrances of stylized iron. In a short while they came to a stop before a wide gate centering a high white wall, streaked with moss and crumbling brick. Two tall jacaranda trees made blue fountains over them. Behind the wall a fringe of palms.

The wallah leaped from the rickshaw, grabbed Hawk's flight bag and carried it up to the gate. A polished brass knob set in an alcove gave off a soft chime when he touched it. The wallah rang twice, stepped back and pointed up to a name cut in the limestone over the gate, indecipherable under layers of time and whitewash. "From the time of the Raj, Sahib," the wallah said, then turned as a small wooden door in the gate squeaked partly open. A frail, very old man swathed in white examined them.

"You are Lieutenant Hawk?" His voice had the cracked quality of one not used very much.

Hawk nodded and found some rupees for the driver.

"Thank you, Sahib." He handed Hawk a small card. "For when you are in the city and perhaps shopping. Very fine cloths."

The ancient gate-keeper stepped out from the doorway and grasped Hawk's flight bag with both hands, straining upward and resisting with surprising strength when Hawk tried to assist him. He motioned Hawk on ahead, nudged the door shut behind them and moved quickly ahead across a wide inner courtyard lit by a single faint light and the gathering of evening. Small tides of flowers swirled from openings in the marble. The old man's bare feet made no sound. Then from beyond a blossoming of shrubs -- was it bergamot that filled the air? -- Jamila came running.

In the quietness between love they lay without speaking, the night sounds of the city soft through a high open window where a waning moon hung in a thin net of clouds. They slept and awakened. "Listen," Jamila whispered. "When I was young the muezzin called me to prayer." She, touched him, her hand across his shoulder, came again against him. He pulled her closer. All her body seemed clad in bergamot. Their bodies moved -- explored -- the natural moments of their togetherness. They slept again and toward dawn came to stand before the high window. Jamila pointed and just faintly Hawk made out where the dome of the Taj loomed, its four minarets thin shadows floating in the morning mist.

By the time they rose the small balcony off their room had been set for breakfast, the old man moving silently behind a draped door. Fruit, pastry and tea amid a wide bouquet of bergamot.

"Seems like this is our flower," Hawk said. "This is a hotel, Jamila?"

"No, Alan. It belongs to a very old and once powerful family who were here even before the time of the Raj. Now there are few left. The owner, now dead, was with Major Greystaff in your first great war. His wife is very old and sees few people. She and Molly were close friends. But naturally she could not approve of us and asked no questions when Molly wrote to her about us, merely telling Molly that we were welcome to stay but her age prevented her seeing us. She did not approve, I remember, of the English education the Greystaffs gave me."

"And does Molly approve, Jamila?"

She smiled, reached up and brushed a hand over his face. "I think she approved of you from our first tea at the plantation. But it would not be fair of me not to tell you that for several years she has been concerned about my future. So many great changes are coming to India. How would I fit in to India? To England? I would not even listen to talk of an arranged marriage. When I told her I was in love with you she said flatly love was no security."

"Did you tell her I was in love with you?"

"I told her that each day you flew off to Burma my heart went with you. Are you in love with me, Alan?"

He pulled her against him. "At least there is no more Burma, Jamila."

"Only the days until I return to Molly and the Major and you fly on to whatever your war brings. But this afternoon, my love, we shall journey to a part of India I do not know. I take you to see the Red Stone Palace. It is claimed to be the finest example of pure Huni architecture."

"I was hoping for the Taj Mahal," Hawk said.

"And so we shall but it is proper to begin at the beginning. Which is impossible because India had no beginning. It has always been here, for me the navel of the world."

"I wish I had that faith in my country."

"Oh, not in my country, Alan." She touched him gently on the arm. "Not India but that country we must sometime come to claim. The country we have yet to discover." She paused. "Tell me, Alan, what is your own true country?"

He shrugged, smiled. "You lose me among many borders. Maybe the Red Stone Palace is a place to begin."

Outside the cloudless day offered up only heat, a drift of high vultures, the distant sound of planes. A taxi brought them, after much engine trouble, beyond the outskirts of Agra, a long, dusty expanse of earth shadowed by wide-spreading banyan trees. They left the taxi and came to the low palace which seemed to Hawk dissolving in a sprawl of worn brick and dark openings. They removed their sandals and wandered through a cool, timeless interior where bats clustered the tiered ceilings and sourceless sounds hovered over them.

"Lost voices from another time," Jamila said.

Finally, under the banyan trees again, they sat in the shade a little while. They had not seen a single person. "It is a place to begin," Hawk said. "And I am very thirsty."

Their driver was asleep in his taxi. Jamila questioned him. He nodded and driving very fast, brought them to a restaurant he claimed all Americans liked, but it was too hot and crowded, too many troops and dancing girls.

"We'll go back to our pool and garden," Jamila said. "The caretaker mentioned to me we might use it."

The old man had trouble with the keys to the pool which they reached through a labyrinth of corridors cool and dim. Finally he managed the heavy door that let them by a flight of worn steps into the garden and pool below their room. He cautioned them to leave the door ajar, vanished into the labyrinth and left them in a small patio of flowers and vines from which a frog croaked.

"He's lonely," Hawk said. "Perhaps waiting for us?"

"Perhaps now to change back into a Prince." Jamila kicked off her sandals and dipped her toes in the translucent water where a shadowy carp appeared and vanished.

The water was not deep and they made a pretense of swimming, dried in the filter of sunlight through the trees. Dim lights came on among a climbing veil of vines. Hand in hand they returned to the dim corridors.

"Tomorrow," Alan said, "You will take me to the Taj?"

"No, not tomorrow, Alan." She sat on the bed beside him, ran her hands through his hair. "Tomorrow we visit the Moti Masjid, the perfect example of the Mohammedan style. Memories when you are in some far country."

"I like your style most of all, my love. It shall be with me in all the far countries I fly to."

He pulled her down to him, brought her dark hair about his face. After a while they rose and went to the window. The thin rising moon was barely visible through the haze cloaking the city. He put his arms about her.

"That fragment I brought you from the destroyed Burmese temple. Did you bring it with you, Jamila?"

"Remember? I told you it would always be with me. Why?"

"Something I want to do."

It was nearly noon the next day when they arrived in the English Bazaar and found the shop where he had first asked directions. He placed the small rough fragment on the strip of blue velvet the woman unfolded on the counter. She ran a finger along the curved incisions of red and gold, then lifted it to her nose and inhaled deeply. He glanced at Jamila who shrugged. "It is from a temple. It has the scent of time," said the woman.

"It is from Burma," Alan said. "What was left did look like a temple. I am wondering if it could be bordered with silver and some sort of silver chain? For around her neck." They both looked at Jamila.

"Yes," Jamila said, "that is what I would like."

"In two days, sir," the woman said. "Then you should come back and see that it pleases you."

Once back on the street Alan said, "And now we shall find a gentle rickshaw and continue our journey into ancient India."

There were few visitors at the Pearl Mosque. They came under a spread of old palms and flames of bougainvillea to a side entrance, removed their sandals and moved into the hushed magic of its shadowy interior.

"So beautiful, so sad," Jamila said, taking his hand. "It is like all the things we once dreamed and believed in. All the violence that has come from the once true and beautiful things people once believed would last forever if they built them."

"I wonder why you brought me here, Jamila."

"Because you are a stranger from a far country. And perhaps some day, my love, you will show me what was built in your land."

He put his arms about her. "Yes, I am a person from a far country, holding tightly a woman in her far country. Do we know what we have built or what it will come to? Let us absolve each other of all history."

She smiled, reached up and kissed him, held her lips hard against his, to be suddenly startled by a violent hiss, a long drawn-out sound of malevolence. An old man in white and flowing dress that made him tower above them stood glaring down, eyes wide and fanatic. Hawk took Jamila's hand and they walked slowly, not looking back, from the mosque.

They came to a stop farther on where a pair of Muscovy ducks coasted a green pool. "It's my fault, Alan. I knew better. It should always be the foreigner who commits the transgression."

"I'd like to feel I help, Jamila. Come on, let's go find our rickshaw chap who will discover for us a restaurant with a perfect and cool drink."

Jamila looked down, burst out laughing. "Of course, Alan, but first we must return to the mosque. We forgot our sandals."

"The old man has probably destroyed them," Alan said.

"No, Alan. They will be there. Untouchable forever."

Their rickshaw man found them and they spent the afternoon wandering the bazaar. Here no real sign of war, the mingling of troops and many peoples, music from the shops and even the high distant murmur of planes joining in.

"In olden times," Jamila said, "we would describe what we hear as the music of the spheres. Let us go buy something for one another that would suit the day."

They were passing a news-stand and he pointed to a headline with photos -- ALLIES PLAN FOR ASSAULT ON FORTRESS EUROPE. Jamila singled out a beach scene from Ceylon, bright with umbrellas and swimmers -- BUT ALWAYS TIME FOR A DIP IN THE POOL.

Jamila bought for him a small box carved from mahogany and set with ivory. He found for her a beautifully illustrated copy in leather of the *Rubaiyat.*

"Now we are properly sentimental," Jamila said. "It is moving toward evening and I am hungry."

The evening had cooled by the time they returned to their room above the pool. They swam again. Rain came briefly, then again, with a dawn filled once more with the scent of bergamot.

It was towards noon when they arrived again at the small shop in the English Bazaar. It appeared closed but when they knocked the door creaked open. The woman, unsmiling, let them in.

"So sorry," she explained. "My husband has been ill but insisted he finish your necklace."

"We can return tomorrow," Hawk said.

"Oh no," the woman said firmly. "It is done, as we promised. But he is a foolish, stubborn man, and now is only anxious to learn your judgment of his work."

She pulled open a drawer in the counter, placed a desk lamp on her strip of velvet and lifted out the, temple fragment. A curved molding of silver now enclosed it, its silver cord fashioned of finely worked mesh.

"Oh, how beautiful," Jamila said. "Alan, please." She lifted it. He took it, placing it about her neck and fixing the clasp

"Ah!" the woman said, "My husband asked me to describe the woman who is to wear it. Now I can tell him it completes your beauty."

Jamila reached up and kissed him.

"You must try to be with happiness and love for a very long time," the woman said softly.

It was very late that evening though the thin moon had yet to rise when they reached the pools before the Taj Mahal. The glow of the city lights tented the night, empty a little while of the murmur of planes. Jamila kneeled on the marble rim of a pool, leaned forward, caught up some water with her hands and splashed it over her face -- then stiffened.

"Ugh," she cried out, glanced up at Alan and made a face. "Ugh, ugh, ugh!"

"Which translated from the Hindi," Alan said, "means?"

"Ugh!" Jamila brushed at her face with both hands. "Bloody awful water." She paused. "Sorry, shouldn't have said that."

"Fortunately, being American, your language doesn't leave me completely shocked." He tried the water, made a face. "Ugh!"

He lifted to Jamila to her feet and kissed her lightly on both cheeks. They went on past the walled gardens adorned with dark cypress and small fountains. Above them the minarets lifted magically into the night. By the steps they removed their sandals and went on into an interior lit by an almost sourceless light filtered by marble screens, a-jewel-like glimmer from the walls that faded upward under the high dome. They stood close, silent for a long time.

"Somewhere beneath us," Jamila finally whispered, "the Shah and Mumtaz Mahal lie in their endless sleep."

"But let us postpone that for a little while," Alan said.

He felt her shiver and her fingers tightened hard on his arms. At the sound of a high plane passing they looked up and without speaking went on out into the night and past the pools, walking slowly, hand in hand, through the still-sleeping city, the thin moon now visible where dawn tinged the eastern sky.

The sun was a low red stain in a dusty sky when they were awakened by the old man, knocking loudly and muttering outside their door.

"An American officer comes urgently to see the lieutenant."

Jamila sat up, eyes wide.

"Ugh," Hawk said. "Ugh, ugh, ugh!"

"Ugh," Jamila said. "Bloody ugh."

Hawk slipped on a robe and followed the old man down to the front courtyard. Robby was pacing by the gate.

"Haven't you been listening to the goddamn radio, Hawk!"

"War has been declared?"

"Asshole! It's been on the air since early evening. The invasion! Across the channel into France, they're already on their way! Our orders came in at midnight. Immediate departure. No Cairo party. It's straight back to Sicily. We've got to haul ass to the airfield! I've got a jeep. Let's go!"

In their room Jamila was already dressed and standing by the window. "So, Alan, it's come." She did not turn to him.

He went to her, felt her trembling as she raised her lips to his. "We haven't even talked about this, Jamila."

"Is there any reason to, my love?"

"After it's over, Jamila. We'll -- "

She place a hand across his lips, then stepped back, lifted the red and gold fragment by its chain, pressed it against his cheek. He wiped away the glint of her tears.

"Come on, I've got us a ride to the airfield."

"Maybe if you don't change from your robe they won't let you leave."

Dressing, Hawk found some rupees for the old man. When they went down the gate was open, Robby at the wheel of the jeep racing the engine. Hawk motioned Jamila to the rear seat.

"No way," Robby said. "No non-official personnel allowed on the base."

"If I'd put on my bathrobe I wouldn't have to go?"

"I'm getting off at the gate," Jamila said. "I'll wait and catch the regular flight to England."

A guard opened the gate. Hawk jumped from the jeep and lifted Jamila down. Robby gunned on, slammed on his brakes and hit the horn. The airbase was roaring to life. Hawk embraced Jamila. "I'll be waving from down here," she said. "See you in England."

He glanced back and down as they lifted from the runway. Jamila was already lost in a lifting cloak of dust from the taxiing planes. The Taj vanished below in a haze of clouds. Chavez came to the cockpit, stood between Hawk and

Robby. He peered ahead, abruptly grabbed Hawk's shoulder and pointed. Lifting straight up ahead of them a dark vortex erupted.

"*Buitres*!" Chavez yelled. "Vultures!"

For moments Hawk stared at the empty, endless reach of sky beyond.

"Jesus Christ!" Robby's hands reached for the wheel.

Hawk dropped his right wing and they fell steeply away and past the birds, heading west toward wherever it was they were going.

THE GOONEY

The C47 series was the military version of the redoubtable DC3. It was properly named "Skytrain" but to the British it became the "Dakota" and to the flyers of the CBI it became the "Gooney." The name was borrowed from the informal name of the black-legged Albatross common in the Pacific islands which was slow in getting airborn but could soar for hours.

More than ten thousand C47s were built and they served in every theatre of war in WWII and later appeared in Korea and Vietnam. General Eisenhower identified the transport as one of the four most important weapons that contributed to the Allies' victory.

It had a wingspan of 95.6,' a length of 63.9,' and weighed 26,000 lbs. The maximum speed was 230 mph and it .could transport 35,000 lbs about 1,600 miles. It was the workhorse of the· US Air Force and really was the "train of the skies."